SOCIAL DISTANCING

A Novel

Scott Spires

"You can't even imagine the kind of hell that's about to fall on our heads. Few of us will live through it. Not one stone will remain standing that our generation and our age knew as its own … I feel I am nearing the end, together with this era."

—Stanisław Ignacy Witkiewicz, Polish avant-garde painter, writer and philosopher, 1939

"Who am I? Why am I here?"

—Admiral James Stockdale, U.S. vice presidential candidate, 1992

Part I:
Fragments of a World

My car stopped at the top of the hill. I pushed the pedal gently. Nothing happened. I pushed it harder. Again, nothing happened.

Going back seemed like an option. Grunting, I shifted from D to R and pushed the pedal again. The car grumbled but failed.

The car couldn't go forward. It couldn't go back. I was stuck.

"Home," I said.

"When you reach the top of the hill, go straight," said the voice. Mrs. Van Dorp was my name for the female voice of the GPS, because the voice reminded me of a grade-school teacher I'd had. The original Mrs. Van Dorp was often impatient with me and got snippy when she felt I wasn't living up to my potential. Once, she wrote in the margins of an unsatisfactory piece of homework: "Hey! Get your act together and take it on the road!" Now, I was on the road as she suggested, taking instructions from her programmed electronic double, and feeling guilty when I couldn't execute them.

"I'm on the top of the hill already," I said by way of explanation. "I can't go straight." Redoubling my efforts, I pushed the pedal gently, then more firmly. The car roared but was stuck. An invisible barrier seemed to be holding it back. I looked down the hill, where I saw the public works facility and elementary school that marked the outskirts of

Roverton. The distant town. My home now. The place I'd committed myself to.

"You really can't go straight?" asked Mrs. Van Dorp. She sounded surprised.

"Really, I can't," I said. "I don't know what to do." I revved the engine fruitlessly again. I had something to prove to her.

"You're not trying hard enough," she said.

"You're exceeding the limits of your authority," I retorted. "It's not your job to criticize my driving." It felt good to say that. For once, I'd put Mrs. Van Dorp in her place.

"What are you going to do about it? Reprogram me?" she snapped.

"I'll replace you with another device."

She switched to psychoanalytical mode. "Your answer's a sign of insecurity. You want a device that will cater to your every whim."

"Well, that's how the product is sold, isn't it? You don't want to piss off the customer too much, right?" Her voice was really starting to aggravate me.

I'm almost sure I heard a sigh emanate from the speaker. "You want to get off this hill, but there are two problems. First, you don't know how to do it. Second, you're not certain you want to get to your destination. You call it 'your new home,' but deep down you're not so sure about that. You're hovering in a zone of insecurity, and you have no solution. But that zone of insecurity is the larger problem, the one that contains the other problems you're dealing with."

"Hey, thanks," I said. "But what I really want to know right now is if there's something wrong with my car."

"There's nothing wrong with your car," said the GPS lady, snippily.

I think it's a sign of middle age: I can only confirm that I've been sleeping if I can remember a dream. Since dreams tend to be absurd or adventurous, they're easy to identify as dreams, and recalling them reminds me that I haven't been awake lately. Which isn't to say that, in those hours when I know I've been awake, life hasn't been absurd. It's that waking absurdity feels different from dreaming absurdity. But sometimes, the two forms of absurdity get mixed up in my mind, to the point where I can't remember if something was a dream or the product of my overheated imagination. The appearance of Mrs. Van Dorp in my car was a case in point. After I got dressed and before I had breakfast, I checked the garage to make sure it was there and not stuck on a hill somewhere.

Waking absurdity is something that characterizes the overall arc of my life. At no point in my earlier existence did I believe that I would wind up where I am now. My world was defined by values that might be grouped under the general heading of cosmopolitanism: the city, the university, the research grant, the library, the seminar; travel to Europe and various academic outposts in the Americas. Who would go all the way to Las Vegas only for the purpose of presenting a paper at a conference on some arcane linguistic topic, and not spend even one night gambling or "taking in a show"? I would, because that was my life and (as became clear as my education advanced and the Mrs. Van Dorps faded into history) my destiny. Or so I thought.

Yet that destiny had deposited me in Roverton, population nine thousand and rising, here on the coast of Lake Michigan, high up on the Wisconsin side. This was turning out to be the biggest detour I'd ever made, and it might not even have been a detour, but a terminus point. That's because I came here looking for a refuge, a haven. By abandoning my academic position in the Philadelphia area and relocating here, I retired from my previous life, closing the door on it. Would I die here, in this peaceful outpost?

It was a melancholy thought that visited me often, usually during times of inactivity, such as today—a morning of early summer that found me in the backyard, dawdling over my oatmeal and coffee as the lazy day ahead took shape in my mind. A blissful period of idleness between the remote consulting projects I sometimes undertook put me in a contemplative mood. My only commitment on this day was dinner at my house with Ethan, my son. After breakfast, I took Bruce, my West Highland white terrier, for a walk.

Turning left onto my quiet tree-lined street, I saw something that gave me a shock.

"Hey, Bruce, it's Mrs. Van Dorp!" I said, as a gray-haired woman approached me from a distance.

But it wasn't Mrs. Van Dorp. It was my neighbor, Mrs. Westerberg, the retired former records keeper at the town hall. She waved at me with her right hand, while her left held the leash connecting her to Porky, her Welsh corgi. "Hi there, Fred," she said as she got closer.

"Good morning," I said. To my embarrassment, I couldn't remember her first name. I'd always known her as Mrs. Westerberg. Wishing to avoid formality, I stuck with the impersonal greeting—which triggered a twinge of worry that, by not using her name, I was being formal.

With Mrs. Westerberg, I enjoyed the cordial, superficial relations that typically characterized my interactions with old-time Rovertonians. By contrast, Bruce and Porky were straightforward in expressing their mutual affection, to the point where they'd jump around and chase each other within the restricted radius permitted by our leashes, which frequently got tangled up, while Mrs. Westerberg and I chatted about the weather, or some other light topic.

"The game was great last night, wasn't it?" observed Mrs. Westerberg. Searching my face for a spark of recognition, she said: "The big game!"

"Oh, the *big* game. I didn't catch it. I had a prior commitment."

"That's too bad. Coach Fangbone said it was the most exciting game he'd ever been involved in."

"I'm sorry I missed it, then," I said. I lied. Not only did I not know that "the game" had been on last night, but I also didn't know what sport or league she referred to, and I'd never heard of Coach Fangbone (not a name you're likely to forget). But since I didn't want to come across as a snob, I refrained from broadcasting my disdain for spectator sports.

We concluded our polite, perfunctory dialogue. I admit there was an awkwardness in my interaction with long-term locals. They seemed guarded, as if they wondered if this strange person, renegade professor Frederick Traubert, really belonged here, despite my solid-sounding Germanic name, so redolent of the Upper Midwest. It didn't take long for my new neighbors to notice that I was a different sort of person from them. I didn't talk like them; I didn't share their interests. I was friendly to them, and they were friendly to me. But on both sides, there was a sense of apprehension—like we were fundamentally different people.

Should I try harder to blend in? I sometimes asked myself. Watch the *Farm Report*, do the crossword in the local paper… If I wasn't actually going to watch *The Big Game*, shouldn't I at least find out who played and who won? But was there any point in pretending to be someone other than myself?

I valued Ethan's company even more due to my lack of close local friends. He'd also moved to Roverton, where he'd set himself up in a completely different line of business than mine. His old man was a one-time professor of Germanic languages; Ethan, however, shunned the learned professions and went into craft brewing instead. He'd done a sort of apprenticeship in this field for a few years, working for a brewpub in the Los Angeles metro area. As he learned the trade and became more ambitious, he decided he wanted to run his own establishment, and to do so in Roverton of all places. He'd identified an opportunity here, and what's more, he could crash at Dad's house and mooch off me if necessary. Now, he was the manager and master brewer at Our Lady of Hops, the converted church that had become one of the town's social magnets. Ethan knew all about food and drink, but tonight I'd be the chef, turning the tables on him, so to speak.

There was another reason I valued Ethan's company. My wife of many years, Amanda, had decided to embark on a "trial separation" from me. That was her term for it, but I don't think it was strictly accurate. We made no written agreement about it, or any legally binding document. Basically, she warned me that she was going to take off, and then she took off. She did it in stages. First, she refused to relocate to Roverton with me, preferring to stay at our old place in Philly. We did visit each other from time to time, but she remained ambivalent about getting back together. The next stage commenced when she went to Europe to do "foundation work." At first, this didn't seem so alarming; after all, Europe was her place of origin (if one considers England to be Europe), she knew all kinds of people there, she'd been involved with charitable and educational work for a long time; in short, she had reasons to be there other than wanting to get away from me. But she stayed and stayed and was discouragingly opaque whenever I asked her when she was coming back, or even when I requested details on what precisely she was doing over there. The upshot was that all I had left of family were Ethan and Bruce the dog.

Despite everything, I felt less like an odd duck in a tiny pond. That's because things were starting to change in Roverton. I wasn't the only person escaping the big bad outside world. More people like me were moving in. They'd had enough of the cities and the suburbs. Recent events and their own fears had convinced them it was time to start over, somewhere else. Personal safety, overcrowding, expense—everything was getting worse. It didn't all happen at once—these changes occurred by degrees. There'd be sudden lurches into chaos, then a return to normality. This return to normality would create a false sense of security, only to be followed by another unpleasant lurch. In one part of your life, change would be so gradual you didn't notice it, until one day something you'd only heard about on the news hit you right in the face, and you realized that the crisis had arrived in your living room. If these cycles continue, you start looking for a way out. You start wanting to live in a place where the words "breaking news" don't fill you with dread. When this trend got underway, I was already in Roverton, watching the trickle of refugees swell into a modest flow, and seeing the town change under their influence.

"It's a good thing I bought this house when I did," I thought, sipping another coffee, back in the backyard after our walk. It was one of those small but solid old brown-brick two-story houses, built early in the twentieth century, of the type that the urban refugees liked to purchase and then "fix up." I was in the happy position of being a short walk to the lakefront, a medium walk to our charming little downtown, and a long walk to the pier and its defunct little red lighthouse, or "harbor light" as they called it around here. If I'd waited a couple of years, the house would probably have flown out of my price range, due to the influx of newcomers with money to spend. But as it stood, there was easily enough room for me, Bruce the dog, Ethan if he wanted to spend the night, any visiting friend, and, if she ever decided to come back, Amanda.

Let's rewind. A few years back, when I was still teaching and had found myself with a load of extra money due to the deaths of a couple of close relatives, plus a frugal and prudent approach to savings over the years, I investigated the idea of purchasing real estate far from the usual centers of civilization. At the time, my motivation for doing so appeared to be indistinct, even to me, the person who was supposedly making the decision. But, at least subconsciously, I picked up on something disturbing. Sigmund Freud wrote a book with the title *Das Unbehagen in der Kultur*—a phrase which was inadequately translated into English as *Civilization and its Discontents*. The *Unbehagen* of the title refers to a sense of unease, a disturbing ripple in the soul, a feeling of disequilibrium caused by the clash between our human desires and the demands of civilization. In my case, this word *Unbehagen* got stuck in my head, and I interpreted it more subjectively, as a feeling that a big storm was coming, and that civilization was going to undergo a historic crash, and I should get the safest roof over my head that I could. What intensified everything was that I've always had an overactive imagination. I've never been able to shut with ease the mental window that keeps out the anxieties of living. Other people shut that window naturally; I push at it and force it closed with a strenuous effort, and as often as not, it pops open again.

At this point, I should stress that I'm not an adherent of Freud, or of Marx, or of any individual mind, no matter how brilliant it may be, that attempts to make sense of the world through any all-encompassing or all-embracing theory. Even the greatest mind couldn't truly make sense of this world as a totality; understanding a particular niche or fragment of reality is usually the best we can do. But I must give credit where it is due and acknowledge that obsessive cogitation on one topic often yields fruitful results. In any case, it was the salience of this phrase—the "sense of uneasiness of the culture"—that mattered most of all, irrespective of what Freud meant by that. It was the fragment that lodged in my mind and set me to thinking, and then worrying, and finally looking for a way out.

Before Amanda split from me, we used to talk about this. Both of us were concerned, but I must admit that I felt the anxiety more intensely, to a degree that worried her. At that time, all talk about escape felt purely theoretical. We were part of a trend, though; at least, we were on the edge of a trend, getting tugged into its gravitational pull as it grew. It seemed that every few years, or even every few months, people who feared the future took an interest in some distant, presumably idyllic country to which they could escape. Some people talked about Iceland, but the fad for that died quickly when people realized that Iceland was too cold, too expensive, and unlikely to welcome immigrants. Attention shifted to Uruguay. It was in the Southern Hemisphere, which meant that if a world war broke out, it would probably be spared. It had a friendly Mediterranean-style climate, a high standard of living for Latin America, and Spanish was a lot easier to learn than Icelandic. But as time went by, interest in Uruguay faded as those old favorites, Australia and New Zealand, regained their traditional popularity. Perceived by the less worldly thinkers among us as quasi-magical lands where toilets flushed backwards, the term "counterclockwise" didn't mean what you thought it meant, the supply of natural wonders was as bottomless as an Ivy League endowment, and nothing really bad ever happened, these countries became the future escape valve for the mega-rich who liked to pile up foreign passports and stay a few steps ahead of impending disaster. Best of all, the Aussies and Kiwis spoke English, which appealed greatly to North American monoglots.

Those mega-rich… In disaster movies, or in footage of real disasters like the 9/11 attacks, you see people running desperately to escape the buildings collapsing behind them. If you're worth a billion or two, you don't have to run like those desperate people. You can make plans to escape, or even pay other people to make those plans for you; and when the time comes, they'll whisk you away to your new home, your new hideaway, in your own private plane.

Since I wasn't mega-rich or any kind of rich, I had to make alternate arrangements. This truth was brought home to me one day, in the living room of our house in a placid neighborhood in the northwestern part of Philadelphia. Amanda sat on the couch, with her face scrunched up in a copy of some magazine, while I perused the online news.

"Do you ever want to get out of here?" I asked her.

She put down the magazine, shook her blonde locks, and fixed me with her fetching, pouty gaze, those marble-like silvery-gray eyes. She wasn't smiling. Having seen this look so many times before, I braced myself for a serious interrogation.

"Get out of where?" she asked, visibly annoyed at my lack of specificity. "Refine your question. Out of this house, out of this city, this country, this life?"

"I was thinking this life in the broad sense," I said.

"You're still talking round the issue," she said. I could tell she was about to go into one of her academic improvisations. This was a habit that had been stamped on her decades ago, when she and I both attended the rather distinguished university in England (I won't say which, but it has an animal and a car company in its name) where I got my doctorate. She was the native, I was the foreigner; she was the undergraduate, I was the post-graduate; and I fell for her so hard, I thought I'd crash through the floor. On the present occasion, as on many such, I could tell that the effect of all those tutorials with leading scholars was about to make itself felt. Adopting a mock-professorial voice, she continued: "You haven't stated the question clearly enough to answer it. What is 'life in the broad sense' supposed to mean? A person who suffers from a vague sense of unease about the future, or about life in general, will never get rid of that sense if he can't define it properly. What brought on this mood, anyway?"

"I've been reading some interesting material," I said, gesturing toward my laptop. "People are talking about Uruguay and New Zealand, but the real subtext of all this talk is *escape*. They want to escape this world before civilization collapses."

"I'd quite like to go on holiday in either country," said Amanda. "But move there for good? I'll stay in the Northern Hemisphere, thank you."

"It doesn't mean you should literally move there. It's all part of a trend. There's this billionaire, one of those tech guys, for instance, I was reading about his plan. He's going to acquire citizenship in one or two of those bolt-hole countries—he can probably bribe his way in. But beyond that, he's got an 'exit project.' That's what he calls it. If these countries don't work out for him, he's going to purchase an island and move himself and all his toys there. If even *that* doesn't work out, he's gonna *build* himself an island and make it into his own private kingdom. He's got the money to do it."

"He's talking piffle," said Amanda. "Even if he isn't, what's it got to do with us? We can't buy ourselves an island."

I explained that we didn't need an island. We needed a modest piece of real estate in a safe place. The United States was huge enough that we didn't have to indulge in fantasies about Uruguay and New Zealand. The important thing was to identify and acquire our hideaway soon, before the crisis became acute and all the good places were taken or became unaffordable.

I got support from an unexpected quarter: Ethan. Living in California, the state that was frequently said to launch the trends that would eventually take hold in the rest of the country, he saw the trends before we did, and he didn't much like what he saw. As a total spectacle, life in the Golden State struck him as a comprehensive panorama of the worst contemporary trends. The environmental factors were bad enough: floods, fires and heat waves, with such bureaucratic responses as the "phased" power outages and restrictions on water use. Add to that the tent cities of homeless people springing up; the overcrowding and the absurd price increases on real estate; and on top of everything, the high-handed governance (he referred to the current governor as "a happy-face fascist dictator")—these all weighed heavily on his thoughts. Like me, he started to think about escaping. From where he stood, a remote town situated on a Great Lake sounded appealing.

I had one important stop to make today: a visit to Alvarado's Fine Foods. On the menu tonight was lamb tagine, a Moroccan dish that I'd only cooked once before. If I wanted to impress Ethan with my cooking skills, I had to get exactly the right ingredients. In Roverton, Alvarado's was the only place where I could do that.

I got to know Miguel Alvarado because I liked to cook Latin American at home, and he had set up the local Latin American food mart, back when he first moved to Roverton. As the town grew and attracted new, different kinds of people, Miguel revamped his business. It still sold Latin American food, but now it had become the local one-stop shop for food from all over the world: East Asian, South Asian, Middle Eastern, African. The demographic transformation of Roverton meant that Miguel's business boomed.

The first thing you noticed about Miguel was that his left arm was missing. This appendage had last been seen somewhere in the desert in Iraq, where Miguel had been deployed to fulfill George W. Bush's hubristic quest to turn that country into a facsimile of his beloved Texas. Even with one arm missing, he retained a quasi-military, traffic-cop demeanor, busy and no-nonsense. He once told me that staying active was the best way to deal with setbacks; the last thing he wanted to do was mope about his disability.

"Drinking and depression—no thanks, not for me."

Before moving to Roverton, Miguel ran a *pupusería* on the Southwest Side of Chicago, in a neighborhood abutting Midway Airport. This bare-bones establishment was so much a hole-in-the-wall that customers had to walk through the tiny kitchen to get to the bathroom. In the three or four seconds of their transit of this space, they were treated to the sight of two or three workers molding the corn flour and slapping it together with various fillings to make the round, stuffed patties, shortly to be fried and delivered to patrons as finished *pupusas*. In those few seconds, they might catch a glimpse of a one-armed, mustachioed middle-aged man directing the whole operation, switching between English and Spanish depending on who he talked to. Outside the restaurant, airplanes landed all day, practically scraping against the roofs of the houses on their way down. It was a strange urban panorama, these enormous steel birds whining as they eased their way down, while people went about their business below them; time and habit had made them oblivious to the constant traffic from the sky. Me, if I lived in the area, I'd be worried that one of the planes might eject a big block of frozen sewage onto my house. Imagine sitting in your living room, kicking back with a cool drink in front of the TV, only to have your chill mood shattered by an icy chunk of human excrement crashing through your roof.

I'd traveled via Midway once or twice, and I'd seen this uncomfortably close air traffic with my own eyes. As often happens, it preyed on my mind, and I decided to take steps to calm myself down. I called a representative at the Federal Aviation Administration and asked him if such incidents ever occurred.

"It happens, but it's extremely rare," said the guy.

"Really? Has anyone been killed?"

"No," he said.

"Don't you mean, 'not yet'?"

"If you want to be strict about it, yes. These discharges mostly happen in rural areas, so they crash into the ground. There have been no reported incidents of blocks of frozen excrement slamming into houses or people. Not at Midway, not ever. Why are you asking?"

An awkward question, for which I had a reply ready. "I'm a journalist writing an article about air safety."

"I'm glad I could be of assistance."

I was temporarily reassured. The possibility, however, hadn't been ruled out.

At first, I thought that Miguel might have left the neighborhood around Midway because he had similar fears. It turned out that his principal reason was economic. The Midway *pupusería* was surviving but not thriving. Miguel got word from someone—a relative or friend in Roverton's small Hispanic community, I forget who—that a culinary gap needed to be filled in this small town on the big lake, a place already tingling with the potential of a resort town or a boom town, eventual fate to be decided. The relative or friend turned out to be right, and Miguel's evolving establishment became a town fixture.

Chimes jingled as I opened the door to Alvarado's.

"Hey there, Professor Freddie," said Miguel from behind the counter, barely looking up. The TV above the counter showed highlights from a baseball game; Miguel was a Milwaukee Brewers fan.

"Hey, Miguel." I grabbed a basket and wandered around, looking for the ingredients of tonight's feast. As I surveyed and scrutinized the cuts of meat, the spices, the vegetables, and anything else that caught my eye, my academic past wouldn't leave my brain alone. I'd been reading a book about archeology and the origins of the Aryans and the Indo-European languages; the book said that if you performed the right rituals using the right words, you'd be called an Aryan; otherwise, you wouldn't. I thought that if I was able to cook the right food using the right ingredients, I could be called a chef. Otherwise, I couldn't.

I put the food basket on the counter and Miguel took a close look at it.

He said: "Don't tell me, let me guess."

"Guess what?"

"What you're cooking." He took each item out of the basket and laid it on the counter. "Let's see, we got lamb, we got couscous, we got some dried apricot... Some spices, cardamom, turmeric... It's Middle Eastern, must be."

"North African, actually. Lamb tagine!"

"I'm sure it'll be delicious," he said. I wished I could be so confident. Ethan liked spicy food, so I planned to turn the heat up. On the other hand, he had his limits... Best to opt for a medium spice level that would be acceptable to both of us, I concluded. Which didn't stop another part of my brain from saying: "Don't worry about it!"

The sports had disappeared from the TV screen, and now there was some kind of panel discussion going on, with a host and a couple of think-tank "scholars." I listened to the discussion while Miguel rang everything up. One of the sleek-looking, smooth-talking Washington wonks blathered something about America's duty to police the world and "guarantee the international system." Miguel, upon hearing this, got a look on his face as if he'd bitten into a rotten egg. He put down my couscous and glared at the screen.

"Look at that *pendejo*," he said. "His hair's perfect. He's got a nice suit on. He's really filling out that suit, I bet he goes to a lot of all-you-can-eat buffets. In DC, they put them on for people like him. They go from one event to another. They give speeches on 'guaranteeing the international system' and they scarf up all the free food they can. I'd like to see *him* in the desert, checking for IEDs. Or doing guard duty in Baghdad late at night. I respect a man who puts his money where his mouth is. This guy, he obviously puts his mouth somewhere else."

With Miguel, I knew to avoid platitudes of the "thank you for your service" kind, since they only made him angry. I nodded and grumbled my agreement.

I have my good points. My upside is that I've never done anything truly terrible, like murder or aggravated battery or swindling someone out of their life savings. I shouldn't pat myself on the back for this. Refraining from doing terrible things is merely a minimum baseline standard for evaluating personal behavior. As a form of boasting it's weak, because it implies that my positives are so meager that I have to cite negatives to build myself up. I should have this line at the top of my resume: "An unimpressive guy who can do a job without causing major problems, but don't expect much more than that." Really makes you want to hire me, doesn't it?

The downside was that mediocrity followed me wherever I went. At my college, I was once voted 4th Most Boring Professor in some sort of informal online poll. Admittedly, this was late in my career, when all the enthusiasm had been sucked out of me and I started to go through the motions, with a lazy sense of detachment infecting me in the performance of my daily tasks.

The truth was that I became the 4th Most Boring Professor because, by that time, after years of routine, I didn't give a shit. One of the reasons was that the students didn't give a shit. Most of them, that is. There were always a few exceptions. I taught a couple of sections of lower-level German. Students tended to drop it after they discovered

14

that the grammar was harder than they expected. If they had to fulfill a requirement, they transferred to some easier course. Occasionally, their objections were more practical. Sometimes, the objection was raised that "Germans all speak English, anyway." I heard this often enough that I developed a mental bullet-pointed response, which I could whip out of my memory and repeat as needed to these PowerPoint-addled youths. It amounted to 1) that's not strictly true; 2) you can't really get to know a foreign country unless you know the language; 3) knowing the language gives entry to a lot of places that would otherwise be closed to you. I don't know if this little speech had any effect in the real world. I do know, however, that it didn't do much to stem the attrition in my classes. But I was glad of the remnant, the minority of serious students who stuck around, did the work, and even showed some interest.

Another course I taught was the survey of Icelandic literature. As far as I know, the college never did an online poll to determine its most marginal and obscure course, but if it had, I'm pretty sure my Icelandic course would have won. It was in English, naturally (lucky for me, too, since my Icelandic was basic), and we read some representative works from the Middle Ages, as well as some modern items, with a novel by Halldór Laxness being the centerpiece. This class turned out to be the most rewarding thing I did at the college. The students who found their way into it were notably engaged and eccentric. Some of them had watched TV shows about Vikings and wanted to study the source material, as it were. Others were curious about Iceland or thought there was something enchanting about it. They knew about its unique geology or had listened to Björk or may even have visited the country.

During the class, I pointed out an interesting historical fact: namely, that the medieval society that produced all this literature, which we're still reading today, had a population somewhere around forty to fifty thousand people. A lot of American suburbs have that many people, and as far as I know, none of them have that kind of creative energy. To be significant, cities or even countries don't need to be big. They need to be places where certain people gather, where certain conditions exist, and where certain things have to be done. At the time I taught my Icelandic class, I'd never heard of Roverton; while I was discontented with my life, it hadn't yet occurred to me that relocating to a small town or rural outpost would be the way to put both myself and civilization back onto a meaningful path. Going through the *Laxdaela Saga*, the *Hávamál*, and Laxness' *Independent People* with my students might have helped plant the seed of escape.

By the time I resigned, I was nobody's favorite professor, mentor, or cutting-edge researcher. I couldn't be a *rising* anything, because I was too old and uninterested to be rising; all the air had gone out of my soufflé. If I were going to rise, I would have risen already, a long time ago.

Surely there must be some intellectual achievements that I can point to, some fragments I can shore against my ruins? It's true that if you gathered all my published (or merely written) work, it might fill a single slim volume. Upon opening that volume, you'd find a strange potpourri of scholarly endeavor. One item would be an article on the devolution of two Germanic languages (Scots and Low Saxon) from prestige status to the condition of "common dialects" (or "loser languages," as I cruelly thought of them). I wrote a few other linguistic and literary ruminations, which had cost me much effort at the time, but which I could scarcely remember writing nowadays. I might also include an abortive sketch for an article on the New German Cinema of the 1960s-80s, which I abandoned because I didn't have the patience to watch all those movies. Fragments indeed, and I couldn't make them fit into a coherent whole. Most fragmentary of all was the autobiographical sketch that I began but never finished. I started working on it about the time that I was seized with fear about the future and my relationship with Amanda started to deteriorate.

I could have included my doctoral dissertation. After all, it's the largest single piece of writing I've ever done, and I was officially awarded the degree of Doctor of Philosophy upon completing it. Whatever else one might think about this, we can agree that it was a major personal milestone. The problem is, I don't want to think about the damn thing. When I finished the dissertation, rather than feeling a sense of accomplishment, I felt bitter. So much time and labor expended on 300 pages of arcane, nitpicky argumentation, all of which was destined to disappear into library stacks, to be read or consulted maybe twice over the next fifty years, doubtless by some misguided individual who had, like me, made the fatal decision to pursue the obscure path of scholarship. My supervisor had helpfully put the whole thing in perspective by pointing out that I was, in effect, "writing a book," and that I should be prepared to sacrifice as much of my life as was necessary to make it a *good book*, because the career of an academic could only be properly launched by a good book. The problem with this way of thinking is that good books are generally available to the public and make some kind of impact out in the wider world, even if that impact is frequently quite modest. My book was destined to spend eternity in a sort of black hole, completely unknown to the world.

I didn't expect to turn out this mediocre. I'd done the important things right. I went to the right schools and cultivated the right people. I'd convinced the big-brained beauty queen to marry me, even though I was sure she'd wind up hitched to somebody more important, some celebrity or successful entrepreneur. But no, she settled for this obscure, modest academic, who was destined to rise no higher than untenured associate professor at a decent, middling college in the Philadelphia area. Most likely, she saw a much brighter future for me than the one I saw. I still can't figure out why. But she got wise to her misjudgment, even if she did so too late to extricate herself smoothly. Now, she was gone.

I suppose it's time to give you a few pointers about Roverton. There was a post office here early on, 1840s or even further back, no one seems to know for sure. But it was William Rover who set it up. There are no other claimants because neither the Ojibwe Indians nor the French-Canadian fur trappers used the postal service. William Rover planted the seed of Anglo-Saxondom here, in the inviting loamy Great Lakes soil.

In its early days, it was one of those towns that thought it was going to grow into something important. Other states had such places too; it was a phenomenon of the time, of the booming post-Civil War economy. The people of Port Townsend, Washington, fully expected their town to grow into one of the major West Coast port cities. In Oregon, further south along the coast, immigrants flooded into Astoria at about the same time for the same reasons. The confidence of the local commercial elites that these coastal settlements were destined for a great future had endowed them with an impressive architectural legacy: spacious Victorian houses, imposing public buildings in various shades of brick and stone, schools and libraries and entertainment venues. But in the end, the rail lines went elsewhere, the upstart port cities like Seattle and Portland and Milwaukee grabbed the lion's share of trade, and the great future never arrived.

Just like me, the younger version of Roverton believed in a great future for itself that turned out to be an illusion. Maybe that's one reason why I liked the town. Maybe its nascent revival was another reason: if it could happen to this place, could it happen to me as well?

From that hopeful time, a lot remained. The village green that was also the town square, with its gazebo in the middle and the shops and restaurants on all four sides. The modest, stout, ruddy harbor light, out in the lake at the end of the pier. All those buildings made of some color of brick and bearing a name and a date up at the top. In my early walks through the town, I liked to take note of them, like a birdwatcher or train spotter. I even thought of creating a written catalogue, in my academic way, but laziness prevented me from doing so. Quinn 1897, red brick. Schneider 1888, brown brick. Lewis & Graham 1903, built of the soft golden yellow brick known as Milwaukee Cream City. There was an opera house that wasn't big enough to stage an actual opera, built in 1890. You'd find these places all over the Great Lakes states, in the more prosperous towns, fixtures of an optimistic and expansive age. Even if they couldn't stage an opera, there would be a singer accompanied by a piano, or a brass ensemble, or the local women's choir belting out hymns or folk songs.

As was typical of these Upper Midwest towns, it was the Germans who dominated. They were all over town, they set their cultural stamp on things, but they got *real* quiet when war was declared, in 1917. Best not to stick out. There were incidents. They've been covered up, people agreed not to talk about them too loudly, but you can find the stories if you look hard enough. Carl Braun, or maybe it was Carl Wagner (you hear both names but it's the same person), was a local doctor, but someone took a dislike to him because of his national origins. Maybe they were jealous about something, and Carl being a German was merely the excuse. There's often something personal about these mob actions. Anyway, a few hotly patriotic local fellows kidnapped Carl Braun or Wagner one winter night, gagged him, threw him into a large sack, and took him to the woods. As the story goes, they were planning to tie Carl to a tree and let him get frostbitten until his hands and feet were permanently crippled, or even let him freeze to death, depending on how long they decided to leave him there (one version of the story has them tying a sign to him with the word "traitor" painted on it in Gothic script). One of the kidnappers joked that, since Carl was a doctor, he should be able to cure himself of whatever ailments they caused him. To which one of the other kidnappers—a more sober-minded fellow—said they should rethink their plan, because Roverton could hardly afford the loss of a doctor. To which a third member of the gang said: Wait a minute, I thought we were supposed to kidnap Carl Somebody-Else, the kraut who runs the grocery store; now you're telling me we abducted the town doctor? Carl got lucky: due to all the confusion and second thoughts, they let him go.

The Carl Braun/Wagner incident was one data point in the death of German America. This vast cultural realm that had once stretched from Pennsylvania to the Dakotas eventually vanished and left only certain of its artifacts behind. You can still get a big mug of beer in venues with names like Heidelberger Fass and Zum Deutschen Eck, but good luck finding a large-circulation German newspaper a la the Chicago *Abendpost*. It's also no easy thing to locate a still functioning gymnastic *Turnverein*, but they used to be in every major city and plenty of minor ones as well. In short, the sort of establishments that make up a thriving community have been reduced to a socially insignificant level. But that's the way it goes in this country. No cultural or ethnic or religious establishment is solid. It falls under influences, be they peaceful or violent, attractive or repulsive, which massage and hammer it into a form that fits the generality of the place. You can lament the loss of distinctiveness and the things that went with it. But there's not much you can do about it, except build a museum or a theme restaurant, hold a concert or lead a tour, something to memorialize that loss.

The war made everyone in Roverton an American, by reason or force. The dreams of a bustling future died; perched on its lakeside fastness, the town continued its placid course. It froze into the status of a Classic American Small Town, but I doubt the inhabitants thought they lived in some archetype, or that they had to embody some image of what the town should be. They lived their lives, and Roverton had its ups and downs, good times and bad times, over the decades.

When my fears about the future took over, and my imagination plagued me with fires, floods, earthquakes, and suffocating heat waves, I did my research. I might have previously noticed Roverton on some map or other, but I'd never given serious thought to the place. Yet now it demanded my attention. One night, discussing the situation with Ethan, I realized that it had all the elements I needed.

"It's on a Great Lake," I said. "You know what the climatologists are saying. As the Earth continues to heat up and the whole string of environmental disasters hits us, the Great Lakes region will be the best, most stable place to live. It's a traditional small town that's managed to preserve a lot of its old architecture and atmosphere. It's not some anonymous suburb full of big-box stores and it's not some clapped-out ghost town. It's got that Germanic history, all those Germans and Scandinavians left their mark, so it's culturally compatible with me, the scholar of Germanic languages. It'll be a good place to escape to. Not to escape: to start over."

"I've done some research, too," said Ethan. "I've decided that Roverton needs a new brewpub. They have some traditional bars that serve craft beers. What they don't have is a pure brewpub, where all the beer is brewed right there on the premises. That's a gap waiting to be filled."

Ethan was right, but I already thought along different lines. Bearing in mind what I told the eccentric students in my Icelandic literature class, that such a tiny country had produced so much lasting literature, I thought it was time to give Roverton a second chance to make a name for itself. As the world deteriorated, a few of us strivers would keep civilization going, far from the cities and other centers of decay. Roverton could be our early medieval monastery, where we hid from the barbarians and the plagues, to cultivate things of lasting value.

Hugh MacDiarmid, kick-starting a modern Scots-language poetry early in the last century, "kent that Ecclefechan stood / As pairt o' an eternal mood." I knew nothing about Ecclefechan, so I looked it up. This village in the south of Scotland was the hometown of Thomas Carlyle—who, whatever one might think of his writings and ideas, was a man of some weight and influence. Robert Burns, known all over the world, once composed a song about a lass from Eccelefechan. According to its Wikipedia entry, fewer than a thousand people lived in the village. Roverton was a metropolis by comparison.

Could Roverton be our Ecclefechan? Could it be "pairt o' an eternal mood?" If so, we might one day have things to boast about.

"I like what you've done with the kitchen, Dad," said Ethan. His face became shiny with anticipation as I brought the tagine and hummus and set them down in front of him.

I looked around in mild bewilderment. "All I did was buy the place and move some stuff into it. But I'm glad you like it, anyway."

"It looks austere, but welcoming," said Ethan. "The white walls and marble flooring give it a feeling of both modernity and permanence. But it's fun to sit at this big old-fashioned trestle table. You could have a couple of people here, or up to ten. It works well for both situations." Being in the food and beverage business, Ethan paid closer attention to these things than I did. Ambience was very important to him. He took a long, slow gulp of the red wine; his pale face, with its close-cropped beard the brownish-blond color of amber ale, heated up with a blush. He was dressed in the casual-serious style favored by people in his circle. His T-shirt was immaculately clean and as dark as the blackest stout or porter. He wore cargo pants of a light golden hue, reminiscent of a blonde Belgian ale. Thank God, I thought, that there were no tattoos on him yet. I'd impressed on him the notion that you shouldn't do something to your body that you couldn't undo.

Cool jazz (West Coast division, Gerry Mulligan blowing his mellow sax) played softly in the background as we got to work on our meal.

Ethan expressed his approval of my tagine. This was a relief, because Ethan never lied or softened his opinion about food. Like ambience, it was of fundamental importance to him.

I was glad that the path he'd chosen in life was working out. The brewery was a much more congenial environment for him than the classroom; he'd mastered it and made a home of it, like a medieval craftsman in his workshop. Getting to that point had been a matter of trial and error. Ethan tried college; he really did. That's the word he used, "tried," like a slice of pumpkin pie or an unfamiliar flavor of coffee. It didn't imply a strong intention to succeed. As he lost even the modest level of interest in academics he'd initially manifested, he turned to the bottle for consolation. In fact, he turned to many bottles. He liked beer the best. This was a relief to me because it meant that he avoided the hard stuff that could really bring you down. I had faint concerns that he'd become sedentary and develop a beer belly, but he patiently explained to me that it wasn't the beer that created the belly; it was the food that beer drinkers ate as they drank. Still, no one would say he needed to put on weight.

But it wasn't only beer that caused Ethan to give up on college. There were other factors, both online and in the so-called real world. But is that distinction even worth making any more? The real world and the cyber one have merged; they interact and interpenetrate. Symbiosis has been achieved. In some cases, though, the distinction is still useful.

In the real world, Ethan was skeptical that college would do him any good. He was willing to try it for a year or two, because it was the expected thing for people of our class, and because it wouldn't cost him anything. Not for him were the part-time jobs of exhausted go-getters, who needed good grades in that organic chemistry or accounting class to realize their professional dreams. No, Ethan had grown up in cramped quarters stuffed with books and other arcana of learning, listening to Daddy and Mummy talk about philosophers and writers. He'd absorbed the idea that the pursuit of one's personal intellectual interests was the point of life, rather than the mad scramble to make as much money as possible. His attitude was aloof, lofty, and detached; and that was at least partly our fault, as his parents. The only problem was, he didn't have quite enough of an interest in the world of ideas to make a living out of it. He'd absorbed the polish of our environment without the depth that we strove to impart.

In the online world, Ethan got sucked into a vortex. This was where his real intellectual life took place. That is, if one may dignify it with the term "intellectual." The bland nostrums of the national media and the received wisdom of teachers and mentors couldn't hold Ethan, not after he discovered a world of shitlords, edgelords, dissidents, alt-this and neo-that and retro-whatever. I'd discussed some of this with him, and I got a sense that he'd gone farther into that world, and got stuck in it more firmly, than he wanted to admit. But he was willing to talk to me about a few of his favorites, and the ideas that had rubbed off on him.

"I think we talked about this guy, Boldmug, last time we met," he said. "You said he sounded interesting. Did you ever look into him in more detail?"

"Oh yeah, Boldmug," I said. "How can I forget a name like that?"

"That's not his real name. He came out of Silicon Valley; he had a regular job in the computer world. He used the pen name because he didn't want to be discovered. But somebody blew his cover and now he's out and proud."

"Curious way to put it."

"Yeah," said Ethan. "Anyway, his ideas already had some underground currency. Some of his followers were rich and connected. He had a cushion." In Ethan's telling, this Boldmug character promoted the most retrograde philosophy one could imagine. What's more, he pushed it to ultramodern tech nerds and the like, people who pride themselves on being trendy and up-to-date, but who probably wouldn't last a day in the ancient world, or in some cruel autocratic society, where they'd be hauling massive stones for fortifications and pacifying rebellious tribes rather than hanging out in the coffee shop. The basis of Boldmug's philosophy was the superiority and inviolability of hierarchy. Boldmug stated that hierarchical, traditional societies had mastered the art of sustaining themselves, and were therefore superior to frivolous liberal-minded states like those that made up the modern Western world. He pointed to such examples as the Inca Empire, the Abbasid Caliphate, the Eastern Roman Empire (Byzantium), and various Chinese dynasties, as having upheld tradition for centuries before being destroyed, usually by some outside force. He was particularly fond of the Indian caste system because it had lasted thousands of years, despite being modified by successive regimes in India. He took some of his inspiration also from Latin America, with its quasi-feudal history. Boldmug believed that America was already a caste society and should formalize that reality as a matter of policy. When the Dictatorship finally arrived (he always capitalized this term), it would be the first duty of the new Dictator to declare the caste system to be America's new governing idea, replacing our worn-out Constitution. Boldmug thought such a policy would be helpful to potential immigrants (as he said in an interview: "Wouldn't it be great if they already knew what caste they should belong to when they got here?").

In performance of my monitoring duty as a parent, I looked into Boldmug's works on the Internet, as collected in an extensive archive. I was surprised that Ethan had managed to glean anything at all from them. Boldmug was one of the most incomprehensible graphomaniacs I'd ever encountered (and as someone who once had to read a lot of undergraduate waffle and bloviation, that's saying quite a lot). He believed that one shouldn't use a hundred words when a thousand would do. Plainly, he was one of those authors who believed that opacity and profundity were natural companions, and that turgidity, wordiness, and obscurity were the marks of a great thinker. This might have been the only thing that was clear about him. Already, he'd spawned several bloggers and vloggers who purported to interpret his work for an intrigued but befuddled audience.

"C'mon," I said. "The guy's spouting nonsense. Some of his ideas are interesting, but that's usually the case with self-proclaimed gurus of this type. They use the truth, whether obvious or overlooked, as a way of dragging you into their worldview. Plus, he needs an editor."

"I've gotten over my Boldmug phase, actually," said Ethan. "He did his work for me. He gave me some new perspectives. The rest is up to me."

"The rest being what? You're going to achieve Nietzschean *Übermensch* status by brewing beer?"

"You become an oober mensch by becoming the best at what you do. If I'm the best brewer, why not?"

"But he's going on about hereditary caste systems and everybody knowing their place, from now into eternity. He thinks that's a *good* thing, and that social mobility is an evil that should be suppressed. At least, that's what I think he's saying, as far as I can tell from the word salads he creates. You don't come from a hereditary caste or guild of master brewers. Hell, me and Mummy, we set you up for the college path, since that was normal for people like you. You're breaking with tradition. You're an individualist. What would Boldmug think of that?"

Ethan was quiet for a few seconds, rolling his eyes as if searching for an answer. "Like I said, Boldmug gave me some perspectives. He came out of Silicon Valley, and I lived in L.A., remember. We've both lived in California, we see the trends. The caste society is coming, and it's going to be implemented there first." I must have looked disturbed, because he hastened to add: "But I'm not a disciple of him or anything like that." I could tell from the expression on his face that he wasn't sure about this. He added: "I'm sorry if I let you down."

This was unexpected. "Let me down? How?"

"You know, the whole college thing." Not wanting to make eye contact with me, he stared at the table, at his fork.

"The college thing? You let me down?" I raised my hands in mock surrender. "The deal was that you *try* college; we weren't going to force you to finish. No need to apologize."

I was being sincere. The younger generation already had a different attitude to higher education than mine did. For the young folks, it was a much more fluid concept, more pragmatic and hands-on. Yawning in a classroom made no sense when lectures by top scholars were available on YouTube. Too many required courses were filler material, of no interest to students who already knew what job they wanted. The question of money hung over everything and had become more acute than ever.

Yet at the same time, I felt that Ethan missed out. If he wasn't going to read serious books in college, he should do it in his own time. It was part of being an adult, of having a sound basis for understanding the world. It would—at least in theory—protect him to some degree from the multitude of frauds and charlatans (online as well as off) who captured so many gullible minds.

I told him about a former colleague of mine, a professor. Before he entered grad school, he spent a year working at several low-level jobs. One of them was the night shift at a small hotel, off the beaten track, which meant he had lots of free time. He read so many books on that shift, he told me, that he felt they should give him an extra degree for all that reading. It gave him a depth of knowledge that helped carry him all the way through graduate school.

"That's a nice story, Dad," said Ethan. "But you know, we don't have that much free time at the brewery." He took an ostentatious swig of the wine; it was like a signal he was changing the subject. "In fact, my deep thoughts have been going in a different direction now. More ambitious."

I was intrigued. "Oh, really. What might that be?"

He pointed at his plate. "You did a good job with this Moroccan dish. But I was thinking: what does Morocco have to do with the Great Lakes?"

"Nothing. So what?"

"This big region that we've chosen to live in. Because we want there to be a future worth living in. To have such a future, we need to implement a *strategic vision* of what that future will be. We need to innovate, to be agile in our leadership."

He'd been reading books, after all. But they were books about business. That much was clear from the jargon he used.

I cut in: "What's *your* strategic vision?"

He sat back in his chair, raised his gaze to the ceiling, and pronounced: "The creation of Great Lakes cuisine!"

"Please expound," I said.

"Nobody talks about Great Lakes cuisine. That's because it doesn't exist as a creation, as a tradition, as something that people know about. Look on the Internet. What do people think 'Great Lakes cuisine' is? Mac and cheese, potato salad, Dutch pancakes, baked potato wedges. Stuff you eat while watching sports on TV. Where's the imagination? Where's the innovation? If there's great cooking in this region, it comes from somewhere else. It's French or Italian or Indian. Nothing's rooted specifically *here*. That's an opportunity. That's a big opportunity, because this region is going to boom. Wait till the climate refugees start showing up in large numbers. They'll demand more than potato salad. We have the chance to put our own culinary stamp on things." He paused to take another swig of wine.

"That's a noble ambition," I said. My mind turned over the question of how many things you could do with whitefish. What exquisite creations could be fashioned using simple ingredients: eggs, potatoes, various cheeses. Surely, if Ethan put his mind to this task in a serious manner, he'd make a success of it. It would resonate in the wider world in a way that his craft brewery wouldn't. The creation of a new, distinctive type of cuisine would be a minor triumph for civilization. Wasn't that ultimately what we were trying to do in this little town— keep civilization going, despite all the forces acting against it?

The cool jazz CD came to an end, and I got up to look for a suitable replacement, while removing the dirty plates from the table. I happened to have Mike Oldfield's *Tubular Bells* lying there, so I popped it in.

As the tinkling, hypnotic music started up, I said: "People of my generation associate this music with demonic possession."

Ethan smiled crookedly. "Why?"

"It was used on the soundtrack of a movie called *The Exorcist*. It was about, well, being possessed by demons. When I was growing up, it was considered one of the scariest movies ever." I was pretty sure that Ethan had never heard of the movie. His blank look convinced me I was right.

While the music played and we made small talk, I improvised some dessert from a couple of slices of cake, plus some ice cream. I sat down again, and while we tucked into it, Ethan asked: "Have you heard anything from Mummy lately?"

I put down my spoon. "It's been a while. She's still in Europe, doing whatever it is she's doing. Some sort of 'foundation' work."

Ethan looked sad. The music was working up to the point where the Master of Ceremonies, voiced by Viv Stanshall, named each instrument in sequence as it played the main tune.

Ethan said: "You really don't talk to her very often, do you? I'm probably more in touch with her than you are."

Viv Stanshall announced a grand piano.

"I think you're right," I said, glumly.

"Do you think we could, um, get her to visit us here again? I mean, you're not actually divorced yet, are you?"

I hemmed and hawed. It was a touchy subject, but I owed Ethan an answer. I'd never been totally straight with him about my mental state, and how that contributed to our split. Plus, I didn't know what Amanda had been telling Ethan; perhaps he knew more than he let on. I said that I hoped she'd come and stay with us here in Roverton; and no, we weren't divorced, strictly speaking.

As Viv Stanshall announced the slightly distorted guitars, I looked at Ethan, he looked at me, and at that moment I think both of us felt awkward. Neither of us wanted to go further into the subject. I looked for a way out.

"Getting back to what you were saying earlier. I really like this Great Lakes cuisine idea. It's one of the more creative concepts I've heard recently."

Ethan nodded and spooned the last of the ice cream into his mouth, just as the tubular bells rang out with the main tune.

Let me present to you—in a style probably inspired by Ingmar Bergman—some scenes from a marriage.

Scene 1. You can picture me as a mopey, bespectacled and depressed graduate student, not eating as well as I should, dragging my lanky frame through the streets, clad in a threadbare black topcoat. I've spent a dispiriting day in the library, hunting through documents in various languages in search of some tiny detail I need to include in my thesis. It was something I absolutely had to do, although I often struggle with a nagging sense that nobody really needs to know anything more about the development of German dialects in certain parts of Eastern Europe, a legacy of the *Drang nach Osten.*

Experiences like these—fervid hunts after meaningless minutiae—are causing me to doubt whether I'm suited to academic life. In this state of mild depression, I require some cheering up. I see a flier on one of the university buildings announcing some kind of charity event. Nowadays, I can't recall exactly who the event was supposed to benefit—whether it was the Tibetans or the indigenous people of the Amazon or the underprivileged youth of this very city. But I know that such events tend to attract young people, and that an amount of free food and drink is often laid out for them. Free, that is, if you're a miser who avoids making a voluntary contribution to defray expenses.

I can spot the graduate students easily: they're older, and some of them look awkward as they interact with the undergraduates. Me, I feel too deflated to care about the impression I make. I'm only interested in a snack and some company.

Among the undergraduates, there's one young lady who stands out instantly. She's a tall, athletic-looking girl (a tennis or track look, nothing that requires heavy lifting) with long, wavy blonde hair. She has "presence," in the sense that if you walk into a gathering of twenty or thirty people, she's the one you notice first. She approaches my pathetic self; I see the nametag attached to her fraying sky-blue sweater, with the words "Amanda Harding, Hertford." This last name is her residential college, not her place of origin. That (as I later find out) is somewhere in the West Midlands.

She greets me with a big smile and asks me some basic questions about myself, which I'm happy to answer. From the perspective of today, I can't remember exactly what we talked about. What I do remember is that I wanted to bask in her angelic blonditude for a while—such a refreshing sensation after spending those stale hours in the library. In addition to being friendly, she appeals strongly to my aesthetic sense, with silvery-gray eyes of a shade I've never quite seen before, and a fetching way of crinkling her mouth when she's trying to be humorous.

It turns out she is "reading PPE" as they say—i.e., she's an undergraduate in her second year, doing the most popular degree course at that institution (Politics, Philosophy and Economics). The broadness of the degree means that she can talk about pretty much anything, even if it's often on a superficial level. We talk, mostly on a superficial level, about various things. As I say goodbye (having exchanged contact info), I conclude that the day wasn't wasted after all.

Scene 2. Several years have passed. I've taken up my academic position. Amanda's doing an office job—a corporate communications, training-related thing—but she finds the work environment brainless and would like to get back into the educational world. Outside of work, she finds plenty of outlets for the play of the intellect.

On this occasion, we're sitting in a restaurant in the Old City neighborhood of Philadelphia, a location where 18th-century architecture meets 21st-century culinary trends. We're having a night out with an academic colleague. Let's call him Professor Zilch. He teaches psychology. He's older than we are, and has a classic professor look— gray beard, round specs, tweed jacket. We've wandered onto the subject of his professional specialization.

"Do you ever really wonder how old psychology is as a real discipline?" I ask. "I think it goes about as far back as Hume's *Treatise of Human Nature*. Most people, if they think of that book at all, remember Hume's argument about causation and the unpredictability of events. But most of the book is taken up with his studies of personality. It has 'human nature' in the title, after all!"

Professor Zilch warns that I've opened a big can of worms, and that to properly answer this question, you have to define your terms strictly before you proceed.

"I do allow that Hume wrote a lot about the specific mental reactions of individuals to stimuli, but I wouldn't consider that to constitute the origins of psychological thought in the modern scientific sense. You can trace that thread all the way back to ancient times."

This subject is turning out to be too big for me. I'm regretting having opened my mouth when Amanda cuts in.

"Hume's ideas about personality are mere elaboration," she states. "You've got to go all the way back to Aristotle, to the *Rhetoric*. That's the book where you find the first categorization of individuals into personality types. Remember how Whitehead said that all modern philosophy is nothing more than 'footnotes to Plato'? He should've remembered to add Aristotle as well!"

"Nicely put," says Professor Zilch. "I'm glad you mentioned Aristotle. One could also cite the theoretical work of Thales and Hippocrates. I *do* like that quote from Whitefield."

"Whitehead," says Amanda gently.

"It looks like I was off by only a couple of thousand years," I say.

Professor Zilch flashes a condescending smile at me. "You're a sapient fellow, Fred. For that reason, I'm surprised that you'd make such a bold statement about psychology."

"Oh, I've dabbled in it, you know." I'm more interested in impressing Amanda with my knowledge than in discussing the subject with Professor Zilch. I look over at Amanda and see her stifling a smirk.

Later at home, we're eating ice cream and watching a forgettable movie on TV, like a stereotypical long-settled married couple.

I tell Amanda: "Professor Zilch is from an earlier generation of academics. The ones who use big words to plug the gaps in their knowledge."

"He sounded quite knowledgeable to me," she says.

"His interpretation of Hume is off, given that the *Treatise* has been described as the founding document of cognitive science, by no less an authority than Jerry Fodor."

Amanda gives me an incredulous look. "Why didn't you tell him that?"

"Oh," I say, throwing invisible confetti into the air. "It's what the French call *l'esprit de l'escalier*. Staircase wit. You know, when you think of your response too late."

"Yes, I know the phrase. I also know you have better things to do than get into these verbal duels with Professor Zilch."

She's right. We spend the rest of the evening cuddling warmly on the couch, watching the stupid movie and letting the mellow ambience wipe away my intellectual concerns. It's peaceful enough that I fall asleep there and don't wake up until two o'clock in the morning.

Scene 3. This one takes place much later. We're still together, but it's increasingly clear to me that we're holding on, cruising on autopilot, going through the motions, or whatever cliché you want to apply to our situation. Our one child, Ethan, having rejected the path we planned for him, is brewing beer in California. My career feels as if it's at a dead end. Amanda's been working as a social science teacher at one of the local private schools, the sort of place where modestly affluent parents pay fees to keep their children safely away from the hellish public schools. But she's not too happy there. Discontent with our situation is starting to spill over into our conversations.

We're sitting in the kitchen, where we have finished breakfast. Amanda's preparing to go to the grocery store and asks if I need anything.

"Can't think of anything beyond the usual," I say.

She fixes me with a serious look. "Are you sure? Don't you want twenty or thirty tins of beans, or maybe the same amount of tinned soup? Or perhaps a big bag of rice?"

"Huh?" I ask. "Why would I want all that stuff?"

"Why wouldn't you, Freddie? You've been talking about how you need to prepare for the end of the world. If we have to live in an underground bunker, won't we need those things? You know, non-perishable consumables, or whatever you call them." She fixes me with that look again, demanding a response.

I sip my coffee gravely.

"Don't worry about it," I say.

"It's difficult not to, when I have to hear about it so often. Have you picked out your bunker yet?"

I try to explain. It's not about picking out a bunker, it's about being prepared for the worst. I see I'm not making much of an impression. She's heard it all before. I give up. Then, I remember something that I wanted to mention—a way to change the subject and put her on the defensive at the same time. "You left the milk carton out last night. I sniffed it, and ew! It was awful. Can't be salvaged. I threw it away."

A troubled look crosses her middle-aged yet still attractive face. "It was going bad, anyway. We didn't lose any milk by leaving it out."

"Yeah, well seeing it out here, standing proudly next to the coffee machine, gave me hope. I thought I'd use it. Almost spoiled my coffee; good thing I sniffed it before pouring it in. If you'd thrown it away instead of leaving it out, you wouldn't have raised and then shattered my hopes."

"Your hopes for a *carton* of *milk*?" The sense of disbelief that she manages to put into those last three words is impressive.

"Yes, I had high hopes for that milk. It was a reminder of better times. It carried a hint of promise, a breath of inspiration. It pointed the way forward to a renewal of our joint life—a life that appears to have slipped off the path of righteousness."

The troubled look on her face is morphing into an expression of alarm. "Are you all right there, Freddie?"

"I've never felt better in my life," I say.

She gets up and starts walking away.

"Thank you for another enlightening lecture, Professor Sarcasm," she says as she leaves the kitchen.

"Get some milk at the store," I say. I'm thinking: *why can't I keep my big mouth shut?* My physical self is sitting calmly at the table, but my mental self is experiencing a mix of confusion and embarrassment. Petty arguments and exchanges of this kind have become distressingly common. I know I should refrain from initiating them, but sometimes I can't help myself.

When Amanda decided to take off, I knew it was a serious decision. That's because Amanda was the last person in the world who would make a snap decision and immediately follow through with it. She was accustomed to weigh, ponder, consider, and do all kinds of planning when it came to major life decisions. Resolutions made in the heat of the moment, or under some surge of passion, were foreign to her. For this reason, I expected that our unsettled situation would continue for some time.

Those last few months in Philadelphia imbued me with a peculiar feeling. It was like a slow-growing nausea that began at a very low level and gradually grew from there, to the point where I could no longer ignore it. It was hard to determine to what extent this nausea was the fault of my immediate surroundings, as opposed to a manifestation of my growing fears concerning the world at large.

Ever since I took up my academic post, we'd lived in one of the nicer neighborhoods in the northwest of the city, a long-settled area with plenty of nature and greenery and an almost suburban atmosphere. It was the kind of self-contained urban neighborhood that felt like a small, detached city. In a place like Philly, you have to careful about what streets you walk down at night. That had never been a major concern in our part of the city, but I started to get worried. If social collapse was right around the corner, the rot was bound to spread, even to our zone of relative safety.

It was about this time that I started talking to Amanda more frequently about moving out. At first it was about escape, not about escaping to any particular place. But as I continued talking about it, she showed the irritation at this topic that I've mentioned. What I didn't talk about in as much detail was my discontent with the college where I taught.

One day, I was invited by one of the academic deans to discuss some matters of personal and professional concern. This individual—whose last name, coincidentally, was Dean—was someone I didn't know very well, although we'd interacted previously on a couple of occasions. Dean Dean was a completely respectable-looking middle-aged white guy who was bald on top and wore heavy-looking horn-rimmed glasses. When you talked to him, he had a habit of hunching his head down defensively and giving you a blank look, which reminded me of a turtle. I launched the meeting with an attempt at some light humor.

"Dean can also be a first name," I observed. "It's too bad your parents didn't name you that. Then you would be Dean Dean Dean."

He stared at me and said blankly, "No, they named me Charles." It seemed that Dean Dean was not in a joking mood on this day. We passed on to matters of substance. Dean Dean laid it out for me straight: the Germanic Department was going to have to cut some courses. I was destined to become even more irrelevant than I already was.

"I'm afraid New German Cinema will have to go," said Dean Dean. "Today's students aren't as interested in film as an art form anymore. At least, not the way they used to be." Sadly, I had to agree. The handful of students that I counted on to show up for that class seemed to be there only because they regarded it as an easy A. They didn't strike me as the types who would have crowded into the ramshackle art-house cinemas of my youth. They lacked the required sense of artistic camaraderie. It was difficult to imagine them sitting on folding chairs and watching blobby prints of badly subtitled movies, as I and many others had done, all those years ago. They also seemed to lack an understanding of chronology, or of history in general. More than once I was asked why the course was called *New* German Cinema when all the movies we watched dated from the 1960s-80s. Surely, I could find some interesting German movies that were newer than that?

"That's what the movement was called at the time," was my canned response. "It was new in the sense that it was a reaction against the older way of making movies." They didn't seem convinced by this explanation. To them, new meant new, and nothing else. As if that weren't enough, they seemed disengaged when watching visual images on anything but a computer screen, or preferably a smartphone.

One occasion stood out in my mind. I screened a DVD of Werner Herzog's *Aguirre, the Wrath of God* for the class. I told them they should watch this high-quality DVD release on a big enough screen to appreciate the visual effects. About fifteen minutes into the film, one of the students raised his hand and asked me if we could watch it at double speed, because the film's pace was too slow. I hit the pause button. I asked the student if he would be glad to spin a Beatles album at 45 rpm. This turned out to be an ineffective counterargument. I think the student vaguely knew who the Beatles were, but he had no idea what "45 rpm" meant.

I tried again: "Do you want all the people in the movie to sound like they're on helium?" This got a laugh, but I had the feeling that nobody was really on my side. None of the students spoke up for aesthetic values, for taking the time to appreciate the film as it was meant to be experienced. They wanted to get through the assignment as quickly as possible. Perhaps I'm libeling the youth of today with these generalizations, based merely on a small sample. I make no apologies for that, because by that time I'd lost interest in the youth of today.

We discussed the literature courses. At least one of them was destined for the chopping block. I was invited to give my own input on which one would be the victim, but I had a hard time deciding. Dean Dean hit me with something that I should have expected but didn't think would ever happen. He suggested axing the Icelandic course, my personal favorite.

"We doubt there's enough student interest to keep it going. We've gotten some complaints that it's not diverse enough, in terms of the course content. 'Just a bunch of old Viking-looking white guys,' was one of the objections."

"Of course, it's not diverse enough," I sputtered. "What do they expect? Iceland is one of the least diverse countries on earth. That goes double for the Middle Ages, when most of this literature was written. There's nothing I can do about that."

Dean Dean hunched his head down a couple of inches in his turtle-like manner, and looked warily to the left and to the right, as if concerned that somebody might be listening.

He said, in a voice softer than before: "I know it and you know it. We both know it. But I can't say that flat out to the faculty senate and—God forbid—any student activists on this campus. They'll rip my head off and play soccer with it." In that moment, I felt sorry for Dean Dean. He was the very model of a modern academic administrator. He was someone who enjoyed certain perks of office—a decent salary, a feeling of importance in the community, subsidized travel, and various other bureaucratic benefits—and the only things he had to give up were independence of mind and any desire to stand out. I'm no hero, and I could see myself taking that deal if someone offered it to me. Running away from difficult situations is more my style. I saw that I and the Dean formed a small community of interest, rooted in timidity; we had reasons to help each other out.

After we'd engaged in a little more mutual commiseration, I began, in my fumbling manner, to improvise a way back to contemporary relevance.

"Actually, now that I think about it, Iceland is a little more diverse historically than you may think. Uniquely among Nordic populations, Icelanders have a lot of Irish in them. It's my understanding—you can correct me if I'm wrong—that Irish people weren't considered 'properly' white until quite recently, at least in America. The reason there were Irish people in medieval Iceland in the first place is because they were taken there as slaves by their Norwegian masters. In fact, one of the characters in the *Laxdaela Saga*—which is one of the texts in my course—is Melkorka, an Irish slave who turns out to be the daughter of a king back in Ireland. You've got the slavery angle there. Melkorka is a strong woman character, the kind who would appeal to a feminist readership. Also, there's Norwegian and Danish imperialism, if you want to play the post-colonial angle."

When I'd finished my creative massage of historical facts, Dean Dean looked at me quizzically. "You're telling me that Icelanders can be spun as 'non-white'?"

"Sure. Why not? Remember what I said about students having no understanding of history. This means they see everything through the lens of the here and now. Spinning Icelanders as non-white will be easier than you think."

Dean Dean was silent for a few seconds. He spoke. "Fred, you may be a clever guy to come up with something like that, but I really don't think the faculty senate is going to go for it. I mean, it's so obviously absurd."

"Hell, if the president of Mexico—who's a white guy, as far as I can tell—can be spun as a so-called person of color, why not do the same thing for the Icelanders?"

"I had no idea," said the Dean. "Icelanders are a bunch of paddies. Who ever thought of such a thing?" He burped out a laugh. He seemed more relaxed, as if he didn't have to wear a mask. Abruptly, he turned serious again. "The problem is that I would have to make that case in front of the faculty senate. You know these people as well as I do. Be honest: do you see them going for it? I sure as hell don't."

I had to agree with him. Playing by their rules could only get you so far, but refusing to play by their rules, in a setting where they made the rules, could get you ostracized. If I stayed where I was, I would be looking at an even more marginalized and increasingly precarious existence. I comforted myself with the thought that I'd already identified an avenue of escape. I had to bear in mind that Dean Dean may not have had such avenues available to him.

We talked further, and it turned out that Dean Dean was a working-class guy from South Philly. His father had been an electrician, while his mother stayed home and took care of young Charles ("Hey, you can call me Chuck") and two other children. A family could live on one income in those days, I thought wistfully. His parents encouraged him to get on the track to a profession and go as far and as high as he could manage. Such was the concept of the American Dream, as it was believed in and pursued by people of his class. It was a practical ethos that could still be found among many of the college's students, especially those of immigrant and working-class backgrounds.

Dean Dean had made the system work for him. His choices had paid off. He'd reached the upper levels of an admittedly modest hierarchical structure.

"At this point in my life, I can't rock the boat," he said. "No, sir. No boat-rocking for me. If the boat needs to be rocked, let someone else rock it. My personal boat has to make it to shore in one piece. Retirement's a few years away, and I don't need the hassle." He was trapped in his silver cage.

I told him "I understand," and we left it at that. Shortly thereafter, I said goodbye to the city where I'd lived for many years. I parked my car in Old City and took a walk for about an hour. My plan was to look at the historic buildings and monuments one last time, but scenes from my own life kept intruding. Walking past Independence Hall, I was reminded of Amanda's joking comments about the "traitors to the King" who established a new nation in that building (at least, I think she was joking). In front of Christ Church, with its towering white steeple, I thought about the gatherings we'd enjoyed in nearby restaurants and bars, with friends and academic colleagues. I've found that moving is always a melancholy experience even if you're glad to make the move. That's because you always leave something of your life in the place you're moving from, and the feeling of separation can be bittersweet. I topped off this farewell tour by heading to my favorite cheesesteak vendor on Market Street, because I knew there would be no proper cheesesteaks in Roverton or anywhere else in the country, and I wanted the last food in my mouth in the City of Brotherly Love to be a righteous and irreplaceable sandwich with all the fixings.

When you order a genuine Philly cheesesteak in genuine Philly, you're likely to be asked a question consisting of one word: "With?" This word, as spoken in this specific context (and usually pronounced *wid*), means: "Do you want grilled onions with it?" If you want to take the initiative, you ask up front for a "Whiz with." This means "I want my cheesesteak to be made with Cheez Whiz rather than provolone, and yes, I'd like onions with it." The last words I pronounced within the city limits of Philadelphia were: "Whiz with, please."

On the long drive to my new home in Wisconsin, I had a Werner Herzog film on my mind once again. This time it was not *Aguirre* but *Stroszek*, a film which had some disturbing parallels to my own situation. The title character and his girlfriend live a precarious life in the big city (Berlin in this case). He's an eccentric street musician who's been in and out of institutions, she's a prostitute. They suffer harassment and violence. With another eccentric, they move to America (specifically to small-town Wisconsin) to start over and make a new life for themselves.

In Wisconsin, there's no violence inflicted on them, but this time it's lack of money that ruins their lives. One scene that stuck in my mind was the banker's visit to Stroszek, to tell him that his mobile home is being repossessed. The banker is like a banking version of Dean Dean: brisk, polite, a stickler for rules, and clearly hating what he has to do. On the run from his troubles at the end of the film, Stroszek winds up in an amusement park, where he fires off a shot. We don't see who or what the shot is aimed at, but suicide is a possibility. Poor Stroszek is a man who can't live safely in Germany, so he tries again in America, traditionally a locus of renewal for European misfits. That doesn't work out either. Maybe he should have gone to a big city instead of the back of beyond, but he fails to explore that option. The simplest and saddest conclusion is that Stroszek is one of those unfortunates who can't make his life work anywhere.

Here I was now, on the road from the big city to the small town, to the same state where Stroszek's last attempt at happiness came to naught. Naturally, I hoped things would turn out differently for me.

My former life would come flooding back to me, in dreams, or in solitary reveries, or when I walked through the town or lay in bed in the morning, too detached from the urgencies of life to force myself up. It was an urban life, a busy world. I'd escaped it, and on the surface, I was glad of it. Yet some part of me wanted to go back.

As I drifted off to sleep at night, I imagined a city. It didn't have to be a city I'd ever experienced. It could be Rome at the time of Christ, or Vienna at the dawn of the twentieth century. But it had to be a city where important things happened, a place that stamped its imprint on my mind. Writers, since they wrote things down and left their impressions behind, were typically the best companions. I walked with Dostoevsky through St. Petersburg scouting the eventual path to be taken by his hero Raskolnikov; or followed Theodore Dreiser as he took notes on the booming industries of Chicago; or tracked gloomy old Herman Melville in Manhattan as he wound his way to work at the customs house, an office drone and an apparent failure in life. (Melville, being only an *apparent* failure, was a particular inspiration to me.) Sights, smells, sounds—horse manure, sweat both animal and human, chatter and cries in various languages, the rough clothing of a working class now passed into history, soot and smoke, cobbled streets, buildings of brick and stone—accompanied me on my way into nocturnal oblivion.

In Roverton, there were other ways to stay in touch with my former city life. I could crank up the loud urban music on my stereo, lie back, and imagine. It didn't matter if it was Elliott Carter's clangorous orchestral works, or some smoky jazz delivered to me from the Village Vanguard, captured on tape in 1961 and thence available forever. It all had the stamp of the Big City on it, the turbulent life and motion, the sights, smells and noises. While it played, I might take the occasional glance outside and see old Mrs. Westerberg slowly walking her dog, who poked about in the clumps of grass. Across the street some kids had set up a lemonade or orangeade or something-ade stand, keeping the age-old tradition going. Every two or six or nine and a half minutes, or whenever, a car would go drifting by.

It was the life I'd chosen. By and large I was happy with it. But when you foreclose on the city, the metroplex, even the suburbs, you rule out possibilities. This didn't upset me. I'd made my decision; I was determined to live with it.

Still, those evenings when it was just me and Bruce at home could get boring and dispiriting. A visit to Jackie O'Reilly's emporium was always a good idea when I couldn't think of anything else to do. In any case, I needed some entertainment for tonight, and maybe some company as well.

Jackie's Light & Sound stood on a gentle slope above the local state route, where you entered Roverton's downtown. The road led to the outside world, which meant that traffic could be intense at times. Mostly it consisted of the locals' cars and pickup trucks, but occasionally you saw a big tractor-trailer lumbering along, bringing its goods to the other towns along the coast. Once or twice, I saw platoons of motorcyclists roaring down the road—whether gangs or clubs, I don't know the proper terminology—zooming at high speed and high volume. Possibly these groups were from around here, although sometimes we got adventurous cross-country riders coming through.

Light & Sound had originally been a video rental place, back in the nineties. Due to the entrepreneurial vision of its owner, you could still rent movies there, even though video rental places had become extinct in most of the country. Jackie had expanded the store in several ways to keep it going. Light & Sound survived not because it was a place to rent videos, but as a nod to nostalgia. Jackie sold used books and records; she also sold various random knickknacks, like homemade art objects, old theatrical and movie posters, peculiarly shaped lamps, and hats of various sizes and styles. Personal eccentricity joined with business imperatives to take us down familiar, distantly remembered pathways. There were a couple of hundred DVDs, neatly organized on shelves near the entrance, and reflecting the eclectic tastes of the shop owner and her friends.

Jackie O'Reilly was originally from Boston. She retained a trace of that city's accent in her speech even though she'd lived in Roverton for ages. She once told me that her faint accent was the only thing that still connected her to her home city. She was a bit like me: middle-aged, with a wrecked relationship (unlike me, she'd gone for the finality of divorce), and one child. She moved to Roverton after the divorce because she liked the town and the surrounding countryside and thought it would be a good place to raise her child.

I entered the store and said hello to Jackie. She puttered around, cleaning up, and putting things in their proper places. Her look was that of an aging countercultural veteran, with long auburn hair slowly turning gray, and a big baggy T-shirt that was a riot of clashing colors. I immediately went to the movie section. It was an odd assortment. There were several classic films; some children's cartoons; a couple of documentaries; and a pile of Hollywood films from the 90s and 00s, some of them good (or at least not bad), some of them trash. In the small, haphazardly accumulated foreign language section, I spotted the Criterion Collection release of Michelangelo Antonioni's 1960 film, *L'Avventura*, sitting there forlornly in the incongruous company of a Hong Kong gangster movie and the French-Canadian art film *Jesus of Montreal*. I'd seen the Antonioni once, many years ago, and both the film and its exalted historical reputation had left me puzzled. Maybe it was time for another viewing?

Jackie smiled as I plopped the DVD of *L'Avventura* down on the counter.

"You like this one, Jackie?" I asked.

"I've never seen it. But there's something funny about it."

"Funny? How?" I asked as I fumbled with my wallet.

"For years, nobody took that movie out," she said. "I regarded it as a decoration in the store. But in the last year, it's been taken out three, maybe four times."

"Things are changing," I said. "Roverton is becoming a cultural center."

"That must be the reason," said Jackie.

"I'm trying to improve my knowledge of Italian cinema," I said. "I got lucky that you have this one in stock."

"I should watch it myself, maybe," said Jackie. "I used to like Fellini's stuff, back when I was in college."

"We should discuss Fellini sometime."

She nodded, and we both left open the questions of when, where, and how we should discuss Fellini. It was a signal rather than an actual proposal.

However, since Amanda's departure, I'd been spending more and more time in Jackie's place, and having more interesting, in-depth discussions with her, than ever before. Partly this was out of boredom, partly out of a desire for the kind of meaningful companionship I'd enjoyed with Amanda, who certainly wouldn't have been averse to discussing Fellini or watching *L'Avventura* with me and talking about what it all meant. I took Jackie's comment about the increasing popularity of that film to be a positive sign. It was proof that, in this idyllic backwater, there were other people like me now—other refugees from the metro regions. If so, we might consider banding together against the coming apocalypse, or at least having a few fun get-togethers. We could invite Jackie along, to show we weren't prejudiced against the long-timers.

But when I got home, I didn't really want to watch *L'Avventura*. Not on this beautiful and peaceful night, full of the lazy seductiveness of summer. Since I only had Bruce for company, I decided we'd take a stroll along the lakefront.

Bruce, fully and officially Robert the Bruce, was always Bruce for short, a West Highland white terrier and therefore a true Scot. Bruce and I set out as the sky turned purple with the dying sunset, and the lake started to darken and fade.

A velvety summer night hovered over us as we approached the edge of the water; the great inland sea rumbled with its steady and heavy lapping against the shore. The stars appeared as pinpricks of light far above us. When we got to the beach, it was mostly deserted, except for a small group of revelers in the distance, who'd rented one of the shelters for some party or gathering. Otherwise, Bruce and I had the place to ourselves. We sat down on a bench to watch the last of the light fade. It was a panorama that validated my decision to move out here. No noise, no fear, no hurry—me and the beach, and the stars. And the dog.

If you talk to the dog long enough, the dog starts to talk back.

"What do you think, Bruce old boy? It's great to be here on the beach on a beautiful summer night like this one."

"No squirrels to chase," said Bruce. "You didn't even bring any treats with you." His voice sounded different from what I'd expected. It was a whiny tenor, like that of a stand-up comedian. Not really what I expected from this dog.

"Whoa there, buddy," I said. "You'll get treats at home. I've still got some leftover lamb. How do you like that?"

"Lamb's great, but do I have to listen to you moan about your personal problems? I'm a dog, for God's sake. Running and barking and eating and sniffing other dogs, that's what floats my boat. I don't need all the other crap. I had to listen to you and Ethan moaning and groaning about all kinds of stuff the other night. *Boring*, is the one word I can apply to that." He looked up at me. His dark eyes, in contrast to the sarcasm in his voice, were imploring, earnest.

"I forgive you, Bruce, for that outburst," I said.

"No problem, dude," he said. "When we get home, I want my bowl of water and soft bed. But first, you have to give me a duck chewie. That's non-negotiable!"

"Don't worry about it," I said. Unbidden, the German word *Sinnstiftung* came into my head: creation of meaning, creation of sense, means of inspiration, meaningfulness, endowment with meaning, signification: it covered all these and more.

"Hey Bruce," I said. "From what do you derive your *Sinnstiftung*?"

"Oh, please," said Bruce. "Don't try to impress me with those German compound words."

"Okay, no worries," I sighed. My mood turned Schubertian; this was the fragment that lodged in my mind:

Schreib' im Vorübergehen
Ans Tor dir: gute Nacht
Damit du mögest sehen
An dich hab' ich gedacht

Loosely translated and updated for our technological age, this is what I was thinking: I'm going away, but I'll write "good night" on your gate, door, whatever—I'll even text it to your phone, or write you an email message—and that way, you'll know I was thinking of you, whatever else was going on, wherever you are, no matter what's keeping us apart.

An dich hab' ich gedacht

Part II:
Sheltering in Place

One of the things I sucked at was playing the piano. I struggled with it, but I persisted, and after a few years I was able to navigate my way through a handful of pieces. I was almost never able to avoid hitting numerous wrong notes; I took to treating tricky bits with the caution of a sailor looking out for hidden rocks, slowing down and peering intently at the score, which wrecked the steadiness of my tempo. Despite my ineptitude, it was something I enjoyed doing, a worthwhile exercise for mind and soul. To minimize my embarrassment, I only played when no other people were in the house. This meant that my sole listener was Bruce the dog, who'd stare at me with wondering eyes while I punched sounds incomprehensible to him from the keyboard.

Today I played one of my show-off pieces (showing off to myself, that is)—Bach's Sinfonia in F Minor. It's a cliché, but there really is something timeless and cosmic about Bach at his best. You understand why Bach's music was blasted into deep space on the Voyager probe; more than anything else, it's the sort of thing that could get across the essence of human intelligence to space aliens with whom we have no other means of communicating. That's what NASA must have thought, and while I admit I have no way of verifying this hypothesis since I don't know any space aliens, I'm tempted to agree.

The Sinfonia is a so-called three-part invention, which means I needed to reproduce three independent lines running simultaneously, crossing and diverging at various points. I played the piece with a grand slowness that sounded appropriately cosmic to my ears, though in reality it probably would have struck listeners as stumbling and lurching, due to my poor abilities. What made this occasion special was that, with only a handful of bars to go before the end, I'd hit all the notes perfectly. I was on the verge of playing the whole piece without hitting any wrong notes, and my excitement mounted. But before I reached the coda, the phone rang, and I muffed an E flat.

"Damn," I grunted, picking up the phone.

"Hey, it's Noodles Fontaine," said a curt, gruff voice.

"Hi, Noodles. What's up?"

He wanted to know if we could meet, right now. He suggested that we get together at Wally's, an old-fashioned bar on the edge of downtown. Wally's was the sort of place that would likely soon be replaced by a hip restaurant with a name like Pablo's Mediterranean Grille or a shop selling hundreds of varieties of olive oil with a name like The Olive Branch. But for now, it was still old, unpretentious Wally's, and Noodles wanted to meet me there.

The occasion for this meeting would be an ongoing project of mine, which had the provisional name of the "Noodles Fontaine Oral History Project." I planned to change the name later, after I'd milked Noodles for everything he knew about local history and the character of the town. The finished version would need a less Noodles-centric title, like "Roverton: History and Culture" (if I wanted to be serious and anthropological), or "Roverton Forever! The Story of a Great Lakes Town" (for a more populist approach). The deeper meaning was that once again, my academic history wouldn't leave me alone. I couldn't live in Roverton like a born-and-bred local, taking everything for granted. I had to do some kind of research project on the place, recording the dialect and the local legends and every other relevant thing. I felt a minor twinge of disappointment at having to abandon my session with Johann Sebastian Bach ("that highly talented and entirely respectable man" as H.L. Mencken described him), but duty called.

You won't be surprised to learn that Noodles Fontaine's first name wasn't really Noodles. His real name was Henry, but nobody called him that. Once I heard somebody call him Hank, but that was a new arrival, a transplant like me. The next time I heard these two persons interacting, the newcomer called Noodles Noodles, as was right and proper. It was a sign that the new guy was integrating.

Why was Henry Fontaine called Noodles? It was one of those dumb things that starts in one's youth and clings forever, like a tattoo. When he was a teenager, he insisted on having noodles for dinner almost every night. He couldn't recall the exact reason why he started doing this, but it was probably a manifestation of adolescent revolt or a desire to stand out. It might even have been a way to fend off boredom by creating his own entertainment. Whatever the reason, it drove his parents crazy.

"Henry," his mother would say, "I made a nice dinner of pork chops for all of us, with some creamy mushroom sauce on the side, and French fries. I know you like fries. Why don't you partake like the rest of us?"

"Thanks, Mom," Noodles would say. "But as you know, I'm on an all-noodle dinner diet right now. Don't you worry about me, I'll cook 'em myself. It's egg noodles tonight. I'll add some kind of sauce. Not creamy mushroom, though."

"Henry," his exasperated mom would wail. "When are you going to put an end to this stunt? Last night it was rice noodles. And the night before that. And last Saturday."

In response, Noodles would say something like, "At least I changed my noodles tonight. You can be happy about that. Also, I've got a bunch of different types of noodles lined up and ready to go, so sorry, Mom, what you call 'this stunt' will go on for a while. There's Italian noodles, Chinese noodles, Japanese noodles to get through. There are so many kinds of noodles in the world, and only limited time to explore them."

His parents always gave in. What the hell, they thought—adolescent rebellion sometimes takes unusual forms. If their son wanted to eat noodles all the time, it beat drinking or drugs or getting a girl pregnant or starting fights or flunking out of school. But they got their revenge. They started calling him Noodles casually, on a regular basis.

They'd be out in public, going about their business, and they'd say to him, "Hey Noodles, can you park the car while we go inside?" or, "Are you interested in playing softball this season, Noodles?" Other people heard this banter and started repeating it. And thus, the people of the town bestowed a nickname on young Henry Fontaine, a nickname he was never able to shed. But rather than getting angry, Noodles embraced the nickname. Here he was, decades later, retired and gray-haired, still calling himself Noodles, and still known as Noodles by everyone else. Within the restricted confines of Roverton, where news travels fast and rarely leaks to the outside world, he would be Noodles forever.

Noodles was around seventy or a little older. He was still trim, fit, and active. After he retired, he was often looking for things to do. He was one of those people who really can't stand to be idle. This was one of the reasons he was eager to meet with me and help me out with my project. The other reason was that he seemed genuinely interested in it. Putting down the history of Roverton in some concrete, fixed form was a proposal that appealed to him.

"This town deserves to go on the map," he told me at our first meeting. His concept of the map was a little vague; he meant something like a permanent record, a memorial.

I'd met Noodles through my barber, Old Earl Anderson, who was about a hundred years old (or so it seemed to me). I never thought of him as plain Earl Anderson; the adjective had, in my mind and in the speech of some other Rovertonians, become so permanently affixed to the man's name that it became a part of it, capitalized like an honorific. Old Earl was one of those people who'd lived in the town so long and, due to the nature of his business, got acquainted with so many people that he was an obvious source of personal recommendations. He was a skinny, wizened fellow with only a couple of tufts of white hair sticking up on his head. Like most barbers, he liked to chat. A slow worker, he'd regale me with lengthy stories about his life while bits of my hair gradually piled up on the floor. I heard an amazingly convoluted and vague story about his "service during the war" (he talked at great length without ever divulging what war he had in mind, what branch of "the service" he'd been in, and what precisely he had been doing—a masterpiece of storytelling avoidance). I learned about the fate of his four children, all of them scattered to the cities, with one coming back eventually to settle in Roverton ("He couldn't stand to live without the nature we have around here, and without Erda's [Old Earl's wife's] apple pie.").

It was during one of these leisurely cuts that I first conceived the idea of doing an oral history project about Roverton.

When I asked Old Earl if he wanted to contribute, he joked, "I thought I already did." But he said he'd allow me to use him as a source, and since he knew so many people in town, he'd be glad to suggest others as well. Noodles Fontaine was his first suggestion. Not only had Noodles lived his whole life in Roverton, but he'd also worked various jobs (handyman, hardware store employee, volunteer fireman), and he knew all kinds of local people. To use the academic lingo, Noodles would be an ideal informant.

I found my informant at Wally's, sitting in one of the booths and nursing a beer. My beer-snob impulses, picked up from Ethan, pinged when I saw that Noodles was drinking a glass of mass-produced mega-swill (none of that fancy craft stuff for him). I ordered a cup of coffee and a glass of water. Noodles wore a baseball cap with a bird logo on it. Wearing a cap indoors was another odd habit of his.

"I'd like to talk about dialect today," I said, switching on my recorder. "In a lot of small towns and other isolated places, people have peculiar words and phrases that they use. I haven't noticed anything like that since I've been here. What was it like when you were young?"

Noodles got a faraway look in his eyes, as if he were reminiscing. He rambled—what time period was I thinking of, what people precisely?—but then righted himself.

"One thing I remember was that some folks would change basic words in certain ways. A lot of older people would say like, 'those'n' or 'these'n,' stuff like that."

"Can you give some examples?" I asked.

"They'd say, 'Do you know those'n kids from down the block?' or, 'I was talking to this'n guy at the grocery store.'"

The linguistic researcher buried deep inside me rejoiced at these examples. They were most likely reflexes left over from the time when a lot of German had been spoken in Roverton. I thought I was done with academia. But the thrill of discovering some tiny detail that nobody else had noticed was still there.

"People used some strange words, too. Like, if you were under pressure or pressed for time, you'd say 'I'm feeling a little eng.'"

"Eng."

"That's right. A little eng, a little tight." Noodles took a sip of his beer. "But nobody talks that way anymore."

Finding such nuggets of local dialect was part of my Roverton research project. Any place that existed for a significant length of time before the homogenizing influence of mass media became ubiquitous is likely to have such local quirks. Sometimes, it goes way beyond mere quirkiness. A classic example is the small town of Boonville. This village, which consists of about a thousand people living in a remote part of the Anderson Valley of northern California, developed its own dialect starting in the 1890s. This dialect, known as Boontling, includes such picturesque terms as "oshtook" (a one-eyed person), "horn of zeese" (cup of coffee), and "breggo" (sheep). Boontians don't speak the language; they *harp* it. As with any well-developed dialect, the influences on Boontling are many and varied. In addition to the languages of the people who settled there (including Spanish and both Scottish and Irish Gaelic), it drew on colorful local characters. Thus, syrup is known as "Bill Nunn," after a Boonville resident who put syrup on almost everything he ate. Coffee is "zeese" after a certain Z.C. (pronounced "Zeese") Blevens, famous for his love of strong coffee.

Imagine a Friday night in old-time Boonville. Jack is a young *kimmie* who wants to have a little fun after a hard day *killing snake* in the fields. Assuming he has some *higgs* in his pocket, he can take his *applehead* Jenny out for a *gorm* at one of the local eating places. Afterwards, the couple goes to a *tidrick* being held at a friend's house. They mingle with the company and enjoy *blooching* with the neighbors about various subjects of interest, fueling their good cheer with a *horn* or two of something strong. But they're careful about it, because they know that too many horns means a visit to the *donicker* for a quick vomit.

Boontling is barely alive nowadays. Current estimates suggest that fewer than a hundred people can "harp Boont," and most of them are old. The dialect is fading into history and taking its speakers with it. It will survive in a few books and academic articles, and (in our present world) probably in occasional YouTube videos. Be that as it may, a word like "donicker" is too good to lose. A public effort should be made to keep it alive, even to propagate it in the wider world.

I doubted that I could find anything that complex in Roverton. But a handful of words is better than no words at all, and they deserve to be written down for posterity.

Noodles was in a mercurial mood and didn't want to dwell on words for very long, so I decided that we should pass on to other subjects.

"I'm curious about the late sixties, early seventies—you know, the hippie era, Vietnam, Watergate, that whole period. What do you remember about it? How did it resonate in this town?"

"To be honest, there wasn't much," said Noodles. "A few boys from the town got sent to Nam, most of them came back alive. I don't remember any protests. I also don't remember any hippies. Roverton was too far off the beaten track for any of that. If you wanted to be a hippie, you went somewhere else."

"That makes sense."

"Hair got longer on some of the boys, and most of the old-timers weren't too happy about that. Some of the girls started wearing miniskirts when the weather was hot, or they got into this Mother Earth look, with T-shirts and jeans and the like. But that was about it." It didn't surprise me to hear that the town was minimally affected by countercultural influences. Most people here were happy to stick to the old ways, no matter what was going on in the big world outside.

Noodles continued: "But you know what's my strongest memory of that time? It's the matchstick sculptures that Bill Diehl used to make."

"Matchstick sculptures?"

"You bet. Bill had a day job—he was a notary, and I think a lawyer—but his real passion was making sculptures out of matchsticks. His favorite subject for the sculptures was architecture. There's a rumor that he wanted to be an architect when he was younger, but that never came to pass, so he took up this architectural hobby. He started small. He made a sculpture of his own house. He showed it to people around town, and they were impressed. He made a couple of sculptures out of neighbor's houses, and those folks really liked what he did. This made Bill popular, and a lot of people advised him to think bigger. He got more ambitious, and one day he took on a big project—the state capitol building in Madison. It's the biggest capitol building outside of Washington DC. Did you know that?"

I nodded.

"You can imagine what a big job it was. People were so impressed by Bill's sculpture of the capitol building that they put it on display at City Hall. All that praise Bill received went to his head. He dreamed even bigger. He started on a sculpture that was going to be his masterpiece. By this stage, he wasn't content to reproduce; he had to put his own stamp on things. He came up with a design for something which was like the Parthenon but also like a skyscraper. That is, it was supposed to have many stories like a skyscraper, but it would also have those columns like the Parthenon. I think it was gonna have a pyramid up at the very top, an Aztec-style pyramid with terraces. It's kinda hard to describe, you have to see his sketches to really understand it. It's like he blended the ancient world and the modern world in one sculpture. This was the matchstick sculpture that was going to make him the most famous matchstick sculptor that had ever lived. He wanted it to be exhibited all over the country and maybe even the world. But you know what happened? One day, after he'd finished the foundation and several floors of the sculpture—he was about halfway to the top at this time—his wife walked in to his studio. She was looking for a match to light her cigarette with. Without asking Bill for permission, she grabbed a match from the first floor of the Parthenon skyscraper. This caused the whole thing to collapse. When Bill saw all his hard work spread out all over the floor, all those thousands of matches scattered every which way, he had a heart attack—or maybe it was a stroke. He fell down flat on the floor and died right there in his studio."

"That's a hell of a story," I said.

The Bill Diehl story was the highlight of today's session with Noodles. I was glad my recording device was running, so I could get it all down. As a local legend, it was gold. Noodles told me a couple of other anecdotes about local characters, but they lacked the tragic grandiosity and touching eccentricity of "The Saga of the Matchstick Sculptures," which is what I already planned to call it.

Notwithstanding the amusement I derived from this oral history project, I took it seriously. Noodles had been an insider all his life, but the town's transformation was turning him into an outsider. New people with completely different backgrounds were moving in, and they put their own stamp on the place. Soon, Noodles would become an object of anthropological curiosity, like the last speaker of a language destined to go extinct. When Dolly Pentreath died in 1777, the Cornish language died with her. It has undergone a revival in recent decades, but the living thread was snapped long ago, and anything that's been "revived" in the present day is bound to be different for that reason. That's how it goes with languages and customs and local history. In most cases, the best we can do is record them for posterity.

Shortly after mining Noodles for local lore, I went back to Old Earl Anderson's barbershop for a haircut. Old Earl's place had the kind of ramshackle charm I looked for in a small-town barbershop. There was the classic candy-striped barber pole. While you waited for your cut, you could pass the time with some of the reading material that Old Earl thoughtfully provided for his customers. A table held a wrinkled, stained copy of *Popular Mechanics* dating from 1975, so I was able to stay up to date on the latest in gadgets and devices. There were also a couple of women's magazines, an odd choice for a men's barbershop. My favorite item was a thin book entitled *Is Putin the Antichrist?*, written by a certain Rev. Lyle Finefellow, and apparently published by him as well (Fine Fellowship Press). I read the good reverend's book and got quickly immersed in a sea of biblical quotations, most of them from Revelation and the more colorful prophetic books of the Old Testament, such as Ezekiel. Old Earl called my name before I decided if Putin was indeed the Antichrist or not.

While Old Earl cut my hair, a question popped into my mind.

"Hey Earl, did you ever hear anyone in this town say 'those'n' instead of 'those'?"

Old Earl put down his clippers and looked at me with the same faraway look that I'd seen on Noodles' face. I had to explain why I asked.

Finally, he said: "Once or twice. I think I heard Crazy Mike Benckendorff say 'those'n.' I remember it because he only said it once. I also remember it because at that time, I had the sweets for Crazy Mike's sister, Eliza. I was always trying to see Eliza, and Crazy Mike, he didn't much like that. For reasons I could never understand, he was against the idea that young Earl Anderson was a fitting mate for young Eliza. This was during the Depression, you know, or the Recession, or some time like that, a time of economic downturn as they call it. I can't remember if the president was Roosevelt or Nixon. Might even have been Ford, no way to be sure. Maybe I didn't have the right prospects as far as Crazy Mike was concerned. You were wise to stay out of the way of Crazy Mike, they called him that for a reason."

I decided not to ask any further questions. As my hair slowly piled up on the floor, Old Earl regaled me with a couple of other anecdotes, but unfortunately, they were so boring and nonsensical that I forgot them as soon as I left the barbershop.

When I got home, I checked my email. The main item of interest was a new message from Amanda.

Dear Freddie,

I'm sorry I haven't written in a while! A lot has been happening chez moi back home in England/Europe. Now I'm in Belgium. With your love of good beer and food you'd like it here! I can now tell you what sort of foundation work I'm doing. I'm one of the group leaders for the Responsible Citizenship course currently being held outside Brussels. It's an interdisciplinary course for students from some of the newer EU member states, and even some from outside the EU (Turkey! Egypt! Nigeria!). We teach them about the Acquis Communautaire and other fascinating topics! They learn something about how we're dealing with environmental challenges, and migration and other subjects!

I have to say that I DO miss you, but I needed to get away for a while, from Philly and that wretched school where I taught and from America in general, which started to exhaust me, too much noise and too many people and all of its problems are getting worse (mind you, things aren't so wonderful in Europe now!), and there were loads of people on this side of the ocean that I wanted to see, I was afraid I'd lose touch with them forever if I didn't go. I've been talking with Ethan, too, it sounds like things are going well for him. I've got another commitment coming up this summer, but after that is over, I DO hope we can see each other again.

Reading between the lines, it struck me that the second paragraph explained the first. She needed a break and didn't quite know how to go about getting one and justifying it to me. I suspected that when she left for Europe, "foundation work" had merely been a goal and an excuse; it didn't materialize until she'd been there a while. Even though she didn't say, "and I needed to put an ocean between the two of us for a couple of months," I sensed that was part of it. (Which didn't bother me at all—if I had to live with me on a permanent basis, I'd be looking for excuses to get away every now and then.) I was glad to get this explanation. It partially assuaged my nagging fear that she'd shut the door forever on our joint life and would stay over there and never return. Still, the phrase "see each other again" wasn't totally reassuring. Did she intend to visit me briefly and leave again? Why not say something like, "I look forward to joining you in our new home for a fresh start?" I had to force myself not to over-interpret her words. I wrote back:

Dear Amanda,
Thanks for writing—it's always good to hear from you and learn about what you're doing. It sounds like you've found something worthwhile to do over there, even though the Acquis Communautaire sounds like about the most boring thing in the world, unless you're a lawyer I suppose.
I would say that my life and things in Roverton in general continue to get more interesting and stimulating. I'm doing some remote work for a couple of firms on the West Coast, and I've started a local history project that's turning out to be fun and (I hope!) educational. Who knows, it might even lead to something bigger, somewhere down the line. I'm even making some friends and improving my social life a little, believe it or not. The town is changing, more people are moving in from the big metro areas, and it feels less like a quaint outpost than it used to. Of course, a lot of people move here precisely because it's a quaint outpost, and by moving here they change the character of the town, and it's not so quaint anymore. It's a

delicate balance, I hope we can preserve the best aspects of both sides, but who knows.

I'm glad to hear that you DO miss me, and of course the feeling is mutual! You were only here a couple of times, and your visits were short. I really do think you'd like the town a lot if you stayed longer, especially in the summer and fall when the weather is so nice. Please tell me you'll do that this year!

Looking over this message, I decided to revise the last paragraph. The pleading tone of the last line struck me as pathetic, and my argument was focused more on her liking the town than on wanting to get back together with me. I rewrote it as follows:

I, of course, miss you too, and I hope you come back refreshed from your travels. Be aware that your new home is waiting for you, right here! With me and Ethan and Bruce, all together in the same place! And growing opportunities in a very nice traditional town for a sophisticated person like you. (This isn't the America that exhausted you, and so far, we've got our problems firmly under control!) Hoping to see you while the weather is still good here, on the idyllic shores of Lake Michigan!

I was satisfied with this version and pressed Send.

Perhaps there was a subtext to my own message, something I'd leave Amanda to tease out on her own. Simply put, Roverton was becoming enough for me. From my steadfast perch on the lake, I watched the outside world collapse. It was a painful and regrettable process, but not one that I'd helped to bring about. Rather, by pursuing the values of frugality, sound judgment, and respect for the power of the intellect, I'd made a modest contribution to preventing it. But now none of that mattered, and the inevitable crisis was upon us.

My best way forward, I decided, was to suppress any worries related to Amanda, and get on with my life here. Immerse myself in work, the town, and whatever relationships I had locally. Take my hobbies and projects seriously, because if you choose to do anything, there's no point doing it lackadaisically or sloppily. In short—make the most out of the small world I now lived in.

This is America, and it's *supposed* to be a free country, dammit, and a man *should* be able to live wherever he likes, and don't let anyone tell you different. Some of us strive to put this theory into practice. There are barriers to doing so. We have jobs, families, real estate, and our own personal preferences to limit our ability to live where we want. Even if we manage to achieve our geographical dream, there's no guarantee that anyone is going to like us or welcome us into the community. Which may cause some of us to reconsider our decision to replant ourselves in this rural idyll.

Many of my new neighbors were former urban Robinson Crusoes. Crusoe lived on an island where he had no one to talk to. My neighbors lived in big cities and sprawling suburbs, where they had no one to talk to, either. They lived in their tiny worlds demarcated by the demands of the lives they'd chosen. Those lives had proven less fulfilling than they'd expected, or grim realities had forced them to consider a new mode of living. Now these people tried again, in a town with a small fraction of the population of their previous municipalities.

When I moved to Roverton, I chose Reinhard's Diner on the central square (Franklin Square) as one of my preferred hangouts. Depending on where you sat, you could listen in on other people's conversations. Initially, I heard people talking about fishing, the weather, and sports events. I heard a couple of impassioned discussions of college football, a subject about which I knew nothing, and cared even less. I listened to people argue about local politics in a much more measured tone than they used for college football. I got some good fishing tips, which I've never had occasion to use. I learned that Leslie was coming out of the hospital tomorrow and we were going to bake her a cake. I found out that some teenagers had gone "walrus swimming" in the lake in the winter and emerged from the icy cold water feeling like heroes.

Gradually, over the course of the next couple of years, the subject matter of these overheard conversations changed. Now, they were about art exhibits, farm-to-table restaurants, and wellness programs. Rebecca's looking for some gallery space but is concerned because prices on the square are going up, and she might have to find a place further out. A community garden is being set up on Harper Street; get your plots while they're still available! After this big breakfast, we'll be fueled for that nature hike in the woods out of town. Don't forget that we have pottery class tomorrow!

Real life changed in accordance with the conversations. Dave's Bar went out of business because Dave couldn't pay the rising rent. Shortly thereafter, a new Italian restaurant called La Bocca della Verità sprang up in its place. In a town with few Italians historically, it immediately stood out as something exotic, a blast of warmth and spice from the

Mediterranean. Changes in the local grocery stores were also noticeable. At the big chain supermarket and later at Miguel Alvarado's establishment, I'd watch people putting their purchases on the conveyor belt or counter. When I was new in Roverton, these purchases would often include six-packs of Coke or some mass-produced beer, Miller, for example. There would be Oreos and Twinkies and various other snack foods. If they were buying fresh un-processed food, it tended to be familiar cuts of meat, meaning pork and beef and chicken, as well as potatoes and other vegetables, and (this being Wisconsin) lots of cheese. But nowadays, the conveyor belt would be full of surprises. You might see packets of quinoa or fresh bunches of arugula. Beef wasn't just beef anymore; now it had to be grass-fed or have a name in front of it (Kobe or Angus). Cheese remained a pleasing constant, although it had proliferated into some odd varieties (Blue Castello, anyone? How about water buffalo cheese?). Beer, of course, more frequently meant craft beer, Ethan's department. Not to mention that we started to see the products of Wisconsin's wine regions, one of the world's newest wine-growing areas. Yes, America's premier dairy state was now home to imitation French châteaus and Italian villas, with their grapes mostly imported from California. There was something fake about it, but on the other hand, it did make the state feel a little more open to the world.

I watched this flux of activity from a privileged position, right in the middle of it. As usual, intellectual titans from the past gave me a way of understanding what was going on. Karl Marx, for example, talked about class consciousness (*Klassenbewusstsein*). Something like that was emerging here in Roverton, where different groups of people were developing a new collective concept of themselves.

Maybe I shouldn't mention Marx to my fellow Rovertonians, though: they might react with hostility, unless they think I'm talking about Groucho and his brothers. Very well, let's consider the perspective of my fellow Great Lakes resident, Thorstein Veblen. He devised the theory of conspicuous consumption, whereby higher social status was indicated via the purchase and display of luxury goods. I saw a variant of Veblen's argument play out in the grocery stores and restaurants and real estate market of Roverton, right in front of me. Veblen based his theory on the behavior of the newly rich industrialist class in Chicago— the sort of people who hired the era's leading architects to build their houses and who endowed glittering cultural institutions.

Maybe it's personal, but I have other reasons to cite Veblen. He spent his summers on a small island off the Wisconsin coast, not far from where I now lived. In that remote place, he even went to the trouble of learning Icelandic, as the island had a lot of Icelandic immigrants. Veblen learned the language well enough to translate the *Laxdaela Saga*, one of the standard texts from that Icelandic course I'd taught back in Philly. All of this made me feel a connection with him; it was another instance of someone continuing the work of civilization in an isolated little dot on the map.

In any case, these observations by Marx and Veblen were pertinent in the Roverton of today. The Flight from the Cities catalyzed its own type of group consciousness. Previously, the people who lived in Roverton were simply the townsfolk; sometimes, the more erudite-sounding epithet "Rovertonians" was used. You would see it, for instance, in the name of the local newspaper (*The Rovertonian*) and in the names of some social organizations (such as an amateur choir known as the Jolly Company of Rovertonians). But the idea that Rovertonians could be divided into distinct groups that differed in essential characteristics—a situation which could, in theory, give rise to conflict—never took hold for long. The closest we had to it was the tension involving the town's German residents during World War I; but I wasn't aware of anything similar occurring in the following years.

Now, however, the Flight from the Cities generated its own form of social tension. This tension began to manifest itself linguistically. People referred to themselves using one of three terms. Those who had lived in Roverton for all or most of their lives started calling themselves *old-timers*. Those who had fled from the cities in the last few years—people like me—became known as *nukes*, which was a jocular abbreviation of "newcomers." Rumor held that this term was coined by an old-timer who was so hostile to the new migrants that he deemed them as threatening to the town's traditional character as a nuclear bomb. There was a third group, an in-between group: people who were not native to the town, but who had moved there before the Flight from the Cities really got underway, and who had lived there long enough that they could practically be considered natives. These people were known as the *long-timers*.

It soon became possible to guess, with a reasonable degree of accuracy, who was a nuke and who wasn't by looking at people and hearing them talk. The distinctions between old-timers and long-timers were more subtle, since the two groups tended to blend into each other. We were all Rovertonians, but new distinctions had been established, and their ramifications were playing out socially.

Back in the old days, Our Lady of Hops was known as St. Catherine's. The church was built in the 1880s, for a congregation hailing mainly from Bavaria, Flanders, and Ireland. The original wooden building burned down under suspicious circumstances during World War I—possibly a casualty of the anti-German agitation at the time, although no one was able to prove anything. A new church was built on the same spot, replacing the wooden one, and this time the builders made the wise decision to use brick, thereby ensuring a long life for it. It served its original religious purpose for several decades, until the number of parishioners declined to the point where it made no sense to keep it open anymore. After being properly de-consecrated and spending a few years in a derelict condition, it was restored to life as a brewpub. The influx of nukes to the town meant that it was thriving.

It was early afternoon, before opening time, when I entered Our Lady of Hops. Ethan was there, sitting up at the bar on the dais, where the altar had previously been. He wore the brewery's official black T-shirt, with its name emblazoned on the front and the words *And God said: "Let there be beer!"* on the back. Next to him sat Miguel Alvarado, holding a glass of something in the one hand still available to him. I looked around at the white walls, the lofty windows, the sacred headspace of the former church. It made me glad they had preserved the original building so well; it was easy to imagine generations of hymns and incense and sermons ascending to heaven in this building, an atmosphere that endowed the brewing and drinking of beer with a certain solemnity and reverence, as was truly right and proper. All those medieval monks who were also brewers would have recognized and respected the fact that good beer was a joyful utilization of God's natural bounty upon the earth. (And—let's face it—they probably really enjoyed the occasional piss-up in their monasteries.) I snatched a menu from one of the tables to see if any new beers had been put on tap. Sure enough, there were a couple of recent arrivals: Tsar Bomba ("a Russian imperial stout so powerful, it will blow up your world") and Pirate Dan's Private Stash ("named after legendary Great Lakes pirate Dan Seavey, this risk-taking pale ale smuggles in a whole load of fruity and hoppy treasures").

"Hey, Dad," Ethan shouted at me from his perch. "I've got a brand new one, an IPA, so new it's not on the menu yet. We call it Old Fart. We named it after you. You should try it for that reason."

"Thanks, that's so thoughtful of you," I said. "Pour me a cold one." While Ethan did so, I made my way up to the bar, where I realized I'd interrupted them in the middle of a conversation. But that was not a problem, because I knew that Ethan wanted me there.

"The situation is as follows," said Ethan. "The both of us are trying to work out how this Great Lakes cuisine project should take shape. We've had some preliminary discussions. We disagree on a few basic things. We wanted you to be here to adjudicate, so to speak."

"I'm flattered. What's the main issue here?"

"I'll start," said Ethan. "I believe that Great Lakes cuisine should be firmly rooted in the history, geography, and available foodstuffs of the Great Lakes. A lot of people don't respect mac & cheese, or potato wedges, or burgers. But these are the building blocks. There's no reason to believe that a burger can't be a gourmet burger—there's plenty of examples, all over the country, to prove that. If a burger can be a gourmet burger, can there be such a thing as gourmet potato wedges? I'll leave that question hanging in the air; you two can take a stab at answering it."

Miguel put down his glass, hunched his shoulders a bit, and stared at Ethan, as if responding to a challenge. "Burgers. Potato wedges. Mac & cheese. Where's the excitement? You talk about history. You talk about geography. Everything's in flux. You've lived in this town for how long? I've been here longer than you. Okay, not so much longer, but I see changes as they happen, because I'm, like, the observer of such changes. My business depends on it. What I see, based on who comes into my store and what they buy, is a lot of people who aren't gonna be satisfied with the basic foods you're talking about. New people come to Roverton. I was one of them. They bring their own ideas about what's good food. They have expectations, you know. This is a chance for you to be dynamic, to get on top of history like a surfer on a wave. You take your potato wedges, and that's fine—I got nothing against potato wedges—but to make it exciting, you're gonna need something else. That something else doesn't have to come from the Great Lakes. It can come from anywhere in the world, and it can become an ingredient for you. Tell me, where did the potato come from? It came from Peru." He gestured toward the south (I think that's where he was gesturing). "It came all the way up here. It went to Europe and other places also. Your Great Lakes cuisine does not have to limit itself to the Great Lakes. All the foods of the world can come here. It's up to you what you do with them."

"I don't disagree with you," Ethan rejoined. "I've long known that new people come here, and they're going to make certain culinary demands. They won't be content to eat the sort of food that the old-timers eat. But there's this whole question of roots. It applies to food as it applies to anything else. We want to take the roots as our foundation. We don't want to sever them. If someone moves to Roverton from, I don't know, Atlanta, they're looking for Roverton but they're also bringing Atlanta with them. It wouldn't make sense to create a cuisine that's 100% one side or the other."

"That's not what we're talking about," retorted Miguel. "You can't interpret anything I said as meaning that we're going to replace the original food and ingredients wholesale. I'm talking about the historical evolution. As you've said, this is your chance to make your mark on history. On the history of cooking, of cuisine. As for me, I can be your—" he looked toward his one, right hand awkwardly, with a slight grin. "—right-hand man." He waited a few seconds, expecting a laugh, but Ethan and I stayed silent. "What do *you* think, Professor?" asked Miguel.

"I think this Old Fart IPA is refreshing," I said. "Hoppy but well-balanced, with floral and citrus notes and a hint of peach at the back end."

"Cool, Dad's got the lingo down," said Ethan.

I continued: "I also think that any basic food, no matter how humble, can be made into something 'gourmet.' But more broadly, I think that both of you have entered a process that we call Hegelian dialectic. Hegel—that's the guy the process is named after—talked about thesis, antithesis, and the synthesis that derives from the clash of these two forces. You, Ethan, are in effect stating the thesis, to which Miguel responds with his antithesis. Out of this, Great Lakes cuisine will emerge as a synthesis. I can't wait to see what the result is! But I also think you should cut to the core of what you're doing. The core is *good food*. That's what you're aiming at. These influences, whether they be local or from somewhere else, are about creating good food rather than making a statement. When somebody tucks into a gourmet burger, they're not thinking about Hegelian dialectic, or even about whether the burger is a proper representation of Great Lakes cuisine. They're thinking about how good that burger is."

"Which is what they should be thinking," said Miguel.

"But we also want to put our own stamp on things," added Ethan.

"This is the sort of discussion that could go round and round in circles, for hours and hours," I said. "The important thing is, you've both got stuff to think about now."

"Oh, we won't go round and round, not today," said Miguel. "I gotta get back to the store. But it's been a good discussion."

We wrapped things up. Ethan still had some free time, so I lingered.

"What happens next?" I asked. "What's the next step in the creation of Great Lakes cuisine? I'm still a bit mystified by the conversation you guys had."

"We have to lay the theoretical basis first," said Ethan. "Then we'll swing into action."

"Have you two even decided which one of you is the chef? When you decide, what's the other guy going to do?"

"I think we'll both be the chef. We'll be co-chefs. This will allow each of us to contribute equally and form a harmonious whole. If that doesn't quite work out, we can implement a dictatorial model instead. I'll be the dictator, since this whole thing was my idea."

"It sounds to me like ideology is muddling your project," I objected. "Are you still reading Boldmug and those other crazies? If so, keep them off the kitchen table. Go back to your business books; at least they have something to do with business."

Ethan smiled at me wryly, as if to say, *Dad, you're hopelessly out of touch.* "Like I said, I take various perspectives and ideas from these guys. They're not infallible and I don't regard them as role models."

"What would Boldmug think about you pairing up with a Mexican guy to internationalize the food in a classic American small town? I'm guessing he wouldn't approve."

"I don't think he would object at all. In fact, Boldmug applauds the Latinization of the North American proletariat. According to him, this brings us closer to the caste society that he favors. In present conditions, Latinization brings other benefits. Let's face it—based Hispanic cops are the only ones who can keep order in the cities nowadays. Of course, that part's more like my L.A. experience talking, not my online reading. Also, only Miguel's father is Mexican. His mother is Italian, by way of Brazil. And I think there's maybe some Salvadoran in there—he did run that *pupusa* place, you know."

"How is that relevant?"

"You've always stressed the importance of getting facts straight, haven't you?"

"Is Miguel okay with you regarding him as a mere ideological tool?"

Ethan smiled again (*You just don't get it, do you?*). "Miguel is first and foremost a practitioner of the culinary arts. That's what you were applauding earlier, right? What matters is how good the burger is, not if it fulfills certain ideological preconceptions. Didn't Deng Xiaoping say something about how it doesn't matter if the cat is black or white, as long as it catches the mice? I learned that from one of my Chinese sources." He plopped our empty beer glasses into a plastic crate for eventual rinsing. "How all this is going to fit into the larger panorama of social transformation is something we can deal with later."

"You have sources in China?"

"Not personally. It's another of the guys I read online. He calls himself Occidental Renegade. He's not even Chinese, really. He was a professor at some American or British university, and he relocated to China because he's convinced that's where the future is. Chinese civilization is going to become the central one again, this time for the whole world, not just for Asia. He writes these insider reports from China, and think pieces about the future of the Western world. Believe me, he's not optimistic about us. We're too decadent and demoralized to survive."

"We're screwed," I said. "Thanks, but I knew that already."

"Been wondering whether I should brush up on my high school Spanish, or start learning Chinese," continued Ethan. "If the former, I'll be in a better position to profit from Latinization. If the latter, I can have stronger connections with our new overlords when they start taking over the craft beer sector. *Those* are the languages we should be studying in this century—not Icelandic, and not Anglo-Saxon, sorry. But we have to see how the post-USA trend plays out. When the Great Lakes Republic—or Empire, or Dictatorship—starts to look like a real possibility, I'll have a better idea what to do."

"You may have to open another brewpub. All those climate refugees and political refugees will be thirsty."

"We'll need to regulate the population inflow," said Ethan. "Maybe build a wall? But to get back to Miguel for a moment. As you are aware, Miguel has already been treated as an ideological tool by other people. I don't need to tell you how he lost his left arm. Personally, I think it goes further than trying to turn Iraq into a Western-style democracy, or grabbing the oil, or whatever the hell Bush and Blair and their cronies thought they were doing. I think Miguel lost that arm because the elites were trying to disarm the working class. In Miguel's case, they did it literally."

"Good food with a local stamp on it, that's all the ideology you need," I said. "No one's gonna get their arm blown off by that."

"But hey," said Ethan, "aren't you using Noodles Fontaine as an ideological tool? To present Roverton as a kind of idealized American small town with a quirky lingo and some lovable local characters?"

I hadn't thought of it that way, but he had a point. Noodles was just a guy, but I risked turning him into a symbol or a trophy. The same danger existed with the other informants I was using. They were sources, not symbols. Still, Noodles and company had minds of their own; I was confident of my ability to respect that fact.

Leaving aside Ethan's neo-reactionary preoccupations, which struck me as an inadequate response to the civilizational crisis at hand, I was left with the feeling that, if any untainted idealism exists in the world, you can probably find it in craft brewing. I came out of Our Lady of Hops that afternoon in a good mood. Outside, I stopped, looked around, listened, and inhaled. What if we drown the world in beer, I mused. The air is clean, crisp, and invigorating, with hints of nutty toastiness and traces of subtle smokiness on the back end. The sun radiates notes of orange peel, papaya and mango. The grass gives off a deep earthy texture, as well as floral and spice notes. Throw it all in a big glass and drink it down.

It was a lazy afternoon, the sun was shining, I had no immediate obligations, and I decided to take a long walk to Light & Sound. I headed down my tree-lined street, took a couple of turns, and found myself on Franklin Square, where several children were loitering in front of the big relief map of the Great Lakes region that stood on the village green. I smiled to myself when I heard one of them say: "Hey, if Lake Superior is up here, where's Lake Inferior?" I passed from the square and entered Huron Avenue (the town's main street), which was almost bereft of cars at this time of day, and where a few pedestrians went about their business. I wanted to see if any new and interesting items had come in, and maybe to chat with Jackie O'Reilly, assuming she was open to the idea. I crossed the state route and went up the little incline into the store. Jackie was alone; she smiled and said hello. She had a small pile of items—some books and CDs—and she was shelving them.

"Hey, Jackie," I said. "Got some interesting new stuff?"

"For you? Probably not. I've been weeding out my personal collection. A few people donated some things, too." A handful of CDs were laid out on the counter. Most were pop music of some sort, but one stood out as being different. It featured a folkish European-looking cover, with a quintet of musicians—a guitarist, a fiddler, and three individuals without instruments—seated on the ground in some sort of forest clearing. They were dressed ready to work outdoors (jeans, flannel or denim shirts), and sitting in the middle was a young woman with flowing dark red hair and a faint smile. The group bore a peculiar name—McTaggart Family Creamery—and the album title was *Running in Place*.

"Hey, the girl in the middle looks kind of like you," I observed.

"You get one guess as to why that is," she said.

"Oh, really?"

"Yep," she said with a hint of pride. "I did have a life before I came to Roverton, believe it or not."

"I believe it. Why shouldn't I? This just happens to be news to me."

"Let me tell you the whole story," she said. "You're the only customer, so it's a good time for a break. I'm going to the Red Rooster—want to join me?" This was a café on Huron Avenue, a short walk away. Jackie closed the shop, and we headed off.

The Red Rooster was being manned by the rail-thin, pimply-faced young guy I usually saw there—Ted or Todd or Tad or Trig, whatever his name was.

"I'd like a latte, please," I said.

"No worries," he rejoined enthusiastically. "I got you covered." This was his tagline, or some kind of nervous tic, something he couldn't help saying.

"Cappuccino for me," said Jackie.

"*No* worries, Jackie," he gushed. "I got you *covered!* Business slow at the shop today?"

"Yeah, taking a break."

Tad or Trig or Ted or Todd got us our coffees, and when we sat down, Jackie told me the story. "We formed the band in Boston, in the mid-nineties. A couple of us had music-school backgrounds, the rest were amateurs. I was one of the amateurs. I could pick at the piano, I wasn't great at it, but I always had a good voice. I was doing odd jobs at the time and singing when and where I could, in whatever venues would take me. That's how I met Howard—he's the guitarist you see on the album cover—and Leah—she's the fiddle player. They were the professionals, so to speak. They wanted to do folk-fusion: you know, folk plus rock, folk plus world music to use the fashionable term, and so on. They needed a lead singer. That turned out to be me."

"That's funny," I said. "I pick at the piano too, but in no world would anyone want to hear me sing. But what's up with the band's name?"

"The McTaggart Family Creamery?" She took a big gulp of coffee, then continued. "It was meant to create a certain image. None of us was named McTaggart, we weren't a family, and we didn't run a creamery. But it gave you a feeling of tradition, of something warm and comfortable, that continues over the generations." She gestured expansively, like a lecturer. "We even liked the name McTaggart because it sounded kind of craggy and old-fashioned, and it was Celtic, and we played a lot of Celtic music. It was kind of funny, though. We'd be playing around Boston and New England, and people would ask which of us was McTaggart, and where was this famous creamery, and could they go there and try the products? It's a little sad that we had to tell them none of that existed. We were, in fact, getting a pretty good local fan base at the time."

Their fan base was big enough that the Creamery attracted the attention of some of the more esoteric record labels, the sort that specialized in yodeling, or Karelian nature songs, or some ninety-year-old Caribbean guy with a guitar. They signed with one of these labels (it had a name like Squawking Bird Records, something like that, I don't remember exactly), and put out two albums in the nineties. The one I'd seen in Jackie's shop, *Running in Place*, was the second, following their self-titled debut. The title turned out to be fitting, as the band was running and running but going pretty much nowhere in terms of sales and wider recognition.

"At that time," she continued, "there was a modest revival of interest in this type of music. We were folk, but not straight folk. The whole 'world music' thing was in fashion, and we took advantage of that. We mixed Celtic with Middle Eastern and Latin American and God knows what else." Both of the Creamery's albums got good reviews in the specialist publications that catered to that type of music. But sales were poor, and the band members were plagued by doubts about their future. While they continued to play together, no record label was willing to sign them for future albums. Tensions within the group made the situation worse.

"Howard wanted to go more in a pop direction; he thought that was the way to save the band. Leah wanted to stick with our original type of music. They argued about it. Those two were sort of the intellectual leaders of the group, and the rest of us, the three others, we thought they were getting arrogant, trying to impose their ideas on us. We started calling ourselves 'the silent three' because we didn't contribute much to these debates. Not that they would've listened to us, anyway. There were also the usual problems with alcohol and drugs. I still remember Howard coming late to a gig because he'd been drinking heavily, and all the time we were playing, we were afraid he was going to fall flat on his face right in front of the audience and we would have to call an ambulance. It was the most nerve-wracking situation we were ever in, in public. It happened in Ogunquit, Maine—beautiful seaside resort town—but oh my God, I couldn't relax at all, there was such tension in the air. He managed to finish that concert, but right after we finished, he busted out crying. He said: 'If I have to play "Reynardine" one more time, I'm gonna hurl right there on the stage.' That was the moment when I knew a breakup was inevitable."

Strangely enough, it wasn't drinking or drugs or artistic disagreements that formed the proximate cause of the breakup. One of the "silent three" was a certain Lydia Douglas, nicknamed "Onyx" due to her thick, shiny black hair. She backed up Jackie's vocals when needed and played several unusual instruments, such as the hammered dulcimer and the glockenspiel. She was talented but mentally not quite stable. Musicians working in obscure or alternative genres often go down strange spiritual paths, and Onyx was no exception. She got involved with a pagan cult, one that combined nature worship with the adoration of selected Indo-European gods, specifically Thor (from the Norse pantheon) and Vishnu (from the Hindu one). But it was the nature worship that mattered most. The cult insisted that its members get in touch with nature, and they meant that literally, and preferred that you do it alone, without the presence of other human beings to hinder your direct communion with the primeval world. Onyx undertook an arduous hike all by herself in the Canadian Rockies during the winter, both to get in touch with nature and to prove her worthiness to the cult. She came back to the band invigorated by the experience and thirsting for more adventures.

"It kind of amazed me because she was such a slight girl," said Jackie. "You really couldn't imagine her surviving in the cold outdoors. But she did it."

The Canadian adventure impressed the other members of the cult, and they talked about promoting her to a position of spiritual leadership. To do that, she would have to undertake a yet more arduous assignment. They gave her several choices: desert or rocky terrain, mountains or valley, cold or hot climate. She chose to hike across the Arizona desert, believing that the contrast to her previous outing would be a source of enlightenment. The cult leaders gave her a choice of starting points: Tombstone or Tuba City. She didn't like the implications of Tombstone, and being a musician, naturally took an immediate liking to Tuba City. (Curious about the name, I looked it up later. It has nothing to do with musical instruments; the town was named after a 19th-century Hopi chief. But such is the power of words and their associations.) It was at the latter location that a small group of cult members gathered to see her off. At this gathering, she gave a brief speech, expressing her faith that Vishnu and Thor would look after her on the trail, and that the hike would help her attain a clearer understanding of the will of the gods when she returned.

She never came back. Her body was never found, and she left behind a mystery. Tantalizingly, in obscure corners of the Internet, you could find messages from people saying things like "Onyx isn't dead. She wants to live her life in private. Leave her in peace," and "I heard from Onyx recently, she said stop searching guys, give it up." But no proof that Onyx was either living or dead ever surfaced. Lacking an essential contributor, and in view of its already existing problems, the McTaggart Family Creamery closed, and its four remaining members went their separate ways.

"I have a new definition of death," Jackie said. "It's the day when your Wikipedia entry changes from *is* to *was*. Onyx's Wikipedia entry still says she *is* a folk musician. I retain some hope, faint though it might be, that she's still alive."

"Those of us without Wikipedia entries will never die," I said. "That's comforting, I suppose. Or maybe we were never alive in the first place."

"If it makes you feel better, I don't have my own Wikipedia entry. There's a collective one for the band, but only Onyx has her own entry. The only reason she got her own entry is because of her disappearance. People got morbidly interested. Vanishing made her more famous. I think they would call it a good career move, assuming she ever comes back."

"It's a shame you guys weren't around during the vinyl days. We could play the records backwards, and it might tell us what happened to her. You can't do that with a CD."

"Hey, is there anything more I can do for you?" asked the young man with the name beginning with T. He appeared as if out of nowhere, with a big smile on his face.

"No thanks," I said. "I think that's all."

"No worries," he said. He scampered back to the counter without finishing his tagline, though I heard him mumbling something (probably "I got you covered") under his breath as he went away. Jackie said it was about time for her to get back to Light & Sound; we wrapped up our little meeting.

As we went out the door, a thought struck me. "Hey, could I buy that copy of *Running in Place* from you? You got me intrigued. I'd love to give it a listen."

"Oh, you can have it for free. A special for a good customer."

"No, really," I insisted. "I like to support the arts, even in a small way."

"Okay, you can have it for a fiver," she said, as we headed back to the shop.

Since I was now the house's only full-time human resident, I took advantage of the situation to spread myself out. There were two bedrooms on the second floor, and I turned one of them into a home office, transferring my belongings up from the spare room on the first floor. The bedroom was more spacious, and had a decent view of the lake, because the house was situated on the gentle slope that led down to the beach. It was pleasant to pop open the window on warmer days and listen to the faint rumbling of the waves in the distance. This morning, I was preparing for a long-distance meeting. I sat down at my desk, put down my mug of coffee, and started up the computer. Bruce took up his station on the couch nearby. This coffee mug was my personal favorite. It had a picture of a dog wearing dark glasses and smoking a cigar, and the caption *The Dogfather—keep your friends close, your enemies closer, and your dog closest.*

"Good morning, Raj," I said to the computer screen.

"Good morning, Fred," the face on the screen said to me. Rajesh Agarwal adjusted his glasses, looking lost for a second. The office in distant Seattle, as seen within the Zoom browser, looked dark and blurry.

"Can you see me?" I asked.

"Yeah, I can see you. Your outlines aren't real clear, but I can tell that it's you and not the dog. Can you see me?"

"Yeah, same deal."

After going through this little ritual, we got down to business. I had done some work for Raj's firm before. I began by writing content for their website. Then, I created an online presentation for them, one that could also be given in person. The company, Jasher Creativity Partners, specialized in various kinds of training and publicity work: communications, media, cross-cultural, and the like. Jasher Creativity Partners did its in-person work in Seattle and the Pacific Northwest as a whole, but they were looking to expand by creating new material, course modules, that sort of thing. Raj was the creative director. To show how creative he was, he'd anagrammed his own first name and given it to the company.

"We liked what you did with the last communications seminar," said Raj. "It was really funny, too. The cross-cultural people especially liked it."

"Great, I'm glad to hear that." The communications seminar he referred to had actually been a fairly easy presentation to put together. I'd done something that was essentially a linguist's version of a comedy routine, pointing out the perils of branding when you don't have an adequate knowledge of foreign languages. I had used a variety of sources, including Reinhold Aman's legendary academic journal, *Maledicta: The International Journal of Verbal Aggression*, a publication dedicated to "bad language" in all its forms. Aman's journal got me beyond the bland examples you've probably heard many times already (did you know that the Chevy Nova didn't sell well in Latin America because *no va* means "it doesn't go" in Spanish? In fact, this is an urban legend), providing risqué and offensive material that I had to be careful about using. Here's another example, this time a true one: since 1954 the French have been imbibing a soft drink called *Pschitt!* (meant to evoke the sound a bottle of carbonated water makes when opened). Try selling that in any English-speaking country. Apparently, I'd hit the mark, because Raj asked me to do more. The great scholar Reinhold Aman (a Germanicist like me, and what's more, a Wisconsin resident) was a miserable character who spent time in prison for sending death threats to his wife and to a judge during his acrimonious divorce proceedings. He didn't merely collect insults and obscene expressions; he dispensed them liberally to anyone who displeased him. Yet with *Maledicta*, he managed to create a scholarly monument that outlived him. There may be a lesson in that somewhere.

"We've got a new project for you," said Raj.

"I'd love to hear about it," I said.

Raj said: "As you know, we've got the Excellence in Innovation Awards submissions coming up. A bunch of different companies are competing, and we want to make a good impression. Last year we snagged one award, and it would be great if we could do even better this year. We'd like you to help put together…" He went on with the details of this project, with which I will not bore you.

Raj continued: "I realize that producing this kind of inane and fatuous corpspeak—these clichés piled on top of clichés, these wooden phrases coined in a desperate attempt to keep up with the latest trends, these carefully calibrated assaults on the English language, which are designed to smother comprehension rather than enable it—is not what you'd like to be doing, but we all have to make a living. But I'm not going to apologize for it, because frankly, Fred, you're not that important to us. You're not so much our third wheel as a spare tire that we pull out of the trunk on the very rare occasions that we need it. Normally I would've given this job to one of our full-time underlings, but with you it works out cheaper, and you've already passed our admittedly modest quality test."

I responded: "I wish I could say that I'm glad to be given this opportunity, but I'm not. If people paid me the same amount of money to do nothing as your company pays me to do your projects, I would drop your company in a second. I have a mind that would rather spend its efforts studying the poems of Georg Trakl or the evolution of the Ingvaeonic languages. However, I've left academia behind for good, which means that no one will pay me even the modest amounts of money that I used to make doing such things. As a result, I have to write this forgettable material for your shitty company. I'm using your company in a purely mercenary manner, as you are using me, and I ask only one thing: that you not list me anywhere as the author. If you need a name, use a pseudonym. Something like Hasbeen Q. Sellout."

I'll leave it to you to determine what parts of the preceding conversation actually happened. The upshot was that I had a new project to work on, and consequently some money, paid on a per project basis, as was normal with Raj's firm and the other firms that I sometimes did these projects for.

I'd made one business trip to Seattle previously, back when I started collaborating with Raj and his team. It was an illuminating visit on several levels. In a glass and steel office building overlooking misty and tranquil Elliott Bay, I sat on a round, tiger-striped couch while I waited for Raj and a couple of his associates. The young lady who sat me down on the couch (Melissa) presented me with a photo album that the company had recently made for one of their clients, a professional services firm specializing in accounting, law, and management consulting.

"This is a recentish production," said Melissa. "It's a very fresh example of the kind of projects we do. This one is a bit lighthearted, but I think you'll agree it shows off our creativity."

"Thanks, I'll take a look." She went away and I opened the album. It was a collection of photos highlighting certain employees at the services firm, with accompanying captions. There was also a text, which seemed to be about the company's history, but I paid no attention to that. The photos were what grabbed my attention. The first one, which took up an entire page, showed a thirtysomething Asian-American woman staring straight at the camera with a slight frown, wearing a ballet costume and holding a folded-up laptop computer in her left hand.

The caption read: "Mindy Lee dreamed of being a ballet dancer when she was growing up. Now, she helps others realize their dreams as a financial advisor." I turned the page. There was another full-page photo. It showed a youngish, fair-haired man with a vaguely hostile look on his face, clutching a violin case and wearing a business suit.

The caption for this one read: "Peter Janowski was once determined to become a violin virtuoso. Now, he plays at the highest level in the field of corporate law." I turned the page again. This time, it showed a black-bearded man with pursed lips and glaring eyes, wearing a chef's hat and apron, which clashed oddly with his dark business suit.

According to the caption, "Farouk Alameddin once saw himself becoming one of the great chefs of the world. Now, in addition to whipping up a delicious meal, he can make your investments more succulent than ever."

Jasher Creativity Partners may have thought they were showcasing the talents and enthusiasm of this company's employees, but my first impression was that this was one of the saddest displays I'd ever seen. The overriding theme that emerged from it was that of gifted, striving people who for some reason or other had failed to fulfill their dreams, and who had to resign themselves to the mundane demands of the business world. My second impression was a feeling of shame on my part. I realized that only a tiny proportion of us ever managed to realize our dreams, and that the individuals in this photo album were probably living happy and fulfilling lives. In a world where innumerable horrors, disappointments, and absurdities happen every day, it made sense to conclude that Mindy, Farouk and Peter were doing quite well for themselves. They were lucky and probably on the way to being rich. I was sure that they didn't have to worry about where their next meal was coming from, or where they were going to live after being evicted. Upon reflection, I decided to stuff my first impression in the closet. Still, why had the photographer not instructed them to smile?

I was in no position to judge these people. If I were to be one of the subjects of this kind of photo spread, what would my caption say?

"When he was young, Fred Traubert dreamed of becoming... Something, he didn't know exactly... A person who'd be taken seriously, in some intellectual field, possibly being referenced and cited in various places, maybe going on the occasional TV show to explain something, but... Now, he's a middle-aged nobody who enjoys the benefits of a comfortable life, but in other respects, he's about given up.

Is this caption going on too long for the page? Very well, let it go on. Even nobodies deserve to have their stories told. Fred's concerned about how he's going to put his marriage back together, how he's going to get the most out of his new environment, and how he plans to manage his slightly strained relations with his son and the other people around him. He'll never play at the highest level of anything, nor is he going to help anyone realize their dreams."

The Fraternity of the Disappointed that I belonged to was a very large organization. It included visionary architects who never got to build that cathedral or concert hall or stately home, but instead had to design elementary schools or big-box stores, taking care not to show any trace of individuality in the results. It included brilliant writers who dreamed of forging new literary paths but had to settle for writing obituaries for their local newspapers. It included schmoes like me, who once had vague ideas that they would become something important.

Being a middle-aged nobody has its advantages. Principally, those advantages relate to perspective. From midlife, the helplessness of infancy and senility looks impossibly distant. It's a good place to be, a place to get a balanced perspective, like sitting on top of a hill with the landscape spread out in front of you. As you get older, you rise higher—you see the past better. Experiences that felt like the end of the world when they happened (you lost a job, you got sick, somebody died) can be perceived in a more cool and objective manner, as if they happened to somebody else. For young people, these end-of-the-world experiences hit harder, because they haven't lived through them multiple times. They haven't yet developed the proper coping mechanisms.

We live in a series of cages, and when we're released from one of them, we think that we're finally free. You have to live for a while before you realize that this is an illusion, which is why the people who most ardently believe that freedom is possible are the young ones. These cages take various and sequential forms. We're born into the cage of the family, which forms a microscopically small corner of a much larger cage, the world. Within the family is the cage of childhood. The cage of childhood merges with that of school. We dream of escaping the cage of school only to enter a new cage, that of work. Often, during our stay in the cage of work, we enter a new cage, that of marriage, which provides a back entry to the first cage, that of family. We spend most of our lives living in cages within cages, moving back and forth among all these cages. If we live long enough, we exit the cage of work and enter the one of retirement. Exiting that cage leads to death, and paradoxically, to final freedom—the freedom of nonexistence, because only when you don't exist can you be totally free. It's a shame you're not around to enjoy it. (If you're a connoisseur of paradoxes, this one's a keeper.)

This midlife perspective has made me mellow. What's the point of struggling to escape your cage, if the only thing that's waiting for you after you escape is another cage? In view of this reality, it's better to make your present cage happy, comfortable, and amusing rather than trying to escape it. The belief that there's a great life waiting for you around the corner is an illusion. My current cage is called Roverton. It feels better than the previous cages I've inhabited, so I've made up my mind to stay in this cage as long as I can. But it's a temporary stay, I'll admit that. That's because everything is temporary, including my life and this world.

On a positive note, the meeting with Raj and his team went well. If I get too disappointed or gloomy about the fate of humanity or the world in general, or about myself, I find it's always a good idea to spend some time with real people, especially if they're optimistic and forward-looking. Thankfully, the meeting and subsequent lunch lifted my spirits.

After lunch, I had some time on my hands and a new city at my feet to explore. A few hours remained until my flight. I decided to wander around downtown. Watching grown men throw fish at each other at Pike Place Market, down on the waterfront, proved insufficiently captivating. Soon I was back on the street, taking everything in.

Up the hill, away from the bay, the new constructions loomed. A tall building, not quite a skyscraper, dominated. Close to completion, it resembled nothing less than a typical Communist-era apartment block. A *Sozialbau*, of a type that was ubiquitous in East Germany. I'd seen multitudes of its originals in situ as it were.

History moves in cycles and there is no end to its ironies. The Berlin or Leipzig *Sozialbau* housed the New Socialist Man, who dutifully went to work at the office or factory every day, fulfilled the quota or plan, and went home to his family at night. Such was the idea, anyway. The Seattle *Sozialbau* housed the New Capitalist Men or Women. The mega-capitalist masters and overlords were replicating, inadvertently, the structures and aesthetics, the sense of mobilization, of the now defunct communist regimes.

The shock workers of the New Capitalist regime worked at home or at the office or on their porch or on a retreat to a beautiful place in the country or from their laptop while on the beach at Dubai, or wherever they might be. Their sartorial style and bodily ornaments seemed designed to match those of the city's large homeless and mentally ill population, to the point where it was sometimes difficult to tell the New Capitalists from the street people.

Movement was the only thing that signaled the difference. New Capitalists had a reason to be somewhere, so if the tattooed Goth girl walked in a straight line with a sense of purpose, she probably had a home and a job and a schedule. If, on the other hand, she carried around a big plastic bag, bumped against walls as she walked, and muttered to herself, that meant something else.

New Capitalism had succeeded in generating unprecedented amounts of wealth, but instead of the public libraries, museums, hospitals, and architectural wonders financed by the coldly amoral Robber Barons over 100 years ago, it had uglified and vulgarized society to a scarcely believable extent. It had also produced billionaires who, having made the world ugly and alienating, want to escape from it—buying citizenships in faraway isolated countries, creating closed island paradises, dreaming of flying to other planets.

At least the old plutocrats had some respect for aesthetics. I can't imagine Andrew Carnegie or John D. Rockefeller bankrolling these monstrosities. Poverty has a lot of downsides, but it also plays a role in preservation. If you lack the money to throw something out and buy something new, you'll be more inclined to keep it in working order. But nothing prevents the New Capitalists from smashing everything in sight and starting all over, because they have the money to do so. Their execrable taste makes everything worse.

"All that is solid melts into air, all that is holy is profaned," as a certain somebody I've mentioned put it.

Before this trip, I'd never been to Seattle. My understanding was that it had formerly been a pleasant city in beautiful natural surroundings, where one could live a decent middle-class life. Now, it felt like a dystopia ruled by a handful of giant corporations in a neo-feudalistic fashion. More and more parts of America and the world in general seemed to be going in this direction. When the time came to go back to Roverton, I was relieved. Seattleites still had the beautiful nature as an escape from the corporate feudalism and general sense of alienation. I had the nature, and my little town on a human scale, which had been built up with some respect for basic aesthetic principles. But how long could my town hold out?

I thought I'd start work with a little mood music. I took the *Running in Place* CD out of its case and slid it into the stereo mini-system that I kept in my office. I pressed a button, and the instruments started up, a rustic sound dominated by the interplay of guitar and fiddle. Then I heard a voice that was unmistakably Jackie's: "One evening as I rambled…" she began. Yes, they were opening with "Reynardine," the song that apparently drove her bandmate Howard crazy through repetition. I'd never heard Jackie sing before, but I recognized her voice immediately. I let the CD play on as I messed with my computer. The spirited version of "Reynardine" came to an end and was followed by a group instrumental, something mournfully Celtic, a dignified lament. I heard the plink and plonk of a hammered dulcimer, sounding like an overly resonant harpsichord, and I thought of the one they called Onyx, the girl who disappeared and never came back. She seemed to be playing her own funeral march a few years in advance.

My task for the day was much more prosaic. I mean that in the literal sense: I had to create a piece of prose. Much as I preferred to procrastinate, Raj in faraway Seattle expected something from me, and I had to produce it. I found that *Running in Place* tugged my attention away from this unpalatable assignment, so I switched off the CD and turned on the radio instead. National Public Radio seemed like a safe, solid choice. The voices of its journalists, soothing and chirpy by turns, would provide a nice murmuring undercurrent to my labors. They were broadcasting a story about some agricultural project being implemented in a poor part of Mexico. The usual words for that type of NPR story were being pronounced: *holistic, sustainable, elders, indigenous, intersectional, community based*. This was the inspiration I needed for my own work. These soothing words from the NPR reporter opened my mind and let the clichés flow in. In my case, the clichés came from a different sphere of business. I played with them the way a composer plays with chords and a painter experiments with colors. I lined them up, let them clash with each other, chopped them into pieces and made new combinations from them.

Let's see… First we can *accelerate* something. But what specifically should we accelerate? How about *growth*? Yes, everybody loves growth. We can't live without growth; you can't run a business without it. But remember, the overall theme is "excellence in innovation." If we want to adhere to this theme, we can talk about "accelerating excellence," which leads to "accelerated innovation," which in turn results in growth. Yes, that's how I can get to where I want to be.

Don't forget that we need to *execute*. Banish from your mind all images of gallows and electric chairs; what we're going to execute here is a *strategy*. To have a strategy, first we need a *strategic vision* (I borrowed this term from Ethan, who liked to use it when talking about his culinary plans). We execute this strategic vision in the context of an accelerated program of innovation. Excellence in innovation is generated as part of a developmental program for strategic leadership. Collaborative and sustainable business improvements are delivered against a background of creative innovation and in a framework of strategic excellence.

"What do you think about what I've written here, Bruce?" I asked, turning my computer so that the dog could see the screen.

"Awful stuff," he barked, and jumped off the couch.

Our team achieves sustained value creation through innovative integration into a developed leadership paradigm. We execute based on an engaged vision generating client satisfaction through a constant process of results-oriented innovation. Our superior track record of inventiveness, innovative agility, self-aware leadership, accelerated vision, and transformational excellence has been recognized with awards and accolades from numerous industry leaders.

I was off to a good start.

This time, Noodles Fontaine wanted to meet me at a building owned by the park district. This was a versatile space located just off Franklin Square that did triple duty as a senior center, youth center, and general meeting place for various social clubs. He wanted to meet me at this location because today, the company would be larger than usual. Today all three of my informants, plus myself, gathered at the same place. It was the first time that all of us would be meeting together, a milestone, like an important international summit. As usual, Noodles wore his baseball cap indoors.

Although I met with Noodles most often, he wasn't my only informant. If you don't count Old Earl Anderson (who contributed in his own verbose and roundabout fashion), I had two others. One was Christine Vandersteen, whose name was easy to remember because it rhymed. She was a round-faced woman in her late sixties with a pleasant smile. She seemed like the sort of person who'd bring you milk and cookies if you were feeling down. However, she was a former schoolteacher, and in addition to her general air of friendliness, she had a well-developed intolerance of nonsense honed to a fine edge by years of dealing with the antics of children. The third informant, Eddie Donnelly, was the youngest at fifty-five or so. Lean, mustachioed, and dark in complexion, he was an outsider in the town, even though he was an old-timer. He did some kind of job in one of the boat shops and spent a lot of time on the water. He was rumored to have "Indian blood" and to have been in trouble with the law on a couple of occasions. Nobody, however, could prove anything. Eddie had been suggested as an informant by Noodles himself, as somebody who could bring a different perspective due to being on the fringes of society.

"Okay," I began. "Noodles, you remember that we talked about language at our last session. I want to get deeper into that subject, with a particular focus on unusual vocabulary items." (I'd been reading up on Boontling again, and that inspired me to pursue the subject further.) "Do any of you three recall any unusual words you used? I mean, words that were different from the normal terms for things?"

Noodles scratched the side of his head in a contemplative manner. "We had some strange names for animals. For example, squirrels were called 'alfreds.' This was in honor of old Alfred Schmidt, who lived on Van Pelt Street when I grew up, about the time I was on my all-noodle diet. He hated squirrels so much that he hunted them with a rifle. He was a lousy shot, though. I don't think he ever killed a squirrel. Not that I ever heard. In fact, come to think of it, I don't think he ever even *shot* at a squirrel. He just liked to get his rifle out and wave it around while shouting at the squirrels to get off his lawn. Poor Alfred, I don't think he ever got the alfreds off his lawn by his own efforts. He shouted and waved that rifle, but the squirrels kept on running across his lawn and chewing on things. Us young people in the neighborhood, we were amazed to see this. It was funny, but it was also a little bit scary. If he could get so crazy over squirrels, how might he react to other animals or people? It was about that time that we started calling squirrels alfreds in honor of him. Later he got a dog, and that finally scared the alfreds away. There's a moral to the story: if you need to get something done, get yourself a dog."

The whole time Noodles was talking, Christine was looking at him with an expression of increasing wonderment. "I've never heard anything like that at all," she said. "You want to know something, Noodles? I was acquainted with Alfred Schmidt personally. But his first name wasn't Alfred, it was Albert. His last name wasn't Schmidt, it was Smith. He lived on Van Buren Street, not Van Pelt Street. I remember that detail because I knew that Martin Van Buren was the only American president who spoke Dutch as his native language. I knew it because my grandparents spoke Dutch, and they told me that."

"Interesting detail," I noted. "Thanks."

"I thought you said they spoke Flemish," said Noodles.

"It's the same thing, isn't it?" said Christine, looking at the ex-prof of Germanic languages for confirmation.

"Yeah, pretty much," I said.

"Thanks," continued Christine. "I'm not quite done with Albert Smith. Maybe he had a rifle, but I never, ever saw it. I never heard that he hated squirrels. Your story about him waving the rifle around and shouting at the squirrels doesn't ring true to me. And I've never—not once—heard anyone in this town refer to squirrels as 'alfreds'."

Noodles stared at her. I don't think he was offended, just disappointed that someone would question his testimony. I tried to keep things cordial. "If his name was really Albert, then did you ever hear anyone refer to squirrels as 'alberts'?"

"Not once," said Christine. "Strangely enough, we called them squirrels."

"Eddie, what do you think?" I asked.

Eddie leaned back in his chair, cracked his knuckles, and chuckled. "Alfreds and alberts? You gotta be kidding me, Noodles. Never, ever heard that in my life. Squirrels are squirrels, never been anything else."

I turned to Noodles. "I'm afraid I'll have to be a bit skeptical about this one, pending confirmation from another source. Are you sure you're remembering things correctly, Noodles?"

He was silent for a few seconds, then took off his cap and ran his fingers wearily through his close-cropped gray hair. "Now that you mention it, I may be misremembering things a little. It could be that we tried to pin Alfred's name on the squirrels, but it didn't take. It was me and a couple of friends who tried to get that trend going. But it might have died about the time Alfred got his dog."

"Albert," Christine corrected him. "Not Alfred."

"Whatever," Noodles shot back. He put his cap back on.

"Still, it's kind of an interesting story in itself," I commented, trying to salvage the situation. "You've given me something to write about in any case, even if it's not quite what I was looking for." I suggested that we move on from squirrels to something else.

Once again, Noodles spoke up with enthusiasm. "Here's something I remember very well. We used to call rabbits 'buckchucks.' That's right. Unfortunately, there's not a story to go with it. I have no idea where the term came from."

Eddie looked at Noodles skeptically. "It wasn't buckchucks. It was chuckbucks. Hell, that was the term I used myself. You wanna back me up here, Christine?"

Christine looked flummoxed. "I've never heard either one. Maybe it was both?"

Noodles seemed to be enjoying the confusion of his fellow informants. He cross-examined Eddie. "Eddie, it's my duty to inform you that we have actual documentation dating back several decades, decisively proving that rabbits were once known as buckchucks around here. Never as chuckbucks. What do you say to that?"

"Chuckbucks was the word I used," said Eddie, sounding faintly defensive. "That's how I remember it."

"It was buckchucks."

"Chuckbucks."

"Buckchucks."

"Chuckbucks."

"Buckchucks."

"Chuckbucks!" Said Eddie with a laugh, throwing his hands in the air.

"What documentation are you talking about, Noodles?" I asked.

Noodles said triumphantly: "In the form of an elementary school yearbook from the 1970s, listing a children's play group called the Roverton Buckchucks. The yearbook says this was a local slang term for rabbits."

"I'd be very interested in seeing that yearbook," I said.

"I'll see if I can find it," said Noodles.

I said to the group: "Does anyone know the origin of this term?" To my mind, it had a vaguely American Indian ring to it. If so, Ojibwe or Menominee would be the most likely candidates, given where we were located. In view of the "Indian blood" rumors about Eddie, I didn't want to put him on the spot by addressing him directly. But all three of them said basically the same thing: they had no idea.

The conversation went on in this vein for a while. Eventually, we decided to put an end to it, and I headed off to the bathroom. While I was doing my business in the donicker, my head continued to ring with the ongoing debate about buckchucks versus chuckbucks, alfreds versus alberts, and so on. When I emerged, the two men were gone, but Christine was still there. She was waiting for me in the corridor, smiling.

"It was a fun session today," I said in my best diplomatic voice.

"Frankly, what was most fun for me was taking Noodles down. You put way too much trust in him. He's a good man but he's a known confabulator."

"He *is* entertaining, you have to admit," I said.

"No question about it. You'll get lots of entertainment value from Noodles. It won't do your scholarly work any good, though. If he remembers something correctly, it's probably by accident." She laughed. "The kids where I taught had a nickname for me. They called me 'Mean Christine Vandersteen.' That was because I didn't put up with any nonsense from them. But you know what? They learned something in my classroom."

Mean Christine had a point. If I wanted to produce a valuable piece of work, I probably shouldn't be relying on a man past retirement age who continued to call himself by a silly teenage nickname, which he'd only received due to a ridiculous culinary experiment undertaken as a form of adolescent revolt.

"Well," I said, "today was a learning experience for me. My earlier meetings with Noodles all took place one on one. That meant there was no one around to raise any objections to what he was saying." A question popped into my mind. "Say, did you ever hear people, when they were feeling under pressure, say 'I'm feeling a little eng'?"

"Eng?"

"Yes, eng. German for 'tight' or 'narrow'."

"Hmm… I think I heard that a few times, when I was growing up. But later—meaning late sixties, early seventies, I'm not sure—people stopped saying it. Did Noodles tell you that it was a common expression?"

"He did."

"He may have been right about that, but if so, it stopped being common a long time ago."

"Thanks," I said. "Nice to have some confirmation, even if you're not very confident about it." I left our session in a mild state of confusion and doubt. Was this project even worth pursuing?

Let me tell you the story of a dog called Wesley. That name, by itself, was enough to mark out the dog as belonging to a nuke, not an old-timer. The dogs of old-timers had names like Jack or Rusty or Champ. The dogs of nukes were called Paloma or Galadriel or Lancelot. Or Wesley.

Wesley was a smooth fox terrier and the companion animal of Ashley and Alex Henderson, a pair of nukes who'd relocated from Chicago suburbia. They were in their late thirties, had no children, and worked at jobs that they described, in a phrase that made no literal sense, as "self-fulfilling." I think they meant that these jobs made them (Ashley and Alex) feel fulfilled, not that the jobs fulfilled themselves.

Alex was engaged in some form of "remote consulting," which put him in a situation possibly like mine. It had something to do with finance, supply chains, and other things I didn't understand. Ashley was a graphic artist or designer. They heard about Roverton through some personal connection, decided they liked the town well enough to move here, and relocated to a newly built, rather sterile-looking white house up on the bluff, with a good view of the lake.

I knew them a little. Dog-walking was the catalyst. They lived only a block away from me, so when I was out with Bruce in the morning, I'd sometimes run into Ashley walking Wesley. Ashley was blonde and scrubbed and the very picture of a modern healthy woman. Wesley, by contrast, was about fourteen or fifteen and manifested a range of canine infirmities. He was blind in one eye, and losing sight in the other, which was afflicted by a cataract. He limped, slowly. Any attempt to speed him up was met with resistance; anything faster than very slow was evidently painful. At one point during this time of our morning excursions, he couldn't walk at all, because he was recovering from a hip operation. For a couple of weeks, Bruce and I would be greeted by the pitiful sight of either Ashley or Alex (or sometimes both) carrying Wesley from place to place up and down the block, planting him temporarily at various locations so he could do his business and commune with nature for a little while. Bruce tried to engage Wesley in dog-to-dog friendship, doing the usual sniffing and jostling, but it was clear that Wesley wasn't all that interested.

One day, as I watched Wesley struggle to take some tentative steps near the end of his recovery period, I decided on impulse to go over to Alex. He was a smooth-looking guy with a full head of springy brown hair and horn-rimmed glasses. Just like Ashley, he had a clean and scrubbed appearance, as if he'd never been seriously harmed by the physical world, never been cut, burned, scraped or bitten.

"Hey there, Fred," he said with a smile, as I walked over.

"Wesley's looking better," I said. "Taking some actual steps. On the road to recovery."

"We sure hope so. The vet was optimistic."

"That so?"

"Yeah, we might have another year with him. He's such a great guy."

"The vet's a great guy?" I asked.

"No, I meant Wesley. But the vet's also a great guy."

I couldn't find the right words for what I really wanted to say, which was that Wesley's time was up, and keeping the dog alive much past that point would be a trial and a burden for him, and for God's sake and the dog's too, it was time to accept that fact and stop tormenting him. But I couldn't say it.

"Hey, I'm wondering about something," said Alex. "Back in Naperville, we used to go to a Pet Parent Circle."

"A pet what?"

"It's a kind of social club. People who have pets gather to share the latest news about them, and they can also ask for help and advice. We found it very useful. Is there anything like that here?"

"Never heard of it myself," I replied. "I believe Naperville is a big suburb, is it not? You would have had a lot of options there. Roverton is nice, but it's a small town. Also, I don't know if the sort of thing you're looking for would really fly here. Not yet, anyway. Maybe in a few years." This last part was my way of saying that most Rovertonians still regarded their children as children and their pets as pets. The idea of "pet parents" would have struck them as absurd.

I don't know if I succeeded in making my point. Yet I needed to communicate what I wanted to say about Wesley's health and prospects to his "parents."

At this time, I still shared superficial pleasantries on a regular basis with my fellow dog-walking neighbor, Mrs. Westerberg. Bruce always perked up when he saw her and Porky the corgi coming down the street. One day while we were out, I saw them approaching, and I was seized by an idea.

After a brief discussion of the weather, I said: "You've met the new dog, I suppose? Wesley, or whatever he's called."

As soon as I mentioned Wesley, sadness spread across Mrs. Westerberg's autumnal, bespectacled face.

"Oh, that poor doggie," she said. Then, the response I was hoping for: "Why are they keeping him alive? It's time for him to go. That should be obvious."

"Wesley must be a great companion for them," I said. "I've talked to them, to Ashley and Alex. They don't have any kids of their own, so I think they regard Wesley as their substitute child." But, not wanting to commit myself explicitly to this thesis, I added: "At least, that's what it looks like to me."

"Their child, eh? Well, you wouldn't put your kid down. Even if sometimes you feel like doing it."

"But you see, that's the great privilege dogs have. We're not obligated to keep them alive as long as we can. If they could express their opinion, I'm sure most dogs would agree with me. Don't you think Wesley would?"

"I'm certain he would," she said, nodding vigorously.

"Yeah, if it was up to me, I'd make that vet appointment right now. Unfortunately, I can't do that."

A sudden change of subject. "What do those two do for a living, anyway?"

"I'm not entirely sure," I said. "He does some kind of consulting, but I'm not sure what he consults about. She's a graphic something, an artist, I think." Here, I was telling less than I knew. In giving only the broad outlines, I'd encourage Mrs. Westerberg to fill in the rest according to her prejudices. I could tell what she was thinking: *nukes*. Not the sort of people I grew up with. Probably nice enough in their own way. But in a sense, aliens. Driving real estate prices up. Replacing our old dive bars (which had plain honest names like Wally's) with that fancy "craft" stuff (like Ethan's place with the vaguely blasphemous name, Our Lady of Hops). Opening art galleries and artisanal food shops and sustainable wellness centers. With their holistic fusion studios, their organic recycled cuisine, their multiple varieties of lemon butter. If they had kids, those kids were demanding and overly sensitive and had a sense of entitlement foreign to our simple, honest old-time people. If they didn't have kids, their kids were dogs, cats and parrots. Overall, the adults are fine folks, I'm sure. But do we really need them here?

My mission had been accomplished. I'd dropped the seed of an idea in Mrs. Westerberg's receptive head. She was a lady known for her plain speech and her open, straightforward approach to everyone. She'd be the proper courier to convey my message, my plea for mercy, to the Hendersons. I couldn't force myself to do it. I was from the same milieu as Alex and Ashley; I was one of the dreaded nukes. Much as I sometimes regretted it, I couldn't break with my class conditioning. I wanted to do so—I wished for the natural eloquence that old-time Rovertonians took for granted—but I didn't know how. I left it to honest, frank Mrs. Westerberg to tell the Hendersons the truth they needed to hear.

One morning several days after my conversation with Mrs. Westerberg, as I was walking Bruce, I saw Alex coming down the street toward me. He was alone—no dog with him—and looked distraught. His pace slowed as he approached me. I put on a face expressing concern. After the usual greetings, he said what I was expecting, indeed hoping, to hear.

"Wesley's gone."

Inwardly I was relieved; outwardly I offered my condolences. "Was it natural causes? Or did you take him to the vet?"

Alex frowned with anger.

"Neither. You won't believe it. We're furious about it, Ashley and I both. It's—it's—it's hard for me to describe. Can I show you something? I need to show you this. It's unreal. Wait here." He strode off quickly toward his house. I stood there on the sidewalk, turning over different scenarios in my mind. Did a hit-and-run driver get Wesley? Had he been accidentally shot by a hunter? Had he drowned in the lake? While I was pondering these possibilities, Alex came back, holding a piece of paper.

"Read this," he said, thrusting it at me. It was a standard A4 white sheet, containing a printed letter with no signatures, no contact information, and no handwriting of any kind. It read as follows:

Dear Alex & Ashley,

We are a small group of concerned citizens. Like you, we love animals, especially dogs. One way we show this love is by knowing when a dog's life is no longer worth living and taking the proper steps to end it. We have made the decision to end Wesley's difficult life. If it's any consolation to you, we can tell you that Wesley's last moments were peaceful, and he died surrounded by people who cared about him.

We know you are angry or sad or some combination of both right now. But we're sure you will understand in time that this was the only good solution for Wesley. He is now in a place where life is no longer a painful struggle. Someday you will thank us, even if you don't know who we are.

With love & compassion
Three Good Samaritans of Roverton

"Shit," escaped from me. My shock wasn't feigned. This was not at all what I'd wished for. When I dropped that seed of an idea in Mrs. Westerberg's mind, the plan was that she would tell the Hendersons, in her old-timer Rovertonian way, about the need to put Wesley down. Thus, Alex and Ashley would feel some social pressure to make the decision to end his life. No respectable person wants to get a reputation for being cruel to animals, and in Wesley's case the solution was obvious. I was also disturbed by the idea that there might be freelance dog murderers roaming about the town. The thought that I might have inadvertently caused this was even more disturbing. For now, I would have to watch what I said. It was important not to betray any sense that I approved of this—even though, on a certain level, I did.

"That's horrible, Alex. I mean, I can see why—well, it should have been your decision, not theirs."

"We were going to talk about making that decision this week," said Alex. He looked as if he were about to cry. "Now, these cowards who won't show themselves have taken that decision away from us."

We stood there for a little while, both of us quietly fuming. I think he was fuming; I was trying to look like I was fuming while thinking very hard about the situation and how I should avoid getting involved any further.

I said: "But how did they get him? You both work from home, don't you?"

"We had to leave the house for a few hours yesterday. When we came home, Wesley was gone, and this piece of paper was on the kitchen table. I called the cops immediately, but they haven't come up with anything yet. We're used to leaving the door unlocked when we go away for a short time. You can do that around here, right? That's what we thought. We won't do that anymore." He paused and looked around. "I have to ask. Did you see any suspicious behavior on this street yesterday, between about noon and three?"

"Can't say that I did," I replied truthfully. "Didn't notice anything out of the ordinary. But then, I wasn't watching the street very much." I ended the conversation quickly, while trying not to say anything that would excite suspicion.

In the following days and weeks, I treated the Hendersons with the sort of cordial superficiality I usually deployed toward the old-timers. Fine folks, nice and professional; conscientious contributors to the revitalization of Roverton, but I wasn't interested in having closer relations with them for the time being. I feared that in their quest to discover who had euthanized their beloved child, they'd seize on anything I said and allow their suspicions to boil up into questions that I, being a bad liar, would have a hard time answering.

As for Mrs. Westerberg, the next time I ran into her while walking the dog, my heart jumped. I put on a casual yet concerned face (I think that's what it was) and walked right up to her. As Bruce and Porky started sniffing and teasing each other, I said hello. I wanted to avoid the subject of Wesley altogether. Would she oblige me? We engaged in some small talk, but she said nothing about Wesley's fate. As she walked away, I thought I observed a faint, sly smile cross her face. I searched my memory for any indication that she had smiled that way before. I couldn't come up with anything. It was the sort of smile that is shared between keepers of an awkward secret—a smile that tells you something without telling you anything at all.

It was Saturday morning, and I was in Reinhard's Diner on Franklin Square, having breakfast with Jackie O'Reilly. While Jackie told me about the latest humdrum goings-on in her life, I toyed with my pancakes, smearing too much butter and pouring too much syrup on them. It was supposed to be that way. I consciously acted within a small-town American paradigm of neighborliness, quaintness, and good cheer, a paradigm that encompassed the public eating of pancakes. The pancakes were also proof of civilization, of the continuity of life. Urbanists, and the more intellectual kind of small-town leaders, spoke of the organic community. They probably spent a lot of time eating pancakes in places like this.

Reinhard's Diner had more than pancakes; it had *authenticity*. It was a real diner run by a real person named Reinhard. It was exactly the sort of place nukes looked for when they moved to Roverton. Most of them didn't know that even though Reinhard's name was on the diner, Reinhard had died of lung cancer several years before. His son sold the diner to an entrepreneur from suburban Milwaukee, who kept Reinhard's name on the establishment while upgrading the diner with all the newest equipment and furnishings. To sum up, the diner wasn't *authentically* authentic, but it was authentic enough, and that was what mattered.

I didn't care about authenticity, not after living here for a couple of years already. The cult of authenticity was for the real nukes, the freshly arrived who knew what they were looking for. I was at Reinhard's because they had the best coffee in town, a deliciously dark roast which, with the addition of cream and sugar, conjured up vistas of tropical paradise while infusing my declining middle-aged carcass with some necessary vigor. Reinhard's pancakes were also spongy and filling, which was more important than their conformity to an ideological paradigm.

"I wish I had an infinite stomach, and infinite cash to go with it," I said. "I'd start the day here, and drink coffee and eat pancakes and waffles and all the other stuff on the menu. I'd shovel it all down without a care in the world for about three hours. Then I'd go to Our Lady of Hops and drink beer and eat pub food till six o'clock. Then I'd finish up at that new ice cream place, Jorgensen's or whatever it's called. Then I'd collapse exhausted on my bed."

"That sounds horrible," said Jackie. "Moderation in all things. It's still a good rule."

"You have to admit it would be entertaining and fun. Achieve Nirvana by over-consumption."

"Not how it works in the real world. I went to a Catholic high school. We read the *Spiritual Exercises* of St. Ignatius Loyola. One of the methods he uses is called 'application of the senses.' You use your imagination to put yourself into a scene of the Gospels, or experience the sufferings of a martyr, and so forth. I still make use of this. If I feel like stuffing myself, I imagine in detail what my stomach will feel like afterwards. To overcome temptation, it works pretty well. Last week I was in Alvarado's Fine Foods, and I saw some yummy-looking chocolate cheesecake. I was tempted to buy it, but then I visualized myself bringing it home, being by myself, gorging on it in front of the TV and having a stomachache afterwards. I literally felt my stomach hurting, and not from hunger, but from overeating. I resisted. I stared right at that cheesecake, and I held myself back and felt proud about it."

"Something to feel proud of, eh? That's nice."

"We all need to feel that way from time to time."

"On the other hand, I'm glad to be talking to you, because I feel a need to unburden myself," I said. She looked at me with wide-eyed receptiveness while drinking her coffee, as if to say, *Oh goodie, this will be juicy.* "I don't want to tell Ethan, because he'll probably make fun of me. But I think you'll understand and not be too judgmental." I told Jackie the story of Wesley the dog and my ambiguous role in his demise. "I need to be honest about it. On the one hand, I didn't intend for it to play out like this. On the other hand, I'm relieved that Wesley has slipped away peacefully to Doggie Heaven, and I'm proud of the fact that I might have played a humanitarian—or rather, dogitarian—part in making it happen."

"If it's any comfort, you can't be charged with criminal liability," said Jackie. "You were voicing a suggestion. You can't be held responsible for anything other people decided to do based on what you said."

"Yeah, I know. But there's one thing I'm kicking myself about. I thought I could read people. After all, I've been reading them and reading about them since I was a child. I thought I could figure them out. I knew Mrs. Westerberg. I'd interacted with her. I figured that she was a plain-speaking old-timer. I had no idea she was as sneaky as that, to tell a 'small group of concerned citizens' to take care of Wesley and how to do it. I really misread the situation."

"At least the dog benefited from it," said Jackie. "You can take some comfort from that fact."

"I suppose that's the most important thing. Meanwhile, maybe I should give up on the idea that I can interact with old-timers in any way but superficially."

"But I'm practically an old-timer myself. I think I've lived here almost long enough to be considered one. Here you are, unburdening yourself to me."

"Do you ever think they'll formalize these categories? Like, if you've been a long-timer for a long enough time, you can graduate to old-timer status. Then they'll give you a certificate, and you can have a ceremony at the village hall, celebrating your graduation."

"Going back to Mrs. Westerberg for a moment," said Jackie. "How do you know she didn't come up with the idea of euthanizing Wesley on her own?"

"Well… You have a point. I don't know. I guess I'm extrapolating. I make a suggestion to her, she tells the wrong people, the dog dies. It's a logical sequence of events. But I have no proof that it happened that way because of anything I said. Maybe I was helping to build consensus. You know, Mrs. Westerberg wants to kill the dog, and she's seeking social support for that idea. When I support her, she realizes that she can get away with her nefarious plan, because there are enough people who agree with her."

"You're never going to know for sure. I think you should let it go. The important thing is that Wesley is in a better place."

"Like the note said." I paused to slice my remaining pancake into little bite-sized morsels, a way of making it last longer. "I think I'm going to lie low for a while with everyone involved. I don't want to put ideas and suspicions into their heads. I'll be the friendly guy who waves and says hi, but that'll be all. By the way, the chocolate-chip pancakes here are also really good. Yummy and decadent."

"A little too heavy for me, I'm afraid."

"Got any big plans for the weekend?" I asked.

"Rehearsal."

"Rehearsal?"

"Yes, rehearsal," she said. "No, we're not putting the band back together, if that's what you're wondering. I joined the Jolly Company of Rovertonians recently, and we've started rehearsals for our fall concert at the Opera House. I'm singing again, first time in ages."

"That's hardly a surprise. In fact, the only thing that surprises me is that you didn't get back to singing earlier."

"I thought I was done with it forever. But I missed it too much. Hey, Christine Vandersteen is also in the Jolly Company, and she told me about your project. It sounds like an absolute hoot. Can't wait to read it."

"I was hoping it would be a little more than an absolute hoot. Believe it or not, I have a semi-serious scholarly purpose here. Most of the hooting is due to one informant in particular. Henceforth I'm going to check and cross-check everything he says rigorously."

"Which one particular informant is that?"

"Noodles Fontaine," I said with a heavy heart. Jackie let fly a laugh. "You know him?"

"Oh, come on! He's a legend. He's known as the village idiot. Scratch that. He's not an idiot, far from it. He's more like the town clown. He's the guy who gets the Santa Claus jobs at Christmas, because he makes up these rambling stories and the kids like it. Hey, did he tell you that great story about Bill Diehl and the sculptures made of matches?"

I was devastated. "You're telling me he made that up, too?"

"If he told you about any sculptures larger than Bill's own house, that was made up. And Noodles' made-up story had a bad effect in real life. Poor Bill's wife—people blamed her for causing her husband's death, because all she wanted to do was light up a cigarette. Remember, this was about the time that campaigns against smoking were becoming a big thing. A lot of people latched on to the story for that reason."

"Damn," I said. "I really wanted to see that awesome sculpture of the Capitol Building in Madison."

Jackie put the coffee cup to her mouth, started drinking, then choked and splattered. She put the cup down, laughing.

"What's funny now?" I demanded.

"Sorry, I can't help it. It's just that Noodles got you to take him seriously."

"Yeah, well, I think I learned my lesson," I grumbled. "What was I saying about how I shouldn't interact with old-timers? This is the second story today to prove it."

"Yes, and I'll repeat what I said earlier—I'm practically an old-timer myself. Don't beat yourself up." Jackie excused herself to go to the donicker. I sat there, nursing my delicious cup of coffee, or horn of zeese as they called it in Boonville, and wondering (not too seriously) what was wrong with me. I was having some major trouble with misreading people—particularly Rovertonian old-timers. Perhaps it wasn't something I should worry about, but it made me wonder if my cognitive abilities were as sharp as I supposed. Who was the real village idiot—Noodles Fontaine, or me?

When Jackie came back, I asked: "What was it like with you, when you first moved here? How long did it take before they accepted you as one of their own?"

She stirred her coffee and took a long sip before answering.

"It was a gradual process. But if I had to pinpoint one incident, it would be the Fourth of July, maybe two and a half years after I moved here. I was walking around in the evening, watching people relax and celebrate, and they hung out in their yards and houses and on the village green. While I was walking around—and my son was with me—we got invited to two different house parties. One was at a neighbor's place, a guy who knew me a little already. The other was a bunch of folks we ran into a few blocks away. I recognized a couple of them, but I can't say that I knew them, and I don't know if they knew me, but they invited us into their yard for some drinks and snacks. They asked me all kinds of questions about who I was and what I was doing. That shows how much social trust there was here, that they were willing to invite this person they barely knew into their homes. It really made me feel part of the community, in a way I hadn't quite up till then."

"That sounds nice. I guess I have to wait for my Fourth of July moment."

"That said… I moved here long, long before the new wave. It could be that the tribe accepted me because there was just me and my son, not a whole huge wave of people. A single mother moving all the way from Boston was a little exotic. It wasn't perceived as a threat. I was Jackie the folk singer and I was a taste of the counterculture for them, but that was all. Now, people are coming in from Chicago and Los Angeles and," (she pointed her pinky at me) "Philadelphia and Minneapolis and God knows where else. The old-timers feel swamped by the newcomers. Mind you, old-timer Rovertonians are peaceful people. They aren't going to burn a cross on your lawn or throw a brick through your window if they disapprove of you being here. But they won't invite you to parties, and they probably won't give you a funny but endearing nickname."

"It's now a two-tribe town," I concluded. "Probably makes things more interesting."

"And more expensive for everyone," she pointed out.

We rounded off our morning with a visit to Fabelhaft Bakery, a few doors down on the square. The bakery was a real survivor, a true old-timer establishment (as a local travel guide put it, "founded by Paul

Fabelhaft in 1924, it's a Roverton institution"). I had my doubts about that, mainly because of the name (which means "fabulous"), but odd names do exist in this world, so perhaps the story was true. It was cute and old-fashioned enough to be popular with the nukes, and it seemed to be flourishing.

I bought a mixed selection of donuts, and Jackie succumbed to a luscious-looking cheesecake (no *Spiritual Exercises* for her today, apparently). As in Central Europe, the bakery had chairs and tables lining its pale cream-colored walls, and the chairs were all occupied by locals enjoying their coffee, tea and sweets. Leave aside the fact that English was the only language being spoken, and you could fool yourself into thinking you were in Prague or Vienna. A calendar from the year 1932 was a permanent fixture decorating one wall; it featured a top page consisting of a black-and-white photo of Franklin Square taken at about that time, with the bottom page showing the months of the year in tiny print. I always wondered if this was meant as a kind of tribute to the last complete normal year in Central Europe before Hitler and his cronies started destroying that world. More likely, the owner simply liked the photo, and thought the calendar provided a nice nostalgic touch.

When I was a kid, we sometimes watched a children's TV show called *Zoom*. The show had one of those inane yet memorable theme songs that would stick in your head, forcing you to hum or sing or whistle it whether you wanted to or not. It was all about how we were going to *zoom zoom zoom* in perpetuity, with apparently no respite for those of us who wanted a break from zooming every now and then. Now that I was having to employ a different meaning of Zoom for work and social reasons, this song, much to my irritation, kept popping into my head.

"What are you singing?" asked Amanda, frowning at me from a few thousand miles away.

"Oh, I'm zooming," I said. "Sorry, I can't help it."

We hadn't talked for a while. I couldn't remember exactly how long it had been—three weeks? A month? In years past, I would have known exactly when we interacted and under what circumstances. I wondered if my current lack of specificity meant not just that we were drifting apart, but that I had become reconciled to it, even comfortable about it. It felt like the new normal.

After a brief introductory exchange, Amanda finally told me, in detail, what her "foundation work" consisted of.

"You would like it, I think, Freddie. With your interest in traditional small towns and all."

"What is it, exactly?"

"It's an environmental foundation. We get some EU grants and some private money. Mostly, we're helping restore villages and other traditional places. It's a sustainability exercise, you might say. There are a lot of forlorn locations, particularly in the newer member states, that need sprucing up. Now I'm in the eastern part of Poland, close to the Lithuanian border. We helped restore an Orthodox church recently—there used to be lots of Russian Orthodox Old Believers in this region. The nature around here is beautiful. But we do have to contend with groups of elderly German cyclists riding around the roads a lot. They're doing some kind of health tourism. They like to stop at some site we're working at, break out their bottles of water, and talk in loud voices. It's too bad you're not here, you could tell me what they're saying."

"That sounds like lots of fun," I said. "All the more reason for you to come to Roverton. I think you'd like the town. In addition to the fact that you have family here." I probably shouldn't have said that last bit; it made our family sound like an afterthought. I continued: "But if you don't mind, why wouldn't you tell me the details of what you're doing until now?"

"To tell the truth, it's because I only had a vague idea of what I was going to do. First, I spent some time with my Mum and Dad, since I hadn't seen them in so long. While I was staying with them, I was spinning my wheels, so to speak. I wanted to undertake some kind of foundation-based work, volunteering, something like that, maybe even getting paid if they were willing to do that. I know enough people in that field, and they were able to connect me with this program."

"How long does the program last?"

"It'll be over at the end of summer. To anticipate your next question, yes, I *will* come to Roverton when I'm done here. That's a promise. Looking forward to it. Ethan's been telling me about his activities and the exciting plans he's got for Our Lady of Hops. It sounds fascinating!"

"What about me?" I almost whined.

"Oh, I want to see you too, Freddie! It's been too long. Sometimes you just need to get away for a while and gain some perspective. I think I'm ready to go home… Wherever home is. But we can talk about that, too."

That was a relief. I was still in the picture. I wanted to know more.

"How does your foundation work? Are you getting paid, or is this strictly a volunteer thing?"

"Oh, we get a small stipend, I can't buy a car with it, but it's better than nothing. Giovanni—he's the leader, officially they call him the facilitator—makes sure we all get paid something. He's an expert at dealing with the bureaucracy back in Brussels."

"Giovanni, eh? Is he a good cook as well? Does he like wine? Does he sing operatic arias?"

"Oh, there you go stereotyping! The facilitator doesn't cook for us. He's too busy facilitating! Mind you, we get our free time in the late afternoon and evening, and we've had some nice walks and done some outdoor cooking! We like to go for walks in the woods and fields around here, it's beautiful. Yesterday, Giovanni and I visited the pagan burial grounds in the woods. It was just me and him. We brought a bottle of Polish vodka and toasted the pagan tribes that used to live around here. It was fun and a bit romantic!"

"Oh, it was romantic, was it?"

"Yes, but mainly it was fun." After clearing her throat, she changed the subject. "What's this I'm hearing about you and Jackie O'Reilly? Ethan said the two of you are spending quite a lot of time together."

"Ethan said that?" (Damn kid; I'll have to tell him to keep his big mouth shut.) "I don't know what he said exactly, but we've got some mutual interests. She's fun to talk to. Do you know she was in a folk-rock band called the McTaggart Family Creamery? They enjoy something of an underground reputation. Broke up many years ago, though, which is when she settled here. Interesting story, I'll have to fill you in on it when you get back." I kept talking, hoping to convey the message that there was nothing suspicious going on between me and Jackie, we just like hanging out together, nothing to see here folks, move along. While I was talking, I had to contend with this new character, this Giovanni, imagining him as some sort of archetypal Latin lover and manipulator, and wondering, what is going on here? A third layer of my mind was interrogating the idea of building dire fantasies out of random snippets of information that may be related to each other or may not be, and how we build up entire scenarios of suspicion in our minds, especially if we happen to be naturally suspicious.

Amanda brought me back to earth.

"In any case, Freddie, let me say again I'm *so* looking forward to seeing you and Ethan at home. I've heard so many good things about the town and everything you're doing. As I said, I've got some new perspectives on life, I'm ready to move forward. I really think things will work out for us, as a family."

I expressed my appreciation and hope for the future, and we signed off. It had been a good and useful Zoom, imbued with a spirit of optimism. It had confirmed one thing: I wasn't comfortable drifting away from Amanda. Our conversation acted like a spoon stirring a horn of zeese, bringing up the dregs from the bottom. Those dregs were feelings which I'd thought were gone. But at the back of my mind a couple of thoughts lurked that I couldn't banish. Jackie? Giovanni? Really?

I scolded Ethan gently the next time he came over for dinner.

"I know you're talking to Mummy, but please don't put silly ideas in her head!"

"Not my fault," he objected. "I stated a few facts. She drew unjustified conclusions from them. Anyway, Dad, she's probably glad you're acquiring some local friends."

I decided to give him (and her) the benefit of the doubt. My loose imagination had already gotten me in trouble.

After dinner, we took a couple of beers out to the backyard for a nightcap. We were treated to the sort of late summer night sky that promotes contemplation. The last touch of purple faded away, and the pinpoints of light dotted the deep blue nocturnal sky. A bluish-white half-moon shed its light on the scene. The three of us—me, Ethan, and Bruce the dog—sat lazily in the backyard, soaking up the atmosphere and enjoying the silence.

"What do you see up there?" I asked.

"Stars and planets," Ethan replied.

"How do you interpret it?"

"I don't know how I interpret it. That's a strange question. Does it need to be interpreted? It's stars and planets, right?" He enjoyed it as a light show, an opportunity to chill out at the end of the working day. It was something he could rely on. For people of his generation, facing a future of decline and collapse in every aspect of life that mattered, the seeming permanence of at least one part of the natural world provided a modest comfort.

"I see your stars and planets, but I see a lot of things in addition to them." I went into a long riff on the general subject of *What the Night Sky Means to Me*, as if I were giving a school presentation. I see the sky through the eyes of poets and artists and the like, those who made references over the course of millennia to the brightness of the stars and whatever it meant, to the stars shining down on humanity and giving us inspiration and hope. I mentioned Kant's dictum about "the starry sky above me and the moral law within me" as the two things that filled him with awe. I quoted James Joyce's phrase about "the heaventree of stars hung with humid nightblue fruit," as viewed from Dublin on that June night in 1904. I brought up Van Gogh and his starry night splashed and slathered on the canvas. I talked about how moved and intimidated I was by the vastness of the universe. In short, my entire perspective was anthropocentric precisely because it was rooted in the aesthetic.

"Then there's another perspective, the scientific one," I continued. "Since there are no scientists present with us in this backyard, let's imagine that Bruce is a scientist, an astrophysicist, and consider what his perspective might be." From his scientific perspective, Bruce the dog sees something different. He laughs at my reference to millennia of poetry and art, because he understands that on the timeline of the universe, my millennia, so impressive to a humble human mind, constitute a brief moment. Those ancient scribblers who wrote about the stars lived only a few minutes ago from the broad standpoint of the history of the universe. Bruce thinks not in terms of millennia, but of millions of years, of processes with no identifiable beginning and no apparent end. From this perspective, nothing we do matters. This is a melancholy thought. Why should we do anything at all?

"You should take off your glasses and put them on Bruce, so he looks intellectual," suggested Ethan.

"His head's too small, they'd fall off," I said.

I couldn't omit an additional perspective—a metaphysical one. The theologians with whom I was familiar were those representing the Abrahamic religions. They assumed that the physical world would come to an end one day, to be superseded by some other state. This state would be spiritual or some combination of spiritual and material; they didn't agree on precisely what form it would take. Many of these thinkers and mystics were only able to conceive it in vague, symbolic terms. But it was understood that this state would be the final one, and effectively static. There would be no more states after this one—the flux of history, as posited by great thinkers from Heraclitus to Hegel, would reach its terminus, like a train entering a station. Those stars would be gone forever. But we, infinitesimally small beings though we are when considered against the vastness of the universe, had some purpose here on this Earth, something we had to do before that final state arrived and fixed everything in place forever. This would form the basis of our *Sinnstiftung*.

"The basis of our *what?*" asked Ethan.

"Creation of meaning, sense of purpose, and a lot of other things."

"There's that damn word again," interjected Bruce. "God, you're pretentious."

September is a pleasingly ambiguous month in our region. One season ends and another begins, and the change is subtle as they blend into each other. The days shorten noticeably. The purple shade in the northern sky that accompanies sunset, in which direction I enjoy walking after dinner, makes its appearance earlier. The children are back in school, and the town gets quieter. Summer slips away in an atmosphere of melancholy.

On this September day I was attacking the piano again. Today I was going modern. On my music stand was a free download of dubious legality, namely one of the pieces from György Ligeti's *Musica Ricercata*. It featured a folk-like melody unwinding over some busy repetitive rhythmic work in the left hand, and due to its relative simplicity didn't pose too great a challenge to my modest abilities. It was the sort of melody that I would have recommended to Jackie to use in her band if the McTaggart Family Creamery had still been in existence. Ligeti wrote this work in the early 1950s in Hungary, when that country's artistic life was in the grip of a puritanical, unforgiving Stalinist aesthetic. If he included too much dissonance in his music, he opened himself to attack as a "cosmopolitan" who expressed "hostility to the people." Therefore, he wrote his more modernistic pieces "for the desk drawer," as the expression went in Eastern Bloc countries at the time. The good news is that, despite twists and turns and upheavals, the modernistic works eventually made it out of the desk drawer and into public life. Stanley Kubrick was sufficiently impressed by Ligeti's avant-garde works that he included several of them on the soundtrack of *2001: A Space Odyssey*, thereby giving the composer a bigger audience than he'd probably ever dreamed of. Everything changes, and although the good times don't last forever, the bad times don't, either.

I hit numerous wrong notes while I played this thing, most of them in the accompanying rhythmic figure, but I didn't care. My phone rang. It was Ethan. He wanted to know if I could come to a "preview."

"Preview of what?" I asked.

"A food preview. Miguel and I have been working on stuff. We haven't been just talking, as it may seem to you. We've been experimenting. We're thinking about rolling it out at some point soon. But we're going to do it the smart way, like a Hollywood studio rolling out a movie. That is, we invite selected persons to partake before we spring it on the public. You get to be the test audience, or part of the test audience. You'll be the first taster, the pioneer. Consider that an honor. Can you make it today?"

"Sure. I'm not doing anything else. What time and where?"

"My place. Five o'clock."

Ethan's place was an apartment in a newly built complex on the edge of town, one of those projects launched in recent years to accommodate Roverton's increase in population. It was usually a mess, with his bed unmade and clothes strewn on the floor and all kinds of unwashed dishes and glasses in the kitchen, which tended to pile up because he used his kitchen for his culinary experiments. But he needed his own space, and the apartment was cheap and met his needs. I wouldn't have tolerated him making a colossal mess in my kitchen, no matter how tasty the results might be. However, when I arrived today, I found that to my surprise he'd cleaned the place up. There were glasses and plates on the kitchen table, but they looked clean. This cleanliness imparted a solemnity, as if an important event were about to take place. Ethan also wore an apron and a chef's hat, which added to the sense of occasion.

"Make yourself comfortable," said Ethan, indicating a chair. "Your preview's going to consist of three items. You'll give me your feedback. Please be brutally honest. Comforting lies do nothing to further the cause of Great Lakes cuisine."

"You can count on me."

I waited at the table while Ethan prepared the three plates for me. The first one was a concoction consisting of whitefish plus some reddish sauce that resembled salsa. The sauce was off to the side. The presentation was basic, with no vegetables or side dish.

"My kitchen is a laboratory right now," Ethan explained. "We'll make things more complex later. Right now, you're getting the basic elements."

I picked up the fork, poked the food, and ate a couple of bites. The whitefish tasted like whitefish. The salsa tasted like salsa, with a fruity addition that I couldn't identify. I put the salsa on top of the whitefish and tasted them together. It tasted like whitefish mixed with salsa.

I put down my fork. I looked into the distance for a few seconds. I turned to Ethan.

"Do you want my reaction now, or should I wait until I've tasted all three items?"

"However you want to do it."

With great seriousness I took another bite of the whitefish, again with a little bit of salsa on top.

Then I said: "I could quite happily eat this for dinner. I like whitefish, and I think the salsa is an interesting way to spice it up. But beyond that, I don't know what to say. I do have a question. What inspired you to create this dish?"

I could tell Ethan was deflated by my response. I don't think I was being negative, but perhaps he'd been expecting me to respond ecstatically.

He replied: "I did some research. I know that whitefish is a popular Great Lakes dish. I decided to spice it up a little. I took into consideration what Miguel said about bringing the foods of the world here and combining them. You know that dialectic thing you were talking about? I tried to implement it."

"You're trying to create something like Mexican whitefish?"

"I wouldn't call it that. Look, if you go on the Internet, you can find all kinds of fish plus salsa recipes. We got salmon plus mango salsa, halibut plus cherry salsa, God knows what else. Unfortunately, I didn't invent this fish-plus-salsa concept. It was already out there. I have to stand out in my own way."

"It sounds to me like you're suffering from what the literary critic Harold Bloom called 'the anxiety of influence.'" I also thought he looked silly in his chef's hat, but I didn't say that.

"You would've made an interesting food critic, bringing all these academic influences into it," Ethan said with a hint of sarcasm. "And you criticized my so-called ideological approach to cuisine! What on earth is the 'anxiety of influence' and what does it have to do with whitefish?"

"Bloom's argument, boiled down to its essentials, is that when authors—really artists in general—start out on their careers, they're haunted by the influence of their great predecessors. These influences make it difficult for them to distinguish themselves in their own way. Therefore, they have to make bold moves precisely to carve out their own identity. If you spent a lot of time on the Internet looking at various fish-plus-salsa recipes, I'd say you are suffering from the anxiety of influence, because innovative chefs before you came up with these ideas and their influence is making it difficult for you to stand out."

"It's true that I didn't invent the idea of pairing salsa with fish," said Ethan. "I don't know if that has any great significance. I look at it as a building block, something we can develop further."

"The historian Will Durant has a good quote on the topic of originality. He said, 'There is nothing new except arrangement,' or words to that effect. We modern people aren't inventing anything. We're making arrangements of previously existing things. In short, don't torment yourself for your perceived lack of originality." I decided not to torture Ethan further with any literary theories. "What's our next test subject in Food Test Lab today?"

He seemed relieved by the question. "I have a sample of our gourmet mac & cheese for you." Without another word (he was careful not to tell me the ingredients of any of these items, so that I would experience them without preconceptions) he took away my plate of fish and replaced it with a small bowl of mac & cheese. I had to give credit where it was due; this iteration of a familiar comfort dish was a cut above. It added some bacon and some other kind of seasoning which I couldn't identify, and the mix of cheeses that went into it was light, complex, and creamy. It put me in mind of the "loaded mac & cheese" I'd eaten in a brewpub once, except Ethan's was more elegant, though it lacked the faint taste of truffle oil.

"It's good," I said. "It's good mac & cheese. Maybe you have some greater ambition for it. Am I right?"

"Only in the sense that it's supposed to stand out. Okay, it's good, I'm glad you said that. But my mac & cheese has to be the kind you can't get in a hundred other restaurants, in a diner, in your local down-home family restaurant. I want to create a mac & cheese that has my name on it, that is known far and wide as my very own mac & cheese with my own personal stamp on it, the famous kind, the kind that was invented in Roverton during its heyday as the birthplace of authentic Great Lakes cuisine. It's like in Cincinnati, they have their four-way chili and their five-way chili and however many ways to do chili, and it's become associated with Cincinnati. It's not even chili, really! They just call it that. Hell, those disgusting cheesesteaks that you love so much, they're associated with Philadelphia, and real cheesesteak connoisseurs don't trust cheesesteaks from outside the Philly city limits. You see what I'm saying?"

"I do," I said. I felt he needed a dose of encouragement. "Actually, let me revise what I said. It's not just good old mac & cheese. What you've done with the cheese blend here is superior. I could see someone asking specifically for this mac & cheese and not some other kind."

Ethan got a contemplative look on his face for a few seconds.

He asked: "Do you think I'm on the right track?"

"You are on the right track, but you're only a few steps down the road. You have to keep going."

"How, specifically? Any suggestions?"

"You're the chef, I'm the test subject."

"That's part of the problem," said Ethan. "I'm not really a chef, even though I'm wearing this chef's hat for the occasion. I'm a brewer. I'm trying to transition to being a chef. But even though I'm not really a chef yet, I still want to consider myself a culinary pioneer. It's like those guys who tinker with machines in their garages and wind up inventing something."

"You said that you and Miguel are 'experimenting.' I like that word. Those guys in the garage are experimenting, too. This mac & cheese is good, but you're playing it safe. It doesn't taste like an experiment."

"Sounds like I need to apply a little more anxiety of influence," he said, permitting himself a smile. "They should sell that in stores. 'Anxiety of Influence Spice Blend is what you need to make your dishes taste original and not like somebody else's! Ethan Traubert, the famous pioneer of Great Lakes cuisine, swears by it: "Anxiety of Influence was what I needed to give my dishes that very special *zing* you can't get from anyone else!" Want to stand out from the crowd? Anxiety of Influence is guaranteed to put you on the map!'"

"Here's a thought," I said. "Make something new. By that, I mean don't take an existing recipe and dress it up. You could make an exciting new creation out of noodles and call it 'Noodles Fontaine.' Old Noodles himself would probably approve, since you're making him famous. Why stop there? Create a whole range of dishes dedicated to various Roverton people and places and events. That's one idea, right there."

"Hmm," was the response. I'd made him think. That was good.

"Shall we move on to the third and last item?" I asked. The last item looked like a donut. It also tasted like a donut. I suspected, and Ethan confirmed, that this donut-like confection was meant to be dessert. As a donut, it succeeded. I wasn't sure if it could be considered an appropriate dessert and said so.

Ethan summed up his view of things. "Yes, I'm disappointed. The food can't just be good or acceptable or anything like that. It has to stand out. It has to be distinctive. Even if it's a riff on what someone else has already done, it has to have its own quality." He pulled the chef's hat off his head and threw it on the kitchen table. "I can tell you think this hat looks stupid on me," he said. I managed to suppress a smile.

"I think we basically agree," I said, wanting to finish tonight's Food Test Lab in a spirit of harmony. "Keep experimenting, is what I say. The basics of the region should serve as your foundation. I think you can cast a wider net than you've done so far. When was the last time you made a good old-fashioned Wisconsin beer cheese soup, for instance? It's got all the authenticity you want. It's from here, it's beer so you've got that angle covered, it's cheese so you've got the dairy angle. I haven't seen it among your food offerings, but it's a natural. Start from there and build something more complex on it later."

"I'm open to all ideas. Including, you know, constructive criticism."

"Opposition is good for you; it forces you to define and strengthen your position further. As Blake said, 'opposition is true friendship'."

Ethan looked at me skeptically. "Blake said that?"

"Not the guy who subs for you at the brewpub. Different Blake."

"Gotcha." He cleaned up the kitchen. Since I had no commitments this evening and he was taking the day off, I suggested that we go to Light & Sound and rent a movie, and maybe get a pizza to eat while we watched.

"Carlucci's is having a deal right now, buy one pizza and get half off another. This will give me enough food to last the weekend." He liked this idea.

We got in my car and started on the short drive to Light & Sound. We got to the state route that fed into downtown, heading toward the store, located on its gentle slope above the road. We turned onto the road, and shortly after turning, we found ourselves at the tail end of a traffic jam.

"Is there some sort of event going on tonight?" I asked Ethan.

"Not that I know of," he responded. We stood for a minute or so, but the cars didn't move.

"I'll try to cross over here, and take one of the side streets back, and approach from Huron Avenue." Traffic was jammed only in our direction, with the oncoming lane being empty, so I was able to nudge my way forward into the other lane and turned into one of the streets leading to downtown. I went straight, then right, then right again onto Huron Avenue. Something felt different about Roverton's main street on this early September evening. I saw people walking with seeming urgency all in the same direction, toward the intersection where Light & Sound was located. A helicopter hovered in the sky. I saw flashing lights up at the intersection. A fire truck stood in the road, and it appeared that police had cordoned off the area. That explained the traffic jam.

"Is that a police helicopter?" I asked.

"Could be police, could be medical," said Ethan.

"We won't be able to get close enough to park at the store," I said. "Let's put it here and walk." I parked on Huron Avenue, a couple of blocks from the intersection. When we got out, we were confronted by the owner of the hardware store standing in front of his store. He stood as if paralyzed and wore a dazed expression. "What's going on?" I asked.

"There's been an accident," he said.

"What kind of accident?"

"You'll have to see it to believe it. Just incredible."

Ethan and I joined the pedestrians surging toward the intersection.

"I bet it's the damn biker gangs," said Ethan. "A few months ago, they got involved in a collision around here. A car got hit, and there were some injuries. They're a bunch of idiots. I don't see why they're tolerated. The cops should really come down harder on them. At least the last accident happened late at night, so only a few people were involved."

"This looks worse, whatever it is," I said. "You've got the cops, the fire department, a chopper." I heard the scream of a siren. "Now an ambulance. If it's the bikers, they chose a really bad time for their antics. A lot of people out and about right now."

We kept walking. As we got closer, the mass of shapes ahead—the vehicles, the flashing lights, the onward rush of pedestrians, the cops and emergency workers—became more clearly distinguishable. I didn't see any bikers or crashed cars. Instead, I was confronted with the strangest and most disturbing spectacle I had ever seen. It was the sort of sight that, when you see it, your brain takes a few steps back and says: "Give me some space here, I need to figure this out."

I stared at it, speechless.

Ethan said: "What the hell?"

Part III:
The Toilet Paper Situation Is Critical

A few days later, an editorial appeared in *The Rovertonian*. I'm reproducing portions of it here, interspersed with my own comments:

"Jackie O'Reilly got up in the morning and went to work, like she did most days. Because she went to work, she died."

Perhaps nothing sums up the death of Jackie—a Roverton resident for over twenty years, and a well-known and well-loved figure in the town—quite as well as this comment by her son, John. Jackie was minding her own business at Light & Sound, her video, music and nostalgia shop well-known to the people of our town, when a truck hauling tons of garbage lost control and slammed into the store, killing her.

A state police preliminary report tells us that the accident can at least in part be attributed to brake failure. Unfortunately, the report does not deal with the larger question: why was a thirteen-ton tractor-trailer truck, which was hauling trash to a landfill, even allowed to drive on a winding rural road? [Note: I'd seen these garbage trucks from time to time, looking absurdly large and clumsy on this relatively small road, and thought many times, "That's an accident waiting to happen." I know I wasn't the only person to have such thoughts.] …

Police have yet to question the driver, Alhamdulillah Jackson, who is currently in the hospital due to injuries sustained in the accident. [Note: The driver's unusual first name led to speculation. It was rumored that he belonged to an Islamic splinter group, and that the accident was in fact a suicide mission, taking out a purveyor of decadent Western cultural items. It was impossible for me to ascertain whether anyone believed this.] …

Above and beyond the immediate tragedy, Roverton's reputation as a thriving, attractive town—one that can serve as a refuge in troubled times—has taken a hit. The crash calls into question the competence of local authorities, who have been warned repeatedly about the dangers of truck traffic down this route yet have chosen to keep kicking the can down the road. Now, that can has jumped off the road and caused a disaster.

One day, when I was idly scanning the news on my computer, I found a story originating from Tennessee. A camel had escaped from a petting zoo and killed two people. It also attacked a police vehicle. The police had no choice but to kill the camel before it continued its murder spree. The story was vague on the details. Apparently, the camel killed the men by stomping on them. I assume the police shot the camel, but the story didn't say exactly how the rampaging beast met its end.

This surreal event took place in a small town, a town that was probably like mine. I tried to imagine how the camel's two victims reacted when they saw the animal running toward them. Perhaps they thought this was some kind of joke, and they tried to play along until it was too late. Perhaps they were shocked into a state of paralysis by what appeared to be a violent breach of the predictable order of a small town. Perhaps their minds played tricks, telling them that what looked like a camel was actually a large dog, a person dressed as a camel as part of some promotional campaign, or even a giant animatronic device. I have no way of knowing their thoughts and feelings. But when I saw the crash at Light & Sound, I remembered the story about the camel.

As I stood there, my brain adjusted to the spectacle, as your eyes gradually do when you leave a sunlit street and enter a dark interior. Here's what I saw.

Jackie's Light & Sound was normally a white, wooden, square little building. Now, it had been smashed and shoved into a sort of parallelepiped or rhomboid shape, a rectangle leaning to the left. Even the most avant-garde modernist architect would not have designed a building that looked like this; it was pure distortion. The entire front portion (the cab) of the truck had disappeared into the store on the right side, and it had hit the store so hard that I saw the wood splintering on the left side. The trailer had flipped over to the left and spilled its contents. It looked as if all the garbage in the Western world had been spewed and scattered all over the road. Due to the crowd of pedestrians and the police and emergency personnel on the scene, who had cordoned off the area, the garbage was just close enough to tease me visually, suggesting its contents without making them clear to the eye. I had the impression of a multicolored mountain range, most of it in various hues of brown and black and gray. There were bits of white and other bright colors dotting the gigantic mess. They might have been milk cartons, orange peels, different types of food packaging, and God only knows what else, sparkling like minerals in the dark mass of coffee grounds, potato peels, rotten meat, industrial junk, and many other things which I didn't want to know about.

While the professionals went about their business, local people talked excitedly, shouting, and maneuvering to try to get a better look at the proceedings.

Behind me, somebody said: "It's a flimsy structure built out of wood. Too bad they didn't use brick; she would've had a chance." When I heard that, I pushed myself (together with Ethan) to the front of the crowd. We found ourselves standing in front of a sympathetic-looking policeman.

I asked: "Who's hurt?"

"The truck driver," he said. "That's who the helicopter's for."

"Anyone else?"

"One dead in the store. I think she's the owner."

Frozen in place, I stared at the scene. Once again, my brain was failing to process what was going on.

"Hey Dad?" asked Ethan. He tugged at my sleeve.

"She's dead," I muttered.

"Who?"

"Jackie. Obviously. Who else would it be?"

"Shit," was all Ethan could say.

While the emergency personnel worked on getting the truck driver out of his cab and free of the shattered store, I backed away from the scene. I feared falling, so I leaned against a nearby building. Ethan, wearing an expression of supreme disbelief on his face, followed me.

"Let's get out of here," he said.

It was the only thing that made sense. I didn't want to stick around and watch them prying Jackie's corpse from the store. Already, my overheated imagination was succumbing to disturbing thoughts. Would her body even be in one piece when they got it out? Would she be flattened, like a cartoon character crushed by an anvil? I imagined her in Light & Sound going about her business—shelving DVDs, playing with the lights to get the illumination just so, lighting a stick of incense for that special mellow countercultural atmosphere—and wondering, just for a second, about the sudden very loud vehicular noise emanating from one side of the store, and looking in that direction when… What was the last thing she saw before the truck killed her?

I had to force myself to stop thinking. This was difficult. Ethan, who had greater presence of mind, volunteered to drive both of us to his place so we could cool down and collect our wits. The only clearly formed thought in my mind was that pizza and a movie were no longer on the agenda for tonight.

Back at Ethan's place, I had no appetite, I didn't want to drink, and I didn't want to do anything else. Conversation was desultory. It mostly took the form of asking, "How could something like this happen?" and trying to answer the question from different angles. Ethan insisted that I have some whiskey to calm myself. I complied with his request. Eventually I said that I had to get home to Bruce, who was due for a walk.

When life becomes too difficult to figure out and your attempts at talking about it stumble and fail, dogs are much better companions than human beings. They don't ask you awkward questions, and they accept you as you are. Like most dogs, Bruce had a very sensitive meter for reading the emotions of his master and responding to them, and he regarded me with his soulful eyes, expressing deep concern. We snuggled together on the bed, and I clung to his warmth and furriness like a lifeline. I slept badly and fitfully. I managed to nod off several times, but each time this happened, I was jolted awake by a violent dream.

After the unfortunate incident described in the editorial, the following things happened.

It took several hours to clean up the gigantic pile of garbage that blocked the road in front of Light & Sound, and to remove the trailer part of the truck from its resting place on the slope and the cab section from inside the shop. As for Light & Sound itself, it was demolished shortly thereafter.

They put Jackie in the ground a few days later. I didn't attend, because it was a modest funeral for her close relatives, of whom she didn't have many. After this perfunctory ceremony, it was decided to hold a memorial service for the broader public, for her friends, neighbors, and anyone else who wanted to attend. Along with her son John, I volunteered to help put it together. Given that I spent most of my time at home not doing very much, I was deemed a good person to field phone calls and furnish information to anyone interested in attending.

The town council held a meeting with the goal of dealing with the problem of large trucks rumbling through our town. Under the usual lazy circumstances that prevailed in Roverton, only a few people ever attended such meetings, or no one attended them, which meant they got cancelled and whatever happened to be on the agenda was postponed until the next meeting, which (as often as not) would get cancelled as well because nobody bothered to show up for it. This meeting, however, attracted a sizeable audience. Several people expressed outrage at the fact that only an obvious, fatal disaster was able to move the town council to do something about the problem. Such is human nature, I thought; few are the people who see disasters coming before they occur, and who have the presence of mind and sense of duty to take appropriate precautions.

The Jolly Company of Rovertonians found itself in a not very jolly mood. After some internal debate, they decided to go ahead with their fall concert. Life goes on, and Jackie would have wanted it that way, they concluded. They decided that the first song on the program should be dedicated to her. I let them know (via Mean Christine) that any song would be suitable except for "Reynardine," which would have set Jackie spinning in her freshly dug grave.

My behavior in the days immediately following the crash became discombobulated. When getting ready to go to bed at night, I discovered that I'd put my socks on inside out. This was something I'd never done before, ever in my life. The next morning, I made breakfast, and I put my scrambled eggs in Bruce's food dish and plopped some dog food on my own plate. It was only when I raised my fork to begin eating that I noticed my mistake. It was too late to salvage the eggs: Bruce, acting with the typical canine swiftness where food is concerned, scarfed them up quickly, so I had to make myself another breakfast. I went to the mailbox to pick up the mail and found that I'd already done so. One afternoon, I discovered that my right hand was holding a toothbrush. I didn't know if I'd just brushed my teeth, was preparing to brush my teeth, had used the toothbrush to do some minor cleaning job, or was preparing to do so. My mind seemed to be blinking in and out of attentiveness, like an Internet connection undergoing random outages.

I had a thought that provoked a feeling of guilt in me for a moment. I wondered whether they were giving away the DVDs, CDs, and other knickknacks left behind in Jackie's shop, and if I could get some of them for free. Then I realized that these items would be forever tainted in my mind, so it would be better not to acquire them. Later, I found out that most of them had been donated to the local library. Those that were damaged beyond use, or had blood on them, were thrown away.

Jackie's death left me in an awkward place emotionally. She wasn't my wife, and (despite what Ethan hinted to Amanda) she wasn't my late-in-life girlfriend. She wasn't my sister or cousin or any other relative. She wasn't even my work colleague with whom I enjoyed having a few drinks. She was my friend, my long-timer (practically old-timer!) friend. When your wife dies, or your sister, you can expect condolences to come your way. But people don't extend condolences to you when your casual, coffee-drinking buddy passes away. Notwithstanding the fact that you might be more broken up by the loss of that buddy than by the loss of a relative, even more so when death occurred suddenly and violently.

There was another factor that caused me to tremble and lose sleep. If Ethan and I had arrived at Jackie's store half an hour earlier, we would most likely have been crushed to death as well. Perhaps it was only that disappointing donut-like dessert that saved us from Jackie's fate. Maybe it was our argument about the anxiety of influence. Maybe it was my little monologue on the importance of mastering the basics, starting with Wisconsin cheese soup. Maybe it was all these things together, or some combination of them—I wasn't sure how many minutes had passed since the accident when we arrived. Remove those things from our activity that day and we could all have been dead, three fatalities instead of one. It was a distinct possibility that my last words would have been: "Hey Ethan, have you seen this movie?"

I was in a new cage, a cage that really wasn't a cage at all (how's that for a paradox). It was a cage that couldn't be properly classified, unlike the cages of work, home, family, and education. It was a cage of ambiguity, which materialized when a relationship that I valued was severed by an almost unimaginable shock. All these factors combined made it difficult for me to mourn in a straightforward fashion. Instead, I felt fear, loss, and a sense of alienation from my town and from the world.

If you're not bald, you have to get your hair cut. If you're not stupid, you won't do it yourself. I was due for a haircut. Well, I wasn't in great need of a haircut strictly speaking, but I could justify it, and I wanted to get out of the house and do something. Having a particular goal would make me feel better, assuage my restlessness. When I got to the barber shop on the square, I saw that the junior barber, Stanley, was putting out some new reading material on the table in the waiting area. There were some newsmagazines—thankfully, they looked to be recent, none from previous years—and a new self-published production by the Rev. Lyle Finefellow, whose book *Is Putin the Antichrist?* had amused me on a previous visit. It seemed that Rev. Finefellow had some kind of arrangement with the barbershop to promote his work. This volume was entitled *Can America Be Fixed?* I looked forward to digging into it.

"Hey Stanley, is Old Earl available?" I asked.

Stanley informed me that Old Earl was now Dead Earl. If he had a Wikipedia entry, it had been updated from *is* to *was* a couple of days ago. I knew it shouldn't have been a shock. But it came as a shock, anyway. Old Earl was a fixture in town like the Opera House, and probably about as old. It seemed that he would live forever, retailing his endless anecdotes while piling up mounds of hair on the floor. But just as buildings burn down or are smashed to pieces by trucks or get euthanized by demolition teams, people have a shelf life, too. I decided to wait on that haircut for a few days.

Shortly after the day of the accident, I invited Ethan over for dinner. I felt stable enough to discuss matters calmly, and I also looked forward to making a good meal for both of us, something we hadn't enjoyed together for a while.

"I'm sorry," he told me over the phone. "I have to leave town for a few days, starting tomorrow. I'm too busy packing and planning to come over tonight."

"What's going on?"

"I'm attending a convention of craft brewers in Cleveland."

"That sounds like fun," I said. I meant it. Ethan filled me in on the specifics. The convention would take place in the Ohio City neighborhood, which was Cleveland's hipster hood. It had the largest concentration of craft breweries in that city. It was the sort of place where, if you were young, adventurous and could get some seed capital, you could start a business and even have fun running it. Ethan and I had a tenuous connection there: I'd passed through it on my way from Philly to Roverton, and stopped for a couple of hours, to soak up the atmosphere and have a beer or two. The area had a scruffy, antique vibe that I liked, with its old and renovated brick buildings and narrow streets.

"I'm actually giving a presentation," Ethan continued. "It's on the aesthetic aspects of beer packaging."

"That sounds like a great subject."

"Yeah, I think you'd find it interesting. I don't know if they're going to record it, but if they do, I can send you the video. If they don't, I'll shoot you the PowerPoint presentation."

I wished him good luck and told him not to forget my dinner invitation. It would have been nice to have some human company, but apparently that was out of the question for the immediate future. For the next several days, it would just be me and Bruce in the house.

I told you earlier about how Ethan found consolation in many bottles, and how this led him to a career in brewing. Now, it was my turn to find such consolation. I'm afraid the results weren't so positive.

It started innocuously enough. Ethan had gifted me a six-pack of Old Fart IPA. The idea was that we would drink it together. But now he was away in Cleveland, and I was lonely and thirsty. This six-pack of Old Fart was the first thing to go down my gullet. I had a bottle to accompany my meager supper, consisting of some ravioli with marinara sauce that I boiled up and slapped together. I had another bottle of beer before I went to bed. The next day, I got up and made myself some instant oatmeal and coffee. While I was consuming that, the bright idea occurred to me that having beer for breakfast would be an interesting experiment. I opened another bottle of Old Fart and drank it down. The combination of coffee, oatmeal, and beer produced a strange clashing effect—a stimulant, a depressant, and something mushy in between. It made me wonder if it was the sort of thing Ethan would like to experiment with—maybe I ought to suggest it to him? I downed another bottle of beer for lunch with my grilled cheese sandwich, and another bottle with dinner (leftover ravioli), and the final bottle later that night, while slumped in front of the television. That took care of the sixpack.

I moved on to harder stuff. There was a fine bottle of Irish whiskey. I tried to ration that one, to make it last longer than a few days, but I failed. There were also a few bottles of cheap wine. Many years earlier, I'd made a resolution not to drink alcohol alone. "Only in company," I said, nodding firmly. Following the literal meaning of the resolution, I found a clever way out. The original resolution did not state that the company had to be human. Bruce the dog was company. In fact, he was my steadiest, most loyal, most agreeable company, so he'd be an ideal partner for my drinking bouts. He never complained that I drank too much, as Amanda would have, had she been still living with me.

Bruce, as it happened, encouraged my drinking. The aroma of beer and wine aroused his interest. That became clear whenever he got close enough to a bottle or glass to sniff it. As I finished each bottle, I put it on the floor. Bruce would walk up to it, sniff it, and lick the bottle opening, where a faint taste of the beverage lingered. When I finished each bottle or glass, I allowed Bruce to lick the remaining drops out of my hand.

At night, Bruce and I did our drinking while watching TV. Wasting large amounts of time in front of the television was a vice I'd never had. Yet now, I started doing it. I'd turn the accursed box on in the evening, to have some company. Pretty soon, I found myself absorbed in it. I'd flip the remote from one show to another, then back, then to yet another show, soaking everything up. I'd lose track of time, and only if Bruce started whining (his usual signal that he wanted to go out) did I realize it was time for bed.

Tonight, I watched a report from Texas. The nation's fourth largest city, Houston, had been inundated by a hurricane-related flood. There were some remarkable pictures. Expressway ramps rising from the flood like water slides at an amusement park. Suburbanites boating down their own streets as if they were piloting a gondola in Venice. Rescue teams trying to pick people off roofs and cajole them out of second-story windows. The newsreader pointed out that, notwithstanding disasters like this, Texas was one of the states in which the population was increasing most rapidly. People were fleeing towards recurring climate catastrophe in large numbers.

After a few minutes, I decided that I wasn't going to break my brain trying to figure out why so many people were moving to Texas despite everything, so I switched to a different news show. On the New York

City subway, one passenger had been shoved onto the tracks by a passing vagrant, who easily managed to escape from the station. The other passengers stood around in shock as if paralyzed, or—more disturbingly—turned away as if they hadn't seen the assault. The victim was able to climb back onto the platform before the train arrived, but it was a close call. I thought about how I might feel to find myself in the victim's situation and concluded that I could forget about getting a good night's sleep for a few days or weeks afterwards. Sad though I might become every now and then, it was useful to get occasional reminders of why it was a good thing that I'd relocated to Roverton, murderous trucks notwithstanding. But that wasn't the only excitement today from the Big Apple, the City That Never Sleeps. Someone had set fire to a bodega on the Upper West Side; apparently it was some kind of revenge attack, undertaken by a customer who thought he'd been "disrespected." The bodega owner, José Somebody-or-Other (I didn't catch the last name), was in the hospital now, recovering from injuries caused by smoke inhalation.

Numbness and indolence suffused me as the programming induced in me a feeling of helpless melancholy. Slumped on the sofa, with Bruce on one side and the remote on the other, I took in a commercial for some medication. All the people in the commercial lived in a beach resort, wore pastel-colored sweaters, smiled a lot, engaged in tasteful hobbies like painting and cycling, and moved slowly and easily through life. A voice-over listed all the potential side effects of the medication at a breathless pace, sounding almost like an auctioneer.

"Take Quaxinol only as directed. You may feel fatigue and loss of interest in life after taking Quaxinol. It may make you feel sad and long for your childhood, which you incorrectly remember as idyllic. It may remind you of the time when Uncle Al touched you inappropriately. It may take you back to that humiliating moment when you were the first one to be cut from the softball team, and everybody snickered because they knew you were no good at sports. Quaxinol may turn out to be the gift that keeps on giving. It may make you tremble, wobble, and drool. It will make your tongue taste like lead, it will cause a windy rushing noise to howl in your ears, it will make you feel like ants are crawling up your nose. You might find yourself scratching your groin obsessively after taking Quaxinol. It may cause you to fall flat on the floor face down, with your limbs twitching and jerking uncontrollably, while a sudsy pink foam comes gushing out of your mouth, forming a puddle that keeps getting bigger, while you choke and gasp for breath. You haven't seen the end of Quaxinol, no sir. Quaxinol is just getting started. Quaxinol Quaxinol Quaxinol—remember the name, and don't say we didn't warn you! Stay tuned for an Action News update."

"Hey Bruce," I said. "Do you really want to watch this Action News update?"

Bruce snuggled closer to me. "Do you believe that this Action News update will bring us any good news?"

"Based on what I've seen so far, I think it will likely be more bad news."

"Then why should we watch this Action News update?"

"Because we want to know what's going on?" I said uncertainly. Bruce stared at me with the studied concern of a psychoanalyst. I found his facial expression unnerving. Did he believe that I was mentally unstable?

"We already know what's going on," responded Bruce. "It's not going to get any better. What you really need to do is watch a romantic comedy or something like that to improve your mood."

"But," I objected, "a romantic comedy is a placebo designed to distract us from the dire condition of the world today. We can only improve our situation by facing the world as it is."

"Look at it dialectically," said Bruce. "That's what you like to do anyway, isn't it? The dialectics of a human personality must be balanced like anything else. A constant onslaught of bad news, bad news, bad news will turn you into a toxic and impotent personality rather than one that has the capability to make positive changes. The romantic comedy may be a drug in the sense that it erases the harshness of the real world for at least a short while. But it does help you regain your morale and sense of equilibrium. Why else do they send musicians and other entertainers to perform for soldiers during a war? It's all about achieving the right balance, and that's something difficult to do in our world that is constantly in flux, as I'm sure you know."

"You have a point there."

Bruce wasn't done. After licking his paws, he launched into another disquisition.

"Because of the constant influx of bad news into your overheated psyche, you worry a lot about things beyond your control. You should heed the sage advice of the Stoic philosopher Epictetus, who said that the key to happiness was not worrying about things that we can't do anything about. We should concentrate on that little corner of the world where our actions might have a positive effect. Epictetus was in a position to know. He was a slave; his room for freedom of action was tiny."

"I guess we should watch that romantic comedy then," I concluded. I picked up the remote and accessed the pay channels. I located the one where I was piggybacking on Ethan's account and checked their selection. There was one romcom that looked like a good choice, so I clicked on it. It dated from the nineties or early zeros, and it had all the characteristic features of romcoms from that time: an upwardly mobile young professional white woman working in a job related to show business; her wisecracking yet sympathetic gay male friend; the brooding romantic leading man who started out as a bit of a jerk but was later revealed to have a yearning heart and a deep spirit of generosity; a couple of female friends of the protagonist who served as foils; and a fashionable New York setting free of burning bodegas and unfortunate passengers being hurled onto train tracks. I didn't bother to follow the story closely; I wanted to sink into the movie's carefree world, one where setbacks happened but could be overcome with some good-natured striving. I don't remember how the movie ended, because while I was immersed in this comforting spectacle, I fell asleep.

For breakfast the next morning, I had another beer, and I paired it with a cup of coffee into which I'd poured some of that Irish whiskey. While I drank these contrasting beverages and wolfed down a bagel, I received an email that required my immediate attention. It was from one of my clients.

Dear Fred,
I'm concerned because I haven't heard from you in a while. Your contribution to Project Arcturus was expected by midnight last night. But today I got up and found nothing from you in my inbox for the past week or so. You only sent in the first of the three installments that you were supposed to do. We'll have to ask for a deadline extension, and I'm not sure Mr. Chang will be amenable to that. Can you please tell me what's going on?

"Oh, shit," I muttered. I'd totally forgotten, neglected, blown off (however you want to put it) my assignment. I fumbled around the living room, looking for my phone. I picked up cushions and pillows, moved magazines and papers out of the way, even looked under the dog's dish, but I couldn't find it. Finally, I located it in the donicker, sitting on the top of my corner stack of four toilet paper rolls. I dialed the number listed in the concerned email.

"Hey, Ian," I said. "Yeah, I'm really sorry about Project Arcturus, but there's something I have to explain."

"I'm listening," said Ian. His voice was bland, but I could tell that his meaning was "this better be good."

"I'm dealing with a disaster," I said. "A close relative of mine got killed in an accident. I have to deal with the funeral preparations, the last will and testament, all of our relatives coming here… It's such a shock, and amid all this, Project Arcturus slipped my mind. I'm sorry, but it's been horrible around here."

"Oh, I'm sorry to hear that," said Ian smoothly.

I could tell he wasn't entirely convinced, so I continued.

"Look, the story is so weird and horrible that it made the papers and caused a lot of local outrage. The whole town is in shock. If you want to check it out yourself, look at the online version of our local paper, *The Rovertonian*." I didn't mention any day or edition and I left out Jackie's name because I wanted to make it difficult for him to find the information. I hoped that having to put some effort into finding out what had happened would dissuade him from taking an interest.

My ploy worked, or at least it didn't immediately fail. "Thanks, Fred, it sounds like you're going through a really bad time. I'll reach out to Mr. Chang and explain the situation to him. How much time do you need to finish your portion? Is a week okay?"

"Yes, that should be fine."

"By the way, if you don't mind my asking… What happened to your relative? Mr. Chang may need some convincing."

I told him how my "relative" had died.

"Oh Jesus, that is shocking," said Ian. "Never heard anything like that before. Sorry I had to probe."

"No problem," I replied. I got off the phone as quickly as I could. Jackie had briefly taken up residence in the cage of family with me, exiting the cage of the ambiguous relationship which we had actually experienced together. I felt guilty at having to take advantage of her death to excuse my negligence. But she wasn't going to object, and what else could I have done?

I needed another beer.

The world was falling apart. In St. Petersburg, Russia, a radioactive leak killed thousands of people. In St. Petersburg, Florida, a bridge collapsed during rush hour and tossed dozens of cars into the waters of Tampa Bay. In London, England, the Houses of Parliament were blown up so completely by terrorist bombs that Guy Fawkes would have envied the result. In London, Ontario, police and rioters clashed all night, destroying most of the city's downtown. In Berlin, Germany, the government abandoned the city as angry crowds marched on the Reichstag. In New Berlin, Wisconsin, a man carrying a rifle walked into a bar and proceeded to shoot every patron he found. In the sweltering metropolis of Cairo, Egypt, thousands died due to a heat wave of unprecedented length and severity. In the tiny town of Cairo, Illinois (pronounced "K-row" for some unknown reason), the Mississippi and Ohio Rivers over-swelled their banks, carrying people and houses away. In Tokyo, Japan, an earthquake wrecked much of the city and killed thousands of people. In the Little Tokyo neighborhood of Los Angeles, peaceful pedestrians were killed in the crossfire of a gang shootout.

Enormous, world-historical events played out, and I struggled to understand them. The biggest thing for me was that the dissolution of the United States of America had finally happened. Possibly the dissolution of Canada, as well—there was lack of clarity about what was happening with our neighbors in the Great White North. But across the fruited plain, chaos reigned. Families once united were split by new borders. You had to change money if you traveled from New York to Chicago. New flags went up in various places. Authority, however, remained shaky. In many places it wasn't clear who was in charge. Crooks and warlords filled the gaps. Once-reliable institutions faltered or even vanished entirely.

What had only been talked about had finally come to pass. The Great Lakes Republic came into existence. Its boundaries were still hazy and being fought over, but it comprised all the states that bordered a Great Lake (apart from New York and Pennsylvania, which joined the new East Coast Confederation), plus the southern parts of Ontario (that is, the parts of that province where people lived in substantial numbers). A provisional capital had been proclaimed in Windsor, Ontario, on the border between the former USA and the former Canada.

Officially, they called it a republic, but that was a joke. The reality was that the Dissolution had taken place, and the Dictatorship had been installed, just as Ethan's favorite online shitlords had hoped and agitated for. World-shaking events find their first expression in the fever dreams of obscure scribblers, and those fever dreams had reached maturity and burst into real life. It was unclear where the Dictator was based geographically, and the extent of his power was still being determined. It was not yet known if he was going to rule all the area north of the Rio Grande, or only parts of it. But it looked like North America was going to replicate the history of Central Europe, specifically the Holy Roman

Empire. Like that grab-bag of a state, we were heading into a future of fragmentation and confusion. We'd have cities and states that were directly subordinate to the Dictator, as well as "free states" or even "free counties" (their freedoms yet to be defined), as well as states and cities and counties ruled by the modern version of dukes, princes and counts. Voltaire quipped that the Holy Roman Empire was "neither holy, nor Roman, nor an empire." I waited for some modern wag to point out that the Great Lakes Republic was neither great nor a republic. But it did have lakes, no one could dispute that.

The town I'd considered my refuge was infected by the chaos. In Roverton, factions formed and battled. The party of Nukes faced off against the party of Old-Timers. The class distinctions had grown mature enough to sprout capital letters. The Nukes were more tech-savvy and had more money, but being relative newcomers flooding in from different places, they lacked coherence, and their knowledge of the local terrain was superficial. Many of them were "remotes," which meant that they spent more time attached to their computers than to the concrete, physical world, and had stronger connections with managers and colleagues in distant cities than they did with the people around them. The Old-Timers had greater numbers, a better knowledge of the town and its deep structures and history, and a determination not to be displaced. They also had more children and fewer pets. One group represented the "right side of history," while the other stood for tradition and continuity. I struggled to explain to both parties that history didn't have sides and that traditions didn't survive by standing still, but nobody listened to me.

The Nukes had a plan to set up a provisional government in the town hall, to be presided over by Rajesh Agarwal of Jasher Creativity Partners, my client in Seattle. I was astounded by this choice, but on reflection it made sense: many of my fellow Nukes were consultants like me, working for companies that claimed to be creative. This "Seattle Faction" of Nukes was poised to take over and install a New Capitalist regime (they even planned to change the town's name to Jasherville) when the Old-Timers stormed the hall, arrested Raj and his gang, shoved them at gunpoint onto a couple of school buses they'd commandeered, and dumped them on the edge of town. The New Capitalist revolutionaries were warned that if they attempted to return, they would be beheaded in Franklin Square to the cheers of the crowd and their heads would subsequently be displayed on pikes throughout the town. This uprising, which took place under the slogan, "Roverton must not become Jasherville," was destined to go down in history as the

Great Reassertion. The party of Old-Timers set up its own government in the town hall, appointing Noodles Fontaine as dictator. Noodles issued proclamations from his new office, but they were so arcane and meandering that no one really knew what he was trying to say. However, the basic meaning of events was clear: the Seattle Faction had been defeated.

The attempted coup by the Seattle Faction and the reactionary Great Reassertion that followed left me torn. My frazzled mind and my whole way of living were being pulled in different directions. My personality was getting stretched out to the point where either it would snap, or it would become paper-thin and insubstantial. I turned into a walking contradiction. I was a Nuke, but I didn't sympathize with the Seattle Faction. Raj paid my bills, but I didn't want him installing a repulsive New Capitalist regime to befoul my beloved cage. I worked for Seattle, but I liked living in Roverton as it currently existed, and I agreed with the Old-Timers' slogan. Still, I didn't want to see beheadings taking place in the town square.

Ethan faced the same pressures. At Our Lady of Hops, most of the clientele consisted of Nukes. These were people with a genuine love of craft beer and an appreciation of old church architecture, even if a converted church that no longer served God but now served beer was the only kind of church they'd consider attending. Yet Ethan, due to his online readings and various life experiences, sympathized with those who promoted tradition and hierarchy. The instauration of tradition and hierarchy as supreme principles was meant to protect us from the coming storm—except the storm was already here and raging all around us. The storm revealed such "supreme principles" to be mere empty words, incapable of protecting us from anything. Ethan had some hard choices to make in the real world. Would the Great Reassertion insist that Our Lady of Hops go back to being a real church? Would it not be in Ethan's interest to oppose the Great Reassertion for that reason?

Amid all the swirling chaos and disorder, I found myself standing in front of a two-story brick building. It had a couple of eating and drinking establishments on its first floor, and at the top was a canopy-like protrusion bearing the words "1874. Heil's Block." It was the familiar Great Lakes building style. I knew where I was: the Ohio City neighborhood of Cleveland, that city's hipster hood. Somewhere in the vicinity, I'd find Ethan, who was still attending that convention of craft brewers. I hoped to warn him about the events in Roverton, about how lines were being drawn and the social contradictions were becoming unbearable, and that his whole livelihood might be in danger. As I looked around, I saw various people walking here and there, but there was no sign of Ethan. I wondered if the craft brewers' convention was already over—perhaps he was heading home? In confusion, I walked further down the street, toward a busy intersection. I stood in front of the biggest local landmark, the West Side Market, one of those grand old brick arcades that you see in older cities, featuring a soaring clock tower surmounted by a pointy, helmet-like cupola. From the top of the clock tower, a powerful but tinny male voice boomed through a loudspeaker: "Attention citizens. Attention, *citizens*. This is your Dictator speaking. The toilet paper situation is critical. I repeat: *the toilet paper situation is critical.* They've cut off our access to the Atlantic. Some items are getting through but expect rationing to begin soon. Watch this space for further announcements. Also, I'll be signing autographs at City Hall on Friday. Have a nice day."

Around me, hipsters and assorted urban denizens flew into a panic. They say civil wars are the worst, but I can't imagine anything worse than a war over toilet paper. I prayed it wouldn't come to that. People ran this way and that, shouting and stumbling as they ran.

Bells, bells, bells, rang, rang, rang. My feet felt cold and wet, and I looked down. Water was rising from the sewers and spilling out into the streets. The ground rumbled as if an earthquake were on its way, and the blue sky turned iron gray. The water continued to rise and gush, and I ran, desperate to get to some higher ground, or at least the second story of a building. Everyone else had fled and left me to struggle alone. I propelled myself forward as hard as I could, but my legs seemed to be slipping into sticky mud. I ran and ran, gulping the air and puffing it out like some primitive machine, but I was only able to move forward a few inches. The water continued to rise, by now up to my knees, and the rumbling had shifted so that it came from the sky.

As it subsided, I heard the voice of Bruce saying: "You're in a tough spot, aren't you?"

"Get me the hell out of here!" I shouted.

Luckily, I was whisked out of Cleveland by some mysterious power and, with a thump, entered a new phase of consciousness. I was in some sort of underground chamber, half basement, half library, half recreation room (three halves were permissible in this context)—the exact nature of the place kept shifting, although the walls remained a depressing, damp gray throughout. The wind howled outside (or was it inside?), and as I lifted my face to the one tiny window high up in the wall, I perceived in the dim light people I knew. There stood Amanda, who'd finally come home to me; next to her stood Jackie, who'd miraculously survived the accident with only a few scratches and a cast on her wrist; and sitting in a low-slung chair in the corner was Ethan, who looked bored.

"Did you hear the announcement?" I asked.

"What announcement?" asked Amanda.

"About the toilet paper." Amanda gave me a blank look, while Jackie started laughing. "At least you're alive," I said to Jackie. "You can be happy about that."

"Why wouldn't I be alive?" asked Jackie.

"What's going on here?" I snapped. The petulance of my own voice surprised me. "This is supposed to be home, am I right? I mean, we're all together in the same place. It's a safe space for all of us. One more question: where's Bruce?"

Out of the corner of my eye, I saw Ethan looking at me with disdain. He pushed himself up from his low-slung chair, and as he got up, I saw a stash of toilet paper rolls under the chair. Evidently, he'd been hoarding them. He reached down, picked up a roll, and without a word flung it right in my face. The world went black.

Ethan found me lying on the floor of the bedroom, face down and mumbling. As he helped me get to my feet, I heard sighs of disgust emanating from him. It made me regret that I'd given him his own key to the house. If he'd had to bang on the front door and shout repeatedly, at least I would have had time to get up and not look comatose. It might have engendered in him doubts and thoughts of sympathy, thereby mitigating his angry mood. Now, I'd have to deal with the consequences of having been found in a state of collapse, and there was no one I could blame except myself.

"I leave you alone for a few days, and look what you do," he said. "I guess I can't rely on Bruce to take care of you. Where is he, anyway?"

"Good question. Let's go find him."

We found him in the kitchen, cowering in the corner and trying to make himself inconspicuous. The reason for Bruce's reticence was that, being unable to hold it in anymore, he'd left a puddle next to the sliding glass door that opened on the backyard. As a dog with a conscience, he knew that he wasn't supposed to do this. Thankfully, he'd been considerate enough to piss on the bare floor rather than the carpet, which made it easier to clean up.

"Forgive me, Bruce, for neglecting your needs," I said. I got some soap and paper towels and did a quick cleaning.

"Now that I'm here, let's have breakfast," said Ethan. "You need to rebalance yourself. Go take a shower and put on some clean clothes. We'll eat in the backyard." I looked out the window: it was a pleasant late summer (or early fall) morning. I felt better already.

"I insist on one thing—use this particular coffee," I said. Reinhard's Diner sold its own zeese to go, and as I mentioned earlier, it was the best in town. I went off to the donicker to clean myself up while Ethan got to work. I emerged shortly thereafter to find that he'd made us fried eggs with bacon on the side and a few slices of buttered toast. It was exactly the sort of homey breakfast I needed, even more so given that my stomach still felt unsettled. I put some dog food in Bruce's bowl; we loaded everything on a tray and, together with Bruce, made ourselves comfortable in the backyard.

"How was the convention?" I inquired, munching.

"It was good. Everything went well. My presentation on the aesthetics of beer packaging was a hit. Unfortunately, they didn't record it, but I'll send you the PowerPoint. Who knows, you may find some inspiration in it for your own work. But the big question is—what the hell happened to you?"

I snapped off a piece of my bacon and gave it to Bruce.

"To borrow a title from Dostoevsky, it was the dream of a ridiculous man."

"Oh, yeah," said Ethan. "Dostoevsky. Of course." He took a gulp of coffee. "Riddle me this. Why is it that I can't find a poem or a novel that's about people like me?"

"What do you mean by that?"

"All your old literature is about kings and queens. We get the newer literature, and it's about businessmen and suffering artists. That gets replaced by the newest stuff, which is all about racial and sexual minorities. I guess the next stage after that will be writing about the robots that will take over and kill us all. The robots will write it, because there will be no human beings left. Meanwhile, nobody writes about the people who provide food and drink. But without us, all of you would starve to death."

"Your brief precis of historical turning points in the literature of the Western world captures some broad trends but is highly selective by its very nature. Seek and ye shall find, as the one who turned water into wine for the benefit of the wedding guests so truly stated."

"You've had enough alcohol," he barked. He didn't even add a friendly sounding "Dad."

"I'm sticking with coffee today. But I'm telling you, the last couple of days were vivid. I remember them in a way I don't remember most dreams, or alcohol-induced hallucinations, or whatever they were. You see, I went to where you were, where the convention was being held, and started looking for you, because I wanted to warn you about the future. Things are going to turn bad very soon."

"How is that news? Haven't you been saying that for ages?"

"This time it was very specific. I saw the future like it was a movie." I told the story of my dream, vision, psychotic episode, however you want to call it. While he drank his coffee and ate his bacon and eggs, his facial expression kept changing, from wonder to skepticism to alarm. "The scariest thing was what happened in Roverton. I couldn't believe that Raj and his gang would try to take over the town like that. The idea of public executions taking place next to the diner where I like to have breakfast! It made me feel that I can't be safe anywhere."

"The scariest thing is that you take your own dreams as prophetic," he rejoined.

"You'll have to forgive me for making a short digression at this point." I told a story from my graduate school days. A friend of mine had recommended a book called *An Experiment with Time*, by a certain J. W. Dunne. The author was a former British Army officer and an aeronautical engineer. This background is important, because it meant that he had to deal with the hard cold dangers of reality and couldn't afford to indulge in untenable flights of fancy. He adhered to an empirical, scientific approach. For this reason, I was predisposed to take him more seriously than if he'd been some New Age fantasist. Dunne insisted that his dreams foretold events in the real world, and he gave some memorable examples (among other things, he supposedly received advance notice of a volcanic eruption on the island of Martinique). Above and beyond that, he worked out an entire methodology for recording dreams, as well as an explanation for how the various levels of time interact and make it possible to predict future events (a complicated process which he called "serial time"). The book contained technical arguments and diagrams that were hard for me to follow, but Dunne seemed to know what he was talking about, and his book excited a lot of interest on the part of some sober intellects. The upshot was that, while I remained agnostic about the possibility of such precognition, I couldn't rule it out. In fact, the suspicion that Dunne was on to something has haunted me ever since and is probably a factor in my imagination's tendency to overheat.

"Uh, yeah…" began Ethan. "I don't know what to say to that; I haven't read the book. This Dunne guy sounds like a crank, but what do I know? I take note of the trends, and I try to come up with ways to deal with them. I'm pretty sure there's more likely to be a coup in some place like Paraguay than in Roverton. I also know I'm more likely to die a violent death in a bad part of Philadelphia than here. It's all a matter of probability."

"Is the collapse of civilization a numbers game to you?"

"Who said anything about the collapse of civilization? I'm trying to live my life in a creative and productive way. Things are getting worse in general, but a collapse of civilization as we know it? That's too large an assumption. Civilization may collapse in some places, but in others, it'll survive. California has a lot of problems, and I left those problems behind, but I don't think California is going to *collapse*—what does that even mean, really? Like, how far do you want to take this? Are we going to start living in cardboard boxes salvaged from the supermarket? You're not talking like someone who relocated to a nice small town because it was better than where you were. You're talking like a survivalist who lives in a cave in the mountains and has ten years' worth of canned food stacked up in a bunker."

"It could be that you don't want to confront the future in all its bleakness." On reflection, I realized I shouldn't have said that. Rubbing the younger generation's face in the future wasn't a nice thing to do.

He didn't seem disturbed or offended by what I had said. In fact, he had a comeback.

"You know, *I* am the optimist here. You're such a pessimist that you're ready to give up. But I'm making plans. I intend to survive and prosper, however unpleasant it might be. That's why I read these people you're so disdainful about. At least they're *talking* about solutions. What are you planning to do—live out the rest of your life in Roverton hoping you won't get killed by a truck or beheaded on the town square? It's a despairing approach, if you ask me."

I hadn't quite thought of it that way, but he had a point. "Let me ask you something. Why do *you* think I moved out here?"

"Because you thought a worldwide disaster was coming, and you wanted to find a safe place to live. You were scared by global warming, climate apocalypse, however you want to call it. And a lot of other things."

"You're not wrong," I said. "But there's more to it than that. Yes, I was looking for refuge. Yes, Roverton met my needs. But it wasn't just a refuge I was looking for. I thought that no matter how bad things got in the outside world, this was a place where we could start again. I don't mean just me as a person or us as a family. I mean keeping the human enterprise going. Making sure that civilization has some kind of future. That it doesn't get cut like a thread. You can't stitch a thread back together, not really. Once it gets cut, that's it."

Ethan looked into the distance, as if reminiscing. "I think you might have mentioned that once or twice. But my impression about you—and I admit I could be wrong about this—is that your motivation consists of about nine parts fear and one part wanting to keep civilization going. Again, you lack balance. If it was five parts each, at least you'd be in a state of equilibrium. But to be optimal, it should really be nine to one in the other direction. Positive energy, you know?"

"Positive energy," I mused. "I wish they would sell that as a pill; I'd take it. Two doses of Positive Energy a day. Brought to you by the makers of Quaxinol."

"The makers of what?"

"Oh, nothing." I took the final sip of my coffee. "Maybe I need to do something more ambitious than the Noodles Fontaine Oral History Project. I admit I'm envious of you. You're doing great things in the beer world, and you've also got this new cuisine project. Even if you stumble, you're still taking an impressive journey. I'm doing insubstantial jobs for people I don't like. Time to rethink my approach."

"You got something to keep you grounded for a while?" asked Ethan.

"Yes. I have to finish my contribution to Project Arcturus. I got an extension. If I don't finish it on time, Ian and Mr. Chang will be very unhappy and will probably fire me."

"Ooh, Project Arcturus," said Ethan. "Sounds very science-fictiony."

"It's a marketing thing. I have to scan a number of German and Scandinavian publications for the way they use certain words. It's not bad work but there's nothing exciting or futuristic about it. They just like giving their projects these astronomical names. The previous one was called Project Pluto. Hey, are you still reading that Chinese guy?"

"You mean Occidental Renegade? Yeah, I'm still reading him. As I said, he's not really Chinese. He just lives in China."

"What have you learned from him lately?"

"I learned one thing, one important thing. The only political organization I wish to join right now is the Chinese Communist Party," declared Ethan. "It's the only political party that I know of which has a decades-long history of success and is confidently striding forward into the future. Those who are lucky enough to belong already know that they're on a winning team. It's a winning team for China, and eventually, for the whole world. I'd like to join, but unfortunately, I don't think they'll take me. It's not like I'm a slacker about it. I even bought a compendium of Xi Jinping Thought to familiarize myself. This is something we can all learn from. I should read real books, right? That's what you told me."

I burst out laughing.

"Maybe I'm being unfair, but I can't imagine a better cure for insomnia than a compendium of Xi Jinping Thought. If I have trouble getting to sleep, I'll ask to borrow it from you."

Afternoon slid into evening, and I felt happy in a muted way, because I'd finished with Project Arcturus. I sent my completed assignment to Ian, and hoped I was done with that client for the near future. While I sat on the sofa in my office wondering what to do next, the phone jingled. I picked it up.

A frail, tentative woman's voice said: "Hello, could I speak to Frederick Traubert, please?"

"That's me," I said cautiously. Please, not more bad news.

"Hi," she said. "My name is Lydia Douglas. I'm calling you because, as I understand, you were a friend of Jackie O'Reilly's."

"Yes, I suppose you could say that. I was a friend of hers. Do you have some connection with her?" Curious, I thought; I knew that name—Lydia Douglas—from somewhere.

She continued: "I'm calling you because I saw your name in your local paper. It said you were involved in organizing Jackie's memorial service, along with her son. I tried to get hold of her son, but for some reason I couldn't. I'm calling you because I'd like to attend it, if I can."

It hit me. Lydia Douglas was the folk musician known as Onyx. She was the one who played with Jackie in the McTaggart Family Creamery, and later joined the cult and disappeared while hiking across the Arizona desert. The great mystery herself was on the phone right now, talking to me. It was an opportunity I could not allow to slip past.

"I'd be very happy if you could attend. I know who you are, I think. You were in the band with Jackie, right? She told me about you."

"I'm sure she did." A brief, nervous laugh. "I bet she told you some interesting things."

"Interesting things is putting it mildly. I hope you don't mind if I ask you a few questions. In a friendly spirit, of course. Before we talk about the details of the memorial service."

"No, go right ahead," she said. "I'd be happy to answer, believe it or not."

Sensing that this phone conversation might go on for quite a while, I made myself comfortable on the sofa, with my feet extended in the direction of the window. The sun was on its way down, and the roseate sky of early evening slowly materialized. Bruce jumped onto the couch and took up his temporary residence in my lap.

"Yeah, as soon as I heard your name, it came back to me. What Jackie told me, I mean."

"Okay," she said. "Before you ask me any questions, please tell me one thing. What did Jackie tell you about me?"

I recounted the story of Onyx, as I had heard it from Jackie.

Lydia said: "That's mostly correct. There are a couple of inaccuracies in her version. First, the cult members actually worshiped *three* Indo-European deities. We wanted to have a trinity of our own. We also wanted to make sure that the Greco-Roman pantheon was represented. We worshiped Zeus, in addition to Thor and Vishnu. The other thing Jackie got wrong is that I wasn't afraid to start my hike from Tombstone, Arizona. I wasn't spooked by the name or anything like that. We had to change the starting location to Tuba City, because we wanted to spend a fun weekend in Vegas before I went on my hike, and Tuba City is a lot closer to Vegas. But she got the essentials of the story right."

"Okay, thanks for setting the record straight. What happened then?"

"I waved goodbye to all the cult members, and I started on the hike. After I'd been on the trail for a while, the absurdity of the situation hit me. I asked myself, did I believe in any of this stuff? I mean, really believe in it, to the point where you're willing to suffer some adverse consequences in your life and put up with a lot of crap because of your beliefs. I realized I didn't believe in Zeus and Thor and Vishnu after all. But there was also the nature stuff. We were big on communing with nature. I liked that part of it. I still like that part. But you don't need pagan gods or any kind of gods to do that. Also, you have to imagine, it's Arizona, it's early in the morning, but the sun is up and it's already starting to get hot, and I can see that the day's gonna get pretty sweltering and I've got this big desert in front of me, and I'm not sure if I can survive with my pack and my water bottles and my big broad-brimmed sun hat. I'm more of a cold-weather person, and I'd been in the Canadian Rockies for a cult hike, and I enjoyed it a lot, but the Arizona desert isn't doing it for me. I didn't want the jackals finding my corpse there and the cult members going on about how I made such a great self-sacrifice for the cult and how they were all touched by it. I started to sweat, so I sat down, drank some water, and thought about what I should do next. I couldn't go right back to the cult, because I wasn't ready to disappoint them, wasn't ready to admit failure. They'd singled me out to become a spiritual leader, and I didn't want to defeat their expectations. I didn't feel strong enough to do that yet. There I was, stuck between unbelief and the expectations of the people close to me. What should I do? I decided to go right back to civilization. I took a different route back into the town so no one from the cult would see me. I got out of Tuba City as fast as I could without telling anyone. I went straight to the airport in Phoenix. I caught a plane back to New England. I got a job, found a place to stay, and have been living in a small town in Vermont ever since."

"A small town, eh?" That resonated with me. "What have you been doing all this time?"

"I got married, but my husband's dead. He was one of those old hippie granola types who moved up to Vermont way long ago because he wanted to live the rustic life. We lived the rustic life together and we both liked it, but he died. I told him my secret early on; he was one of the few people who knew. His death unsettled me for a while. Since he died it's mostly been odd jobs for me: working at the library, working at the café, doing musical performances here and there. I've made a fair bit of money playing music. I try not to sing though, because I'm worried that someone in the audience will recognize my voice. I'm kind of paranoid that way." A chuckle. "I always thought that singing was a joyous expression of the soul or some such thing. Isn't it funny that I'm afraid to do it."

I said: "If you're trying to stay hidden, don't you worry about coming to the memorial service? I mean, there's a strong likelihood that somebody will recognize you."

"I'm the only member of the Creamery who can come to this service. Howard is dead, so the chance that he'll show up is low, though frankly I wouldn't put it past him, even in his current condition. Leah—she's the fiddler, you know—she lives in Australia now. From what I've heard, she's not doing too well financially, so I don't think she'd be able to make it all the way to your town. Our bass player bought an RV and now he lives on the road, moving from place to place mainly in the Western states, and he's only very sporadically in contact with anyone associated with the band. I doubt he'll be there."

"How do you know what the other band members are doing, if you haven't had any contact with them since you disappeared?"

"Well, some of them were in the public eye, and information is easy to find. Like, I found Howard's obituary on the Internet, in one of the folk music publications. I think a heart attack got him, but really it was loose living. Leah, I tracked her down using some Internet sleuthing, found her on an Australian music forum. She mentioned my story a couple of times. It was weird, this feeling of being talked about, and I'm pretty sure she had no idea I tracked her." Another laugh. "I'm going to tell her what happened. Before *all* of us are dead. Enough time has passed that I think we can laugh about it. Plus, I think she'll be glad to find out."

"But—if you don't mind my asking—why did you hide from them?"

"First of all, I wanted to get away from my former life. The atmosphere in the band had become toxic. The cult looked ridiculous— I couldn't take it seriously. I didn't really want to hang out with these people anymore. I started my new life. Something happened that I think happens a lot in situations like that. Once you've closed the door, you don't want to open it again. It's like leaving a place where you lived, a place you didn't particularly like. Do you want to go back there? Probably not. Not anytime soon, in any case. But as time went by, I became more distant, more like an observer. I became curious about how my disappearance would be seen by other people. I mean, not just the band members, but the public—assuming there was anyone in the public who was still interested in us. I started watching myself. Meaning, I monitored how I was described on the Internet and in publications and so forth. I found a bunch of articles and blog posts. It was like I built a legend by having disappeared. It became almost my personal work of art, something I hadn't been able to achieve as a member of an obscure folk-fusion band."

"Few of us are fortunate enough to have our own legend," I observed. "Fewer still when we're not dead."

"You have no idea of the variety of fates that people have imagined for me. I've seen it stated that I died in the desert and my bones are still out there and people haven't found them yet. I've also heard a story that I was adopted into the Navajo Nation—Tuba City is in Navajo territory—and I live on the rez as an ordinary member of the tribe, studying Navajo language and culture. Somebody else claims that I was kidnapped by members of a drug cartel and whisked off to Mexico, where I give private musical performances for the head of the cartel. You could fill a book with all these made-up stories about me."

"Maybe you should," I said. "Put together a book, I mean. You could even do it under a pseudonym, if you still don't want to show yourself."

"Yes, indeed. I'm the most famous member of the McTaggart Family Creamery. I'm the only one with an individual Wikipedia entry. Nobody, except a handful of people, knows what happened to me."

"Why tell *me* this? Now, I've become one of that handful."

"What's the point of building my legend if I'm not around to enjoy it? I've decided the time has come to reveal myself."

"You just now decided that?"

"Yes, and I'll tell you why. I had made the decision to reach out to Jackie again, after so many years of being incommunicado. Then maybe I would contact Leah and the bassist Andy, assuming I could find him. Then, just like that, Jackie died. Jackie's death hit me a lot harder than Howard's did. I saw Howard's death coming a mile away, his life was basically a slow-motion suicide. Drinking, drugs, you name it. But Jackie got up in the morning and went to work, like she did every day, like we're all expected to do, and she got murdered by a truck. It brought home to me in the most graphic way possible that something like that could happen to me, even while living my peaceful life in a little town in Vermont, which I think is a lot like the town you live in. I didn't want to die leaving behind a total mystery. The truck that killed Jackie convinced me that it was time to make my story public. I had to tell you because you're the organizer of the memorial service. If it's okay with you, I'm planning to give a little speech in her honor, and I'll send that speech afterwards to one of the music publications, and to Leah in Australia. Then everyone who cares will know that I am alive."

After a brief pause, I said, "Thank you for that. That's an incredible story. You know, it's funny. I think my situation has something in common with yours."

"How do you mean?"

"We're both running away from difficult situations." I gave her a brief account of my former life as an academic, and what had led me to settle in Roverton. I told her how much I liked the town, how I was integrating in fits and starts, how I'd experienced a few setbacks, but overall, I was glad to be here. I told her that the death of Jackie had made a similar impact on my consciousness as it had on hers. "It was so crazy and disturbing that I didn't know how to react to it. Finally, I started coping in the time-honored way: by drinking lots and lots of alcohol. Let me tell you, it didn't make things any better."

"Your last name is Traubert? Like the Tom Waits song, right? The drinking might be appropriate."

"Yeah, like that song," I said. "I'm not as desperate as the guy in the song. But I did really let myself go for a short time. I'm better now, though."

We left the personal stuff behind and discussed the practical matters relating to Jackie's memorial service. After I hung up, I understood the feeling of having "privileged information," as the term went. It wasn't the information that was privileged. Rather, I had the privilege of having such information. All the people who knew the full story of Onyx could probably fit into a small room, and I had joined that exclusive company. The fate of this solitary member of the McTaggart Family Creamery may not have meant very much in the outside world, but I knew that there were people who cared enough to follow the story and wonder if the mystery would ever be cleared up. Now, I was one of the people who knew what really happened. Ridiculous as it may sound, this made me feel important.

Our conversation had made me curious about something, so I got on the Internet. I went to various sites that sold used CDs and LPs— Amazon, Discogs, and a couple of others. Prices for second-hand copies of *Welcome to the McTaggart Family Creamery* and *Running in Place* were surprisingly high. Copies in good condition were going for thirty or forty dollars. This wasn't what I expected from Lydia's comment about "an obscure folk-fusion band." I looked for any recent news and information on the band. The most substantial item that I found was a recently posted article on the website of a well-known music publication.

The shocking death of Jackie O'Reilly—the former lead singer of the group known as the McTaggart Family Creamery—has not surprisingly led to a further uptick of interest in that quirky, protean group. This uptick has come about in the most unfortunate of ways. O'Reilly was working in the shop she owned when… [The story of the crash follows.] In its gruesome way, the incident reflects the revenge of the outside world on Jackie O'Reilly. She made a conscious decision to flee from industrial and urban civilization and plant herself in a small town in Wisconsin, where she lived quietly and apparently happily for many years. But there was no escaping the appetites and demands of the consumer society that surrounded her, which created the mountain of garbage that the truck was carrying when it killed her... [The story goes on in this vein for a bit longer. The part about her "conscious decision to flee from industrial and urban civilization" struck me as too ideological, given what I knew about her. But she had a "back to the land" streak.]

We can hope that before she died, O'Reilly took note of a renewal of interest in her long defunct band's work, a renewal which had been percolating for several years. Within the community of folk, roots, and world music fans, the Creamery's two albums acquired something of an underground reputation... [A brief discussion of the group's musical style and history follows.]

Sadly, there's no chance that the Creamery will ever play together again. Only two of its members are currently known to be alive, and they live in different countries. The group's founder, Howard Forster, died several years ago. A total air of mystery surrounds the group's backup singer and multi-instrumentalist Lydia Douglas, nicknamed "Onyx." She was last seen hiking in the Arizona desert... [The well-known story of Onyx is told at this point.]

Meanwhile, the group's growing fandom has been clamoring for proper reissues of their two albums, as well as the release of some of their live recordings that are known to exist. Now the reissue label Leitmotif Records is about to make their dreams come true, with CD and vinyl issues of both official albums slated to appear early next year... [Here follows some information about these reissues, then the article comes to an end.]

It was always a strange experience to read published stories about people I knew. It made them seem so alien and distant, even when the story had a positive slant. But beyond that, reading this sort of material made me feel important and privileged again, in the way I just described. It also put a sneaky idea into my head. What if I bought up all those McTaggart Family Creamery CDs that were being sold used, thereby cornering the market and turning a tidy profit by selling them immediately after Lydia told the world she was still alive (thus engendering yet further interest in the band), but before the reissues were released? I believe this is known as "insider trading," and it can land you in jail. On the other hand, the authorities were unlikely to take any interest in insider trading on such a modest level. After turning it over in my head, I let the idea die—I wasn't desperate enough to do such a thing. But I still felt important, like an authority in some field, even if my importance was difficult to substantiate.

One day early in October, Ethan told me he had to go to Milwaukee. I assumed it was work-related: meeting with contacts, picking up some equipment that he needed for the brewery, or even interviewing potential employees. He told me he would only be gone for a few hours and expected to be back in Roverton by evening.

I was sitting in my upstairs office when I heard his car pull up several hours later. I heard the doors open and close, and little bits of conversation which I couldn't make out. Then I realized that the person talking to Ethan was a very educated-sounding English woman. I put my shoes on and went out the front door as quickly as possible.

Ethan was walking toward me.

"Picked her up at the airport," he said, with a big smile on his face. Amanda was grasping her big suitcase, had a jacket flung over her left shoulder (it was jacket weather now in Wisconsin with autumn setting in), and looked in my direction with a faint smile of her own. I ran forward and gave her a big hug, from which (to my relief) she did not shrink.

"Welcome home!" I said. "Let me get that suitcase for you."

"It's lovely to be here… Er, I mean, *back*," said Amanda. She'd already visited Roverton a couple of times before she took off for Europe, so *back* was technically true. However, she'd never spent more than a few days here. The European "foundation work" jaunt had apparently done her some good. During our late period in Philadelphia, she started to look a tad blowsy and unhealthy, as if she'd become too demoralized to take decent care of herself. Now, she was slimmer and moderately tanned, and moved as if she'd received a shot of extra energy. It was clear that she'd spent a lot of time outdoors, doing some kind of physically invigorating work and getting lots of fresh air. She seemed to have shed not only some weight but also a few years.

Ethan declared that he'd make dinner for all of us. While he got to work in the kitchen, I sat with Amanda in the living room.

I said: "Have you got a slideshow of your travels for us?"

"You know that photography isn't my strong point," she said. "But I'll tell you everything over dinner." I wasn't ready to discuss serious topics, so we continued to indulge in small talk. Bruce jumped on my lap and made himself at home there, but when the smells from the

131

kitchen reached his nose, he jumped back down and made his way into the kitchen, walking with that endearing doggie clickety-clack noise.

"Be careful, Ethan," I said. "Bruce is on the lookout for scraps."

"Don't worry, I've got enough for him too," said Ethan.

"What are you making in there?" I asked.

"Chicken enchiladas." Not quite what I'd expected from the innovative pioneer of Great Lakes cuisine, but it was bound to be good anyway.

We decided to eat in the kitchen, as it was already getting dark outside, and a bit chilly. I promised Amanda that we'd go for a long walk after dinner, all the way to the harbor light, which would be a good way to unwind and give her a look at the town. Ethan supplemented the Mexican food with some beers he had brought from Our Lady of Hops.

"I've got a new one for Dad. It's a pale ale, called Faith, Hops, and Charity. It brings a message of hope—no, I mean hops—well, I mean both."

"Charity, that sounds like what I've been doing," said Amanda. "Charity-type work, in any case. The faith part of the beer, that's for whom precisely?"

"That's got to be for you, right Ethan?" I asked. "You're engaged in a quest for faith, am I right?"

"Er… Sort of."

"Ethan wants to join the Chinese Communist Party," I told Amanda. "That's his latest enthusiasm."

Amanda's reaction was the same as mine had been—disbelieving laughter. Once she had stopped laughing, she said: "Don't you have to be a citizen of the People's Republic? It sounds like you have your work cut out for you. If you want to join a radical sect, I'm sure there are some in Madison that would be glad to have you."

"Ethan wants to join a winning team," I said. "I don't think any of the goofballs in Madison would fit that description."

"On the other hand," Amanda suggested, "you could try catering for the next Party Congress. If they really like your beer, they may give you some kind of honorary status."

Ethan gave her a sour look. "Dad's exaggerating."

We moved on to the topic of Amanda's travels and the work she'd been doing. She gave us a more in-depth account of things she had already told us about in email messages and Zoom sessions. There were no real surprises.

"Giovanni's out of the picture now?" asked Ethan. What a provocateur! I'd suppressed all thoughts of smooth-talking, vodka-toasting Giovanni to keep him from preying on my imagination. Why did Ethan have to dredge him up?

"Giovanni was never really *in* the picture," objected Amanda smoothly. "He was a facilitator, and he was good at his job. He had a sense of fun, of theatricality. He behaved the same way with everyone." I decided to let the matter rest.

As we finished our dinner, we debated whether to take Bruce with us on the walk to the harbor light. Bruce would want to join us because it was a pack activity, and I was sure he didn't want to be left out. However, it would have been quite a long walk. We worked out a compromise solution, where Ethan would drive us part of the way in his own car and take us back home later. The four of us parked downtown, on one of the streets connecting to Franklin Square. We got out, passed through the square, and headed to the beach.

The square showed off its usual evening mood. Most of the stores were closed by this time, and the storefronts were darkened; by contrast, the eating and drinking establishments were bustling with customers. Their interiors were brightly lit up, and the outdoor patios were still open, despite the chilly touch of autumn. I saw that yet another restaurant was slated to open soon, this one with the unbearably precious name of Beyond Yummy (the sign in the window announced: "There's yummy, and then there's *Beyond Yummy*!"). As we walked through the square, I pointed out to Amanda how much it had changed since I relocated to Roverton. I felt like a real estate agent trying to impress a client, with the advantage that I didn't have to bend the truth to make the property look better than it was.

"Half of this stuff wasn't even here when I moved in. Real estate on the square has become hot. I'll have to introduce you to a couple of my favorite places."

"Looking forward to it," said Amanda. We continued on our way, and soon we reached the pier that poked out into Lake Michigan and led to the squat little red lighthouse. Ethan, who'd taken charge of Bruce for this walk, lingered behind, allowing the dog to loiter and sniff. Amanda and I kept going to the end of the pier.

"I don't think you've been out here before," I said. "To the harbor light, I mean." We listened to the never-ending rhythm of the waves crashing, over and over again. "Peaceful, isn't it? I know that's a clichéd thing to say, but that's how it feels."

"Ethan told me about what happened to Jackie," said Amanda. "What a horrendous thing."

"Yeah. I lost a friend that night. And an illusion."

"What illusion?"

"Maybe it was multiple illusions. Or interrelated ones. The illusion of safety, first and foremost. The idea of a safe refuge, a hideaway from the big bad outside world. Everything feels fine until it doesn't. The machine works until it stops working. Your health is fine until one day it isn't. Then what do you do?"

"No idea," she said. "But I'm here now, as you wanted. And Ethan too, and the dog. We can't forget the dog! Altogether, a nice nuclear family. It's as if your fragments have come back together after being scattered apart for a long time. Surely you must be feeling better now?"

"I am. But deep down, I know that's an illusion, too. What's the best way to deal with it? I think it's to realize it's there, stare it down, and don't let fear be your governing emotion."

We were silent for a while. Amanda stared out at the lake, into the deep blue distance where the water and the sky blended into each other, looking as if she were trying to discern something.

"If I'm going to be living here, I need something to do. Education, that's my field. Got any leads? Got any recommendations?"

"Can we talk about that tomorrow?" I asked. I must have sounded weary.

"Not a problem, I can wait."

"Once again, welcome home, and I mean it. Let this be our common cage now."

"Our common what?"

"Home, if you prefer."

Later that night, after Ethan went home, I helped Amanda unpack. She was exhausted from her long journey and wanted to refresh herself with a good long coma-like sleep. After a final walk around the block, the three of us—Amanda, I, and Bruce—settled down together in the bed. I had slept alone in this big bed for so long that I'd gotten used to being able to spread myself out, to the luxury of expansive space. Now, it felt as if I'd joined a commune. It didn't bother me, though. Bruce, happy to have all his adult masters back, lay down between me and Amanda with his head at shoulder height and his body stretched out in the direction of our feet, so we could both lay our hands on him at the same time.

Part IV:
Completing the Picture

It was in 1847 that William Rover came ashore here, at the end of his long journey starting from somewhere in New England. Or maybe it was in 1842. That said, some people have even asserted that he came ashore as early as 1837. Or maybe he didn't come ashore at all; it's possible he took a coach with horses. I have no idea. New York, Boston, and my former home of Philadelphia were already long-established major cities at the time. But out here in what was formerly known as the Northwest Territory, European settlement was just getting started.

There is one thing of which we can be certain. Whatever year he came ashore, and with whatever purpose William Rover founded the town that was eventually to be named after him (although most people claim that he merely set up a post office here), we can be certain that he decided to stay because he was enchanted by the nature all around him. (Actually, we don't even know he decided to stay, and his opinion about nature remains a complete mystery. No one seems to be well-informed about his residence and subsequent activities. But I'll leave that aside for now.) That nature remains as charming today as it was then (in fact I have no real idea about this, so much has happened since then).

We can confidently assert (we can't, but so what) that he found the air crisp and refreshing, like an IPA that is hoppy, floral and citrusy. At the same time, the air was balanced, with a piney aftertaste and distinct notes of grapefruit on the back end. The dense, dark woods all around him were toasty and opulent, bringing smoky hints of caramel and chocolate, with a robust, malty finish. In the morning, the sky was hazy, frothy and fruity, like a heavily juiced ale. The afternoon brought notes of banana, coffee and oatmeal, a deep and satisfying infusion of flavor. The night was like a stout aged in whiskey barrels, with dark notes of chocolate and coffee, and subtle hints of vanilla. In this paradise of flavors and styles, William Rover found himself a home. (Or maybe he didn't.)

Lo and behold, the people of Roverton—they whose ancestors came from Germany and Austria, from England and Ireland, from Holland and Belgium, from Sweden and Norway—built themselves a town, and they expected great things to follow. They held to a strategic vision, a vision that promised a future of innovation, agile leadership, and accelerated sustainability. As a commercial proposition, Roverton had legs. Those legs strode into the future with the confidence of a Chinese commissar. If the citizens sometimes felt a little eng, if they feared that their matchstick sculpture of success would fail to reach its pinnacle, that was only natural. Local kimmies enjoyed blooching about what a great life was in store for them. Drinking their beer and their horns of zeese, they looked forward to a pattern of sustainable growth, undertaken in a spirit of progressive leadership, collaborative togetherness, unstintingly competitive vision, authentically authentic authenticity, innovatively innovative innovation, and adherence to a results-oriented paradigm with a demonstrated track record of excellence.

Here I was, trying to make sense of all this.

Ethan liked to mock me for my lack of skills as a handyman. It was his stated belief that if I wanted to be a serious survivalist, I would have to learn to fix things.

As he put it: "You can only call the plumber or the electrician as long as you've got the money and as long as the plumber and the electrician still exist." I admitted he was right, and I looked for small jobs around the house that would help me improve my abilities in this field.

A clogged bathroom sink gave me an opportunity. I watched a couple of YouTube videos, picked up some basic tools, and got to work. I was able to unscrew the PVC pipes, extract the gunky disgusting clog, and put everything back together without too much fuss and bother. It took longer than I expected, but projects that take longer than you expect are among the basic building blocks of life. As I finished up, feeling virtuous, I heard the front door open. I could tell from the heaviness of the step that it was Ethan. With head held high and shoulders back, I walked down the stairs, intending to boast about my new achievement.

"Hey, guess what I did." I told him the whole story. However, his mind seemed to be elsewhere. He had a disturbed look on his face.

"That's great, Dad. You're making progress," he said in a flat voice. He continued to look glum.

"You got something on your mind?" I asked. "You don't seem too happy."

"Yeah. Can we sit in the kitchen?"

"Sure." We sat down at the big table. Ethan took off his jacket, and while doing so he reached into the inside pocket and took out some sort of flyer or brochure.

He said: "This is from Beyond Yummy, that new restaurant on the square with the ridiculous name. They're handing out these flyers. Look at it." He put the flyer on the table and pushed it in my direction. I picked it up and read the first few lines.

There's yummy, and then there's BEYOND YUMMY!
25 Franklin Sq.
GRAND OPENING
Beyond Yummy is the gourmet experience Rovertonians have been waiting for! Specializing in authentic, progressive, and above all, *delicious* GREAT LAKES CUISINE.
Beyond Yummy is a pioneer in this exciting new field. But more than that—the food at Beyond Yummy is what will keep you coming back again and again!

"I've been scooped," moaned Ethan. "I've been played. I've been cut out of the loop, and I didn't even know it till today. I feel like an idiot. What am I going to do now?"

"Well…" I had no idea what to say. Many potential responses contended in my head. I could point out how most inventions cannot be attributed to a single person, how there's a whole chain of innovation with multiple participants. I could throw out a historical analogy, like Newton and Leibniz inventing calculus independently and at the same time and both getting credit for it. I could laugh at his naïveté and tell him there was no point in despairing. But I got the sense that he wouldn't be willing to listen to any of these things.

Finally, I said: "Have you looked at their actual menu?"

"The full menu isn't available yet. But they mention a few things in their advertisements. You can probably guess what they are. You can expect a Wisconsin beer cheese soup that goes *beyond the yumminess* of every previous Wisconsin beer cheese soup ever cooked. Other stuff like that."

I felt more confident. "You know, this is not nearly as bad as you think. That's what I'm willing to bet."

"Why so?"

My inner academic stepped forward. "Let's do a little textual analysis. The flyer refers to Great Lakes cuisine as 'this exciting new field.' The phrasing suggests that this field already exists; the use of the word 'new' implies that it hasn't existed for very long. At the same time, Beyond Yummy describes itself as a pioneer. A pioneer isn't necessarily the person who comes first. The word can be ambiguous; it doesn't have the clear-cut meaning of 'inventor.' Also, the flyer describes the food at Beyond Yummy as 'authentic' and 'progressive.' These are buzzwords designed to attract nukes who have money to spend. In and of themselves, they tell us nothing about the food they're serving. Thus, my conclusion is—you're still a pioneer. Your job isn't to create this cuisine from scratch, but to put your own spin on it."

"Alright, but there's another thing. According to their website, they're teaming up with—Miguel! It's like he stabbed me in the back. How could he do that?"

"Again, be realistic. Miguel owes you nothing. You don't have a contract with him, you guys talked and talked and made plans, but a real business never came out of it. As an entrepreneur, he has to look out for his own business first. This new opportunity comes along, and he grabs it. In his place you'd do the same."

Ethan brooded on this for a moment.

Then he said: "Let's say you're right. Miguel does what's best for him. I should do what's best for me. But what is that?"

"You say that the restaurant is teaming up with Miguel. I don't know exactly what that means. I assume he's going to supply them with various foodstuffs that they need, because he's the best guy in town for finding unusual or exotic food. Which leads me to another thought. Instead of getting all resentful at Beyond Yummy for scooping you, why don't *you* try to team up with them? I mean, on the beverage side of things?"

He looked annoyed.

"Possibly good advice. I'll have to think about it."

"Sleep on it, and then reevaluate it in the cold light of day. But if you decide to act, do it quickly. You don't want someone else to get that beer contract with Beyond Yummy, do you?"

I said earlier that young people tend to treat setbacks and disappointments as bigger deals than they are, because they lack sufficient life experience to put things in perspective. Here was Ethan, in his mid-twenties, providing me with a textbook example. I was in the midst of telling him this when he interrupted.

"Yeah, that may be true in the abstract. But who found you lying on the floor not so long ago, ranting about the end of the world? Who got you cleaned up and rebalanced? It was me, the young guy without sufficient perspective on life." He smiled in triumph.

He'd turned the tables on me. I had to admire that. "Touché. That said—I'm serious about the idea of you approaching Beyond Yummy. They've already scooped you. Don't let it get you down. This is something you can turn to your advantage."

He frowned. "Maybe."

My turn for a comeback. "Who was the person who told me I should follow my hopes rather than my fears? This is a good chance for you to put your own advice into action."

"I'll think about it." Maybe he would, maybe he wouldn't. He needed some time to work out a strategy. I reminded him that there were no original ideas, so if he thought he was being original, then he was lying to himself.

"Is Mummy around?"

"She took Bruce down to the beach for a walk. Do you need to talk to her?"

"Thought I'd say hi," he said. While we waited for Amanda to return, we got on to the topic of religion. Ethan had accepted that joining the Chinese Communist Party was an unrealistic goal. He was now considering other organizations, other belief systems. We'd raised him in a spirit of cheerful agnosticism; we promoted an openness to spiritual matters without pushing him to commit to any path. Now, he was spending his young adulthood in a quest for something to believe in, some guiding faith or set of principles. However, the situation was more complex and slippery than that. I'd been struck by the discrepancy between his pragmatic approach to the world as he found it and the way his mind flitted from one ideology or belief system to another. If actions are the best indicator of beliefs, I had to conclude that he never really believed in any of these things—not strongly enough to make any concrete changes in his life.

"My latest interest is Islam," he announced.

"That's funny," I said. "You mock me for being a survivalist, but at least I'm consistent about it, even if a little lazy in that respect. You, on the other hand, change your ideological stance about as frequently as you get a haircut. What happened this time? Did you discover some YouTube videos expounding on the Koran?"

"Not YouTube, I've been reading some things. The great thing about Islam is that it's a badass religion that doesn't take crap from anyone. Muslims take their religion seriously. That's why they're gaining so many converts. Most forms of Christianity nowadays are hopelessly polite and wimpy."

I cut to the core of this latest enthusiasm.

"If you become a Muslim, what are you going to do for a living?"

"What do you mean?"

"Isn't alcohol prohibited in Islam? You make a living by brewing beer."

Ethan frowned.

"It's a religion with a billion adherents. I'm sure plenty of them drink alcohol. Beer isn't that high in alcoholic content, anyway."

"Mormons don't drink alcohol either, and from what I've seen, they take that rule very seriously. Why would you assume that Muslims are any different?"

"Because as I said, we're talking about over a billion people. Any religion with that many believers is going to have different sects with different beliefs. I'm sure I can find a more liberal brand of Islam that will let me brew beer."

"But a more liberal brand of Islam would not be sufficiently 'badass,' to use your word. I thought the attraction of the religion was that it takes itself seriously. But here you are, starting on your exploration, and you're trying to bend the rules already. You're trying to accommodate the religion to yourself, rather than accommodating yourself to the religion. That's not what a real convert does."

"You know what… I'm going to explore more deeply, and I'm sure I can come up with something to square that circle. You're being hostile to my exploration of a notably badass faith."

"Not at all," I said. "You can be a comparative religion major in your downtime; I don't care. But I don't want to see my town lose an excellent brewpub."

Ethan frowned again. The discomfort of being pulled in opposite directions was visible on his face. It was a discomfort that I knew well. "I'm sure there's a workaround of some sort. They've had, what, 1400 years to figure out these details."

In a state of mild exasperation, I said: "Why don't you just try to find out the truth?" I wanted to continue, but I heard the front door open, and Bruce charged into the kitchen, jumping up at Ethan and giving vent to his excitement with a series of high-pitched whines. It was clear that the conversation was over.

Reinhard's Diner, with its stellar coffee and succulent food, was my most constant hangout location in Roverton, and I was certain that Amanda would like it, too. One morning shortly after her return, I suggested that we go there for breakfast. I had another reason to be there on this day.

I ordered my usual pancakes and coffee. Amanda had a Dutch apple breakfast bake, which the menu described as "imbued with the deep flavors of autumn—a mellifluous symphony of apple, cinnamon and raisin." These nuke-influenced culinary descriptions were springing up all over town; it was hard to imagine that the original Reinhard's could have had such a poetically eloquent menu.

At one point, I waited for her to start drinking her coffee, then tossed out, in my best half-joking voice: "Hey, now that you're back, shouldn't we have sex or something to celebrate?"

This produced the same splatter effect that I'd triggered in Jackie, back when we were talking about Noodles Fontaine, not so long ago in this very diner. Amanda picked up a napkin and cleaned the spray of coffee from the table in front of her.

"You are quite a romantic fellow, aren't you, Freddie? If that's what you want to do, let's put it on our schedule." (Of course, she pronounced this last word *shedule*.)

"At some point we probably should, to complete the picture of familial harmony. The fact is, though, we're a couple of middle-aged eggheads with vanishing libidos. You know what—life is easier that way. After a certain age, you don't need the complications."

She didn't say anything to this, but I could tell she agreed with me. After breakfast, I suggested we take the short walk to Fabelhaft Bakery.

"Don't believe I've ever been in here before," observed Amanda, surveying the cozy setting. As she walked around slowly, looking at the baked goods on sale and the photos on the walls, I walked up to the counter and discreetly transacted a piece of business. An elongated item wrapped in paper was passed to me, and I placed it in a plastic bag.

Out on the square again, we crossed to the village green, where I invited Amanda to sit with me on a park bench right next to the big relief map of the Great Lakes. When we'd taken our positions, I slid the long object out of the bag and, with ceremonial slowness, started unwrapping it.

"Oh, this looks like something special," said Amanda.

"Something special for you!" I announced. I finished unwrapping and handed the item to her.

"Beautiful," she said, examining the Swiss chocolate and coffee roll I'd ordered for her the day after she returned. Curlicues of chocolate syrup across the top said, "Welcome home Amanda!"

"Freddie, this looks delicious. Thank you!"

"Hey," I said, "if I'd known *when* you were coming, I'd have baked a cake. But I didn't know, so I took the second-best option. I looked at cheesesteaks—sorry, I meant *cheesecakes*—and cakes with fruit on top and other stuff. But this Swiss roll is a European creation of subtlety and complexity, which makes it like you."

"Oh, that's *so* sweet, in multiple senses of the word."

Now that Amanda had settled in, we were confronted with a basic question: what was she going to do? Despite all her complaints about life in Philly, it was a large metro area with a lot of opportunities for a person like her. Living now out in the sticks, she would have to make some adjustments.

One morning over breakfast, I explained the sociology of the town. I talked about the nuke versus non-nuke division that had sprung up recently. I went into detail about demographics, economics, and culture. I was holding forth on Veblen's theories when Amanda interrupted me.

"That's all very nice, Freddie—all very erudite—but it doesn't give me any useful ideas. What do *you* think should be my first step? I'm asking you because you've already lived here for a while."

"You taught school. If you want to do that here, this is the setup. There's the private high school and the public high school. The private school tends to be favored by the nukes. They'll probably regard you as an asset, given your background. In addition to your obvious credentials, you play a role in internationalizing Roverton. They'd like that. The old-timers generally prefer the public school. If you worked there, you might get a different reaction. You'd be regarded as that exotic lady with the high-tone accent. As you know, in America, having that accent adds points to your IQ. This might be something you can spin to your advantage."

"It all sounds a bit cynical," mused Amanda, stirring her zeese.

"I wouldn't call it cynical, just realistic. The fact is, it's a nice town, but for a person like you the options are limited. I don't know if either of these schools would have an opening for you. The academic year has already started. It's unlikely right now."

She gave me a concerned look.

"How are things with you now, Freddie? I mean regarding employment."

"Not too bad. I still have inherited money to live off, and I'm doing okay with these consulting jobs, although I wish they paid more. It would give us some extra security to have two incomes in the house now. I'm saying you may have to settle for less than you wanted."

"If you're a nuke, then I suppose I'm a nuke, as well," she said. "What's a typical job for a nuke?"

"Remote remote remote, that seems to be the main thing. Yes, it's another case of technological change creating a new way of life and a new class of people. But plenty of nukes aren't wired. They might run a store or restaurant, or work for a small business, or they might run an art gallery, or they might take care of the kids while the money comes from somewhere else."

"Anyone growing marijuana?" she asked.

I smiled at the question.

"I haven't looked into it myself. But I wouldn't be surprised. You're not considering that option, are you?"

"Trying to get a complete picture."

"My advice to you is, think about joining the remote consulting world. Don't you have lots of contacts—in Europe and elsewhere? Maybe you can do your foundation work without leaving the living room."

We finished breakfast, and she went off to ponder her future as a small-town resident. I went upstairs to my office, sat down on the couch with Bruce, and vegetated online. There was no pressing business today, but I thought about projects. I don't mean in the sense of Project Arcturus or Project Snoopy or Project Befuddlement or any of the other jobs I'd done lately. I used the term in its existentialist sense, as something to give meaning and purpose to my life. I thought about my oral history project and how I could retool it, given the problems it had run into. I toyed with ideas, flipping them back and forth in my mind, but came to no solid conclusions. I gave up and went back to looking at websites. Occasionally, I'd access the newspaper of my former college in Philadelphia to find out what was going on there. What I read today seemed to confirm the wisdom of relocating to Roverton.

The big current scandal was that the president of the college was now under indictment for embezzlement. It wasn't enough that he already received a remarkably generous salary for an institution that enjoyed merely the fourth or even fifth prestige slot in the Philadelphia area (although that salary had been bestowed based on the president's promise that "I will make this place competitive with Penn"). It wasn't enough that he lived in a very nice house in a Main Line suburb and took advantage of subsidized travel to far corners of the United States and even abroad. No, that wasn't enough (insert "allegedly" wherever necessary). The indictment claimed he overcharged for meals and travel expenses and pocketed the difference. He'd done this consistently for several years, thereby earning himself a tidy amount, in addition to everything else. My mind boggled at the fact that a man who already had his material needs met (and then some) could be so greedy, and what's more, in such a petty way. Shaking my head, I thought about my canceled courses, which were killed to save the administration a meager sum of money.

Scandals also affected the classroom. Not surprisingly, they often had something to do with sex. In an art history class, the lecturer made the mistake of referring to the *Mona Lisa* as "a portrait of a woman." A couple of student activists took exception to this, pointing out that the portrait of La Gioconda (whom they referred to as Lx Giocondx) could have been the portrait of a man posing as a woman. The lecturer compounded her error: she attempted to reason with the activists, pointing out this and that, but they would have none of it. They were only pacified when the lecturer, under pressure from the spineless administration (I imagined my old friend Dean Dean cowering in his office), issued a compelled apology, with the promise to "take some time to reflect" and to "do better" in the future. A similar kerfuffle roiled the English department, but there it was resolved more harmoniously. A student objected to having to read Henry James' novella *The Turn of the Screw*, because she felt threatened by the sexual implications of the title. When it was pointed out that the "screw" in question was not a sexual act but a piece of hardware, the student withdrew her objection. Later, she admitted that the real reason she didn't want to read the book was because she didn't like Henry James' convoluted prose style.

The usual problems of interpreting journalism applied (particularly if the journalism was produced by students without much experience). What was hearsay, what was fact: from my current distance, it was hard to tell. These stories brought no surprises, so I was inclined to believe them, at least their essential elements. Had I stayed in Philly, I'd probably be ingesting tablets of Quaxinol at an alarming rate. These stories filled me with negative feelings, at a time when I'd resolved to be more positive. Like Amanda, I needed to think about my options in more detail.

When Jackie died, she was still officially a Catholic, though a lackadaisical one. She didn't attend mass frequently, but I think it would be fair to say that she didn't feel out of place inside a church. That's where we decided to hold her memorial service: in Roverton's one still functioning Catholic church. (I mean the one functioning as a church, not the one functioning as a brewery.)

A few days before the event, I scanned the Internet, looking for photos of Lydia "Onyx" Douglas. I wanted to be able to recognize her if she showed up without telling me. Every photo I could find was from the 1990s, when she was young and still had the shiny black hair that gave rise to her nickname. That black hair must be gray by now, I thought; and if I add a few wrinkles to that face, I'll get her current appearance. I realized I had no way of knowing what she looked like now and gave up the effort.

Two days before the memorial service, Lydia gave me a call. "I'm glad to hear from you," I said. "There are a couple of logistical issues I want to talk to you about. How exactly are you planning to get to Roverton? I might be able to provide some help if you need it."

She was silent for a few seconds; then I heard a sigh. "I'm sorry, Fred—I can't do it."

I was stunned.

"You can't? You really can't?"

"I really can't."

"Why can't you?"

Another sigh. "Last week I was looking for any cheap flight I could get from Boston out to Milwaukee. I figured I'd rent a car and drive up to where you are. I started to think about whether I really wanted to do this."

"If your major problem is getting from Milwaukee to Roverton, I'd be willing to pick you up, or send my son to do it. It's no problem for us, not at all. You're the honored guest."

"That's not my major problem. My major problem is that I'm not ready to reveal myself after all."

"But you told me the exact opposite when we talked earlier. What caused you to change your mind?"

"I like my life, Fred. I mean, the life I have now. I shut the door on my old life many years ago. If I open that door now, I'm afraid it will put my current life in danger. Around here, I use my dead husband's last name, not Douglas. I don't look like I used to—you'd have to call me Moonstone or Silver or something like that, not Onyx. The people here know me as that nice, eccentric middle-aged lady who does odd jobs and plays those weird instruments. I fit in here. If there's the occasional rumor, I don't mind—as long as the paparazzi don't show up, it adds a little sparkle to my life. I'm comfortable with things as they are. That's what it comes down to."

There was nothing I could say to counter this. She knew her own life; I didn't. Still, it struck me as odd, given her talk about creating a personal legend and how she wanted to be around to enjoy it.

"Do you think there is some possibility you'll change your mind back? I mean, is this a temporary decision, or do you think you'll stick with it for the rest of your life?"

"All I know is I'm not ready yet. You didn't tell anyone, did you Fred?"

"Nope."

"Okay. But you know what… If you want to tell the occasional person about it, I don't think I'd object. I don't mind if the truth seeps out gradually. I may even tell Leah and a couple of other people, as I was planning to do. I'm not ready to return to public life, that's all."

I didn't express disappointment. I told her that I fully understood and sympathized with her decision. What else could I do?

I was disappointed none the less. She would have made something special—a real event—out of Jackie's memorial service. As usual, there was a silver lining. I was very pleased with myself that I had not succumbed to the temptation to corner the market on all those secondhand McTaggart Family Creamery CDs. That would really have left me feeling like a chump.

Still, I felt deflated. Thinking about Jackie and Onyx and everything, I remembered how I had rented Antonioni's film *L'Avventura* in Light & Sound. It was one of the last films I rented there. Jackie and I planned to discuss Italian cinema together, and I hoped to make sense of this classic film on a repeat viewing. The first thing didn't happen. I had more success with the second. I still found it opaque; but now, I could begin to understand why the opening night audience booed the film so badly that the director fled the cinema, and why the critics turned right around and proclaimed it a masterpiece shortly thereafter. The existential ennui of the idle rich was a fashionable subject at the time, and *L'Avventura* delivered on that front. But now, what stood out in my mind was that the entire story was based around a disappearance. A group of friends take a yacht to visit a volcanic island off the coast of Sicily. While they're exploring the island, one of their number (named Anna) disappears. She has said something about wanting to be left alone. Her friends search for her, but they never find her. The rest of the film deals with the aftermath of her disappearance. I thought of the group of friends as the McTaggart Family Creamery, and of Anna as Lydia. I thought about how unsettling it was that this was the film I decided to watch when I was in Jackie's store, in view of what followed. I couldn't help wondering if she kept the movie around as a kind of memorial to her vanished bandmate, even though she claimed that she'd never watched it. Sadly, I'd never know. But in contrast to the people in the film, I did have the satisfaction of knowing what had happened to my own private Anna.

Jackie's memorial service went about as well as I expected it to, except for the personal disappointment, which I didn't talk about at the service. Catholic churches are aesthetically appealing enough to make me forget my natural attraction to stoic and skeptical ways of thinking, at least during the time when I'm in the church, soaking up the art, music, and atmosphere. But then I walk back out into the world, and the tug of the supernatural gradually subsides.

There were a few people from the music biz at the service, including the founder of her onetime record label, a Mr. Frank Newman, one of those endearing old countercultural types who got into the business for love rather than money. There were some Rovertonian friends, such as Mean Christine Vandersteen. A few speakers gave short but moving eulogies, including her son John and the aforementioned Mr. Newman. The latter talked about the history and surprising resurgent popularity of the McTaggart Family Creamery, expressing regret that none of the other members of the band could be there. Naturally, he talked about the "complete mystery" surrounding Onyx. I broke into a nice inward smile when he said that.

When the service was over, I stayed behind to blooch with Frank Newman and anyone else who wanted to talk. Frank was a bald, grey-bearded guy with a paunch and an intermittent twinkle in his eye. He seemed genuinely pleased to be talking with friends of Jackie. I couldn't resist asking him a question.

"What do you think happened to Onyx?"

His eyes twinkled as if receiving some electronic communication. "I don't know. But I suspect she's out there somewhere, lying low. Under the radar. That's how she likes it."

"Why do you think that?"

He raised his hands theatrically.

"Oh, rumors, speculations, occasional bits of information that come my way… Along the lines of, 'Hey, I think I met your missing folk singer, in a café in New Hampshire or somewhere.' Not proven, of course. Maybe we'll find out when she finally dies. If she's not dead already."

"She doesn't talk to many people, does she?" I asked.

"That's it, basically," said Frank before correcting himself: "I mean… I have no way of knowing, do I? Neither do you, right?" He laughed.

"Yeah, let's agree not to know."

Hastily, Frank shifted the subject to the business of recording folk music.

He said, "You know, one of the things I like about these small record labels, a lot of times they're located in out-of-the-way places. Durham, North Carolina. Newton, New Jersey. You must've heard of Paramount Records? Right here in Wisconsin, little town called Grafton. They put out some of the great pioneering jazz and blues records. Isn't that amazing?"

I agreed it was amazing. When our conversation ended, and he walked away, I swear he winked at me.

A couple of days after Jackie's memorial service, I went to the Red Rooster café, ostensibly to get some work done, but really as a nostalgia trip. I'd spent some good time with Jackie there, blooching about all kinds of things. This was, after all, the place where she'd told me the whole story about her life as a folk musician. I also had a vague idea (probably picked up from the literature I'd read) that cafés were good places to do intellectual work. I thought about the wits in eighteenth-century London; the complex network of intellectuals that inhabited the cafés of Vienna around 1900; the existentialists in Paris in the 1950s. And here I was, doing a forgettable piece of marketing in a café in Roverton, Wisconsin.

Ted (yes, that was his name) gave me my zeese and I sat down and worked. It was a quiet afternoon, and there were only a few people in the café. I'd only been there a short time when a new customer entered. I recognized him immediately—it was Alex Henderson, until recently the "parent" of Wesley the dog. He said hello and indicated that he wanted to talk to me about something ("I'm glad I ran into you… Wait till you hear this!").

I was still reluctant to talk to him, but he seemed not at all hostile, so I invited him to sit down. After some preliminaries, he got to the core of the matter.

"You do know that Mrs. Westerberg died recently, right?"

I admitted to not knowing that. "Now that you mention it, I haven't seen her while walking the dog for a while. But I thought maybe she went away or something. Yeah, I had no idea."

"You didn't notice the For Sale sign on her front yard?"

"Honestly, I don't remember if I noticed it or not. Things like that tend to slip right past me. But how is this significant?"

Alex fixed me with the accusing eyes of a police interrogator. "We finally know who murdered our dog."

I hoped that my own facial expression did not betray any signs of fear. "Oh really? Who was it?"

Alex said: "It was Mrs. Westerberg herself."

I felt relief. "Is that so? How did you find out?"

Alex told me the story. Shortly after Mrs. Westerberg's demise, the Hendersons received a letter from an unknown sender. It had been hand-delivered to their mailbox. The letter itself was written by Mrs. Westerberg. In it, she took full responsibility for the death of Wesley. She stated that she'd entrusted this letter to a close friend, who'd been charged with delivering it immediately after her death. She outlined her reasons for euthanizing Wesley, pointing out that such a miserable dog deserved a better fate than the Hendersons were willing to give it. In her initial letter, which was delivered on the same day as Wesley's death, she disguised herself as "Three Good Samaritans of Roverton." In fact, there were not three people involved. There was only Mrs. Westerberg, who watched the comings and goings of Ashley and Alex carefully, and who knew when they were home and when they were not. She kidnapped Wesley and took him immediately to her home, where she euthanized him with sleeping pills. The method proved to be successful, although Mrs. Westerberg became disturbed to the point of tears when she watched Wesley twitching and gasping as the life ebbed from him.

"Wow, Alex," I said. "What a story. I bet you're glad to have some closure."

"Yeah, what a situation. Enough time has passed that I can't really get angry about it. She was willing to confess even though she's dead. A confession from beyond the grave. Seems cowardly, doesn't it? What I can never forgive is that she took Wesley's last moments away from us. Maybe I told you earlier, but Ashley and I were concluding that euthanasia would be necessary. We were going to discuss it, as much as we hated the idea. But he died in someone else's house, and even if it was peaceful, we weren't there. By the way, you may see another For Sale sign going up soon."

"Oh really?"

"Yes indeed. Ashley has an offer from a company in Texas. It'll require her to be on site. No more remote work for her. She's still considering it, but I think she'll take it. The conditions are too good to turn it down."

I thought about the flooding in Texas that I'd seen on the TV. I thought about the general problem of climate in the Southern states. From my point of view, the ice-cold snowy winters of the Great Lakes were greatly preferable to conflagrations, hurricanes, tornadoes, floods, mudslides, heat waves, and earthquakes. However, I knew that millions of people disagreed with me.

"Actually, we're glad to be getting out of here," said Alex. "The Roverton experience didn't work out as we had hoped. That's putting it mildly."

I expressed my best wishes for their bright future in Texas. The Dallas-Fort Worth Metroplex was a booming region, a red-hot center of the new economy, a city (or cities) on the rise. The Hendersons could anticipate a future of dense traffic, endless identikit suburban developments, and the icy hum of air conditioning every time they stepped indoors. They could look forward to the blinding glare of the sun glinting off a thousand silvery automotive heat shields whenever they walked out of their multistory office building and into the parking lot. Not my idea of a healthy environment, but who was I to decide for them? They were probably making the right move.

Nestling deep within my mind was the suspicion that Mrs. Westerberg wasn't telling the whole truth in that letter. She didn't say how she disposed of the dog's corpse, nor did she give any indication of how she managed to inveigle someone else's dog into her house without outside help. But I decided to let it rest, because at this point there was no reason to dig up the whole truth, assuming it could even be discovered.

The Grand Opera House in Roverton isn't especially grand, nor is it really an opera house. This two-story, creamy yellow brick-and-stone building sits right off the square, a typical manifestation of our local late 19th-century architectural styles, and it has never staged a full-scale opera; the stage isn't big enough for that. But it is our best local performance space, and it was where the Jolly Company of Rovertonians held their fall concert.

Amanda and I went together, and it was our plan to meet Ethan afterwards. As expected, the first song was dedicated to Jackie O'Reilly. While I wondered what they were going to sing, the conductor of the choir talked. He said they had done some digging to find an appropriate song, because they felt that Jackie deserved proper commemoration. They had found a song composed by one of her former bandmates—Lydia Douglas, "who seemingly disappeared off the face of the earth many years ago, and has never been seen or heard from since." As he gave a brief account of the disappearance of Onyx, I experienced another inward smile. The fact that she was also a songwriter came as a surprise to me.

The song itself was pleasant, but I can't say it made a great impression on me. It must have been on their first album, the one I hadn't heard. It was about how summer is over, the plants are withering and dying, our youth is slipping away, we're entering the long period of grayness and boredom known as adulthood, and other melancholy sentiments. Luckily, the rest of the concert was more upbeat—they were the Jolly Company, after all.

The concert was followed by another event, a special one in its own way. Amanda and I crossed the square to Beyond Yummy, which had just opened and, in the usual honeymoon style of new restaurants, was enjoying a booming business because all the locals wanted to check it out. We'd be joined for dinner there by Ethan, and by Mean Christine Vandersteen, whom I'd long valued both as an informant on my oral history project and as a friend of the deceased Jackie. For Ethan, the occasion would be doubly satisfying. He'd followed my advice and managed to get the restaurant's beer concession for Our Lady of Hops. It was the first week of their collaboration. He was busy, and he radiated a sense of confidence and contentment that made him a pleasure to be around. (All the more so because he'd followed his old man's advice.)

The chef at Beyond Yummy had moved here all the way from Montreal. He was a thirtysomething Canadian of partial Vietnamese descent named Jean-Louis Tran. I have no idea how he heard about this obscure town on the other side of the border, or why he concluded it would be a good place for a restaurant, or if he'd already experimented with Great Lakes cuisine. There seemed to be a vibe in the air, and he, Ethan, and Miguel all picked up on it at the same time.

Beyond Yummy had installed some big globe lamps out front, which shed their soft yellow light on its entrance. The interior was pleasantly countrified in appearance, with its wood-paneled butter-hued walls and the large photos of Great Lakes scenes on those walls, both monochrome and color. We were seated at a table near the front window and under a remarkably chilly color photo of the Apostle Islands ice caves, up in Lake Superior.

"I'd quite like to try the chislic combo," said Amanda, surveying the menu.

"You'd like to try the what?"

"Chislic, it's called. Deep-fried cubes of meat. It's a combo because they give you three types of cubes—beef, pork, and lamb. Says on the menu that this dish is characteristic of South Dakota."

"South Dakota? That's not on a Great Lake."

"South Dakota borders on Minnesota, which is situated on a Great Lake, namely Superior, up in the north," countered Amanda. "One could make the—fanciful—argument that it has a close relation to the Great Lakes."

"Are you suggesting that Minnesota has annexed South Dakota, so that the latter now has its own Great Lakes coastal region? Even if you want to make this argument, does that mean that Minnesota has also annexed Dakotan cuisine by implication?"

"My, aren't we being puristic," scolded Amanda. "I suggest you take this up with the chef."

"Dad is in academic nitpicking mode again," said Ethan. "The chislic here is good stuff. You should try it."

"Well," I said. "I'm going to stick up for authenticity, even if nobody else does. I'm a nuke after all, I'm supposed to care about such things. I'm going to have the baked shrimp—the Shrimp de Jonghe—which was invented in a hotel in Chicago and counts as an authentic Great Lakes dish."

Christine ordered a gourmet burger of some kind. Ethan had already eaten his dinner, so he stuck with beer. As I looked through the menu again, I had a thought that I wanted to share with Ethan.

"I'm noticing an interesting thing about this menu. All of their Great Lakes cuisine consists of dishes that already exist. Leave aside whether it's Great Lakes or not, it's like a collection of stuff that's already existed for ages. It strikes me that there is still a lot of space for innovation here. That's something you can take advantage of."

Ethan took a long swig from a glass containing his own creation, Pirate Dan's Private Stash pale ale, and responded.

"I've already talked about that with Jean-Louis. He's open to collaboration. Hopefully I won't just be the beer supplier. Miguel wants to be involved, too. You put all three of us together, that's a pretty good team in my view. We come from different places, different backgrounds. We all bring our own ideas to the table, so to speak. Great cuisines incorporate multiple influences from all sorts of places—wasn't Miguel talking about that when we all met, at Our Lady of Hops? The potato from Peru, and all that? Anyway, he was right."

"You haven't really been scooped, as you feared," I said. "You're at the beginning of something, rather than the end."

"That's a way to look at it," he said.

"What do *you* think, Mean Christine?" I asked. (She laughed at the use of her nickname.) "Let's imagine that Ethan is a student in your class. Are you sufficiently impressed with the elementary school book report that Ethan just delivered?"

"Hey, that's not really fair," interjected Ethan. "What book am I meant to be reporting on, Professor?"

Christine said, "It sounds like Ethan has a very good idea of what he wants to do. There's all the excitement of starting a new project—right, Ethan?" She took a bite of her gourmet burger.

"That's right. Admittedly, it's still a little hazy."

"Like a hazy IPA?" I asked.

"Yeah, about that degree of haziness," said Ethan in a deadpan voice.

"I have to admit," said Christine, "all of this sounds rather foreign to me. You're talking about foods I grew up with. I didn't think of it as any sort of 'cuisine.' It was just what we ate around here."

"Good to have the old-timer perspective," I said. "You're planning to incorporate that, I hope?"

"You bet," said Ethan.

Between the concert at the Opera House, the shared mourning for Jackie O'Reilly, the food, the beer, the family all together in one place, the presence of Mean Christine the old-timer, and the conversation, I felt more integrated into the town than ever. Now all I had to do was take Bruce for an evening walk, and the picture would be complete.

In Finland in the 19th century, there lived a doctor named Elias Lönnrot. Like most members of Finland's governing and professional class, he came from the country's Swedish-speaking minority. But he took an interest in the culture of the majority population, the ones who spoke Finnish and lived mostly in rural areas. Their language was not even Indo-European and was genetically totally unrelated to Lönnrot's native Swedish, and they cultivated an ancient folk culture that was little-known in Europe at the time. It was Lönnrot's achievement to collect, record, and disseminate this folk culture, thereby endowing Finland with its own distinctive identity. This was the way it went in Europe at the time: outsiders—typically urban, from the middle or upper classes, and often speaking a different language—took an interest in the culture of the "people of the land," and in doing so memorialized this culture forever. Thanks to Lönnrot's achievements, you can walk into a bookstore and buy a copy of the *Kalevala*, the Finnish national epic, which previously had only existed in the form of tales and ballads told by illiterate bards. You can find manifestations of this phenomenon in other parts of Europe. Due to the exertions of Dublin-based Anglo-Protestant intellectuals with names like Alfred Perceval Graves and John Millington Synge, the ancient Gaelic culture of Ireland lives and thrives. Because of the efforts of mostly Polish-speaking scholars, pagan-era Lithuanian folk culture was recovered from oblivion. At its most basic, it was the city folk reviving and recording the culture of the country folk.

For me, what this meant was that I'd decided on a new paradigm to follow. I was going to be the Elias Lönnrot of Roverton. One day, talking with Bruce while we sat together on the couch in my office, I hammered out a way forward.

"Bruce, I need to take action," I explained. "I need to make a positive change in my life. It's time to get out from under the cloud of dread that drove me to relocate here. I need to be guided by hope and pursue a creative project that will have a meaningful impact in the world." I realized that I veered dangerously close to Jasher-style corpspeak at this point, so I tried to express myself more plainly. "I know all these creative people, who are talented in brewing and cuisine and music. In fact, I envy them for their talents. My strengths are in research and writing, plus some languages that people don't speak here anymore. Those are the things I've been doing for the whole of my career. It's not like I can completely remake myself at this stage. It's hard to break out of my old self. What am I supposed to do?"

Bruce stared at me with those soulful brown eyes. I could tell that he sympathized with my plight.

He said: "If your strengths are in research and writing, that's what you should do. But you should take a different approach now. Your history project stalled because of the unreliability of your informants. Well, of one of your informants. But when a project runs into problems, do we give up on that project? That's the response of a weak-minded individual. You need to rethink what you actually want to achieve and retool accordingly."

"That's insightful, Bruce," I said. "I can tell that you've been thinking deeply about this during our walks together, and when lounging on the floor chewing your rawhide toy. But how do you think I should go about it?"

"I've come up with a plan you can try out. The next time you gather your informants, tell them that the plan has changed. Be upfront: mention that your attempts to find a unique local dialect that you can record have failed, because there isn't enough there. Instead, you're going to carry out a storytelling project. You have only three informants right now. Give each of them a challenge. Tell them that they each have to bring in three more informants. You will interview each of these informants and record whatever stories they tell you about their lives here, whether those stories be humorous, outlandish, tragic, or barely believable. When you're done with those informants, find new ones, and continue setting down their stories. You can ask them probing questions, you can request clarification, but never assume that they're lying and never assume that they're telling the truth. If Noodles Fontaine decides to let rip, you sit there and you record it. You can smirk or smile or laugh but let him have his say. The same goes for everyone else. Eventually, in one year or two years or five—however long it takes—you'll become known as the Roverton Story Guy. You'll have such an inventory of stories that you can put them all together in a big book and edit them. Out of this whole process, a modern classic of oral history will emerge. Prepare for the journey well, because it's going to be a long one."

"Bruce, you're a gold mine of useful advice. I do have to admit though, I find the length and complexity of this project kind of intimidating. Do you really think there are that many Rovertonians who would be willing to tell their stories to me? Would they really want to hang out with Professor Nuke, and disclose their darkest secrets and the intimate events of their lives? I'm not sure about that."

"People like to tell their stories. It's a human universal. That's why you shouldn't talk to the police without your lawyer present. It's in the nature of people to want to tell their story, to justify themselves, to make the world aware of how they see things. Everyone has a story to tell, and they all want someone to listen. You don't even know what's in this town, or in any community, until you start digging. So far, you've barely scratched the surface. Each person you meet is a universe. Explore those universes, to the extent that they let you. In that charming old house, in that renovated store on the main street, in that garden behind the pub on a moonlit night, you'll find histories, dreams, visions. You have to be an explorer and go looking. Nobody cares if you're Professor Nuke—it's not like you just arrived here. You're part of the scene now. They have no reason not to trust you."

"Thank you, Bruce, for these suggestions. I think I'm going to do what I tell Ethan to do when I give him a piece of advice: sleep on it and reconsider it in the cold light of day. But I like your idea, even though it will require a lot of work. It's not a project, it's a whole enterprise."

"I'm glad I could be of assistance," said Bruce. He jumped down onto the floor, shook himself, and fixed me with an earnest look. "As a token of your gratitude, you owe me something."

"Really? What is it?"

"I saw you put a frozen bag of chicken stock out to melt in the kitchen sink. That means you're going to cook with it later. Also, you said something about rice being on the menu for tonight. When you're done cooking, I would like some of that rice in my own personal food dish, infused with some of that nicely boiled chicken stock. Yum!"

"Consider it done."

One afternoon, when I had some business on Huron Avenue, I decided to take a short walk to look at the place where Jackie's Light & Sound had once stood. Nothing remained of the white wooden shack that had been a town fixture for so long. Small, feeble-looking patches of grass had sprung up here and there on the dusty rectangle where the building had stood. From what I'd heard, the town council still had no clear idea what it was going to do with the space. Some people wanted to take it over and build something new there, but it was generally agreed that a barrier would need to be put up as a safety measure first. This patch of ground was likely to remain barren for some time. In the first few weeks after Jackie's death, you might occasionally see flowers lying on the patch as a memorial; but by this day, people had stopped doing that.

Surveying this melancholy scene, I found myself thinking in my academic way about another musician, namely Anton Webern. A composer of the Second Vienna School (those pioneers of atonality), Webern probably set down on paper fewer notes than any other famous composer in history, and those notes got more scholarly and critical attention on a per-note basis than the notes of any other composer. The likes of Bach and Mozart composed so much music that you can put their complete works on your computer or CD player and the music will run for days and days before reaching the end. But you can listen to Webern's entire oeuvre in a few hours. Many words have been applied to the pieces he produced: aphoristic, laconic, compressed, gnomic, and (to quote Igor Stravinsky) "dazzling diamonds." After his death, his influence on avant-garde and modernist music grew bigger than ever.

It was, in fact, the death of Webern rather than his music that was mostly on my mind. That's because, in the academic and literary world that deals so heavily in interpretations, this composer is seen as a representative figure, a terminus of historical processes. Webern's death has been perceived not merely as the death of an important composer, but as the death of a civilization, a tradition, and a way of life and thought.

Webern was the last composer in a Viennese tradition that stretched back to Haydn. Alternatively, if you want to view him in a broader context, he belonged to a tradition that went all the way back to the Renaissance—he was heavily influenced by the polyphonic composers of that era. In 1945, he fled Vienna as the final battle for the city began, as the Red Army approached, and the Wehrmacht's defenses collapsed. He looked for a safe place as the battle raged. He took refuge in a village called Mittersill, up in the mountains.

The problem was that the outside world refused to stay out. Webern's son-in-law Bruno—who also lived in Mittersill—was a former member of the SS, and what's more, he was involved in black-market activities. The U.S. Army arranged a sting operation to arrest Bruno. On the evening when the sting took place, several incidents occurred. As usual, accounts of what happened vary.

One of the American soldiers taking part in this operation was a cook from North Carolina, a certain Raymond Norwood Bell. At one point while the sting was underway, Webern went outside to smoke a cigar. According to one account, Bell mistook the cigar for a gun and fired at Webern, killing him instantly. According to another account,

Bell bumped into Webern, thought the composer was attacking him, and shot him in what he believed to be self-defense.

The exact course of events that evening remains a mystery. We can be certain about two things: Bell shot Webern dead, and ten years later he died of illnesses related to alcoholism. According to Bell's wife, heavy drinking was Bell's way of coping with the guilt he felt at killing Webern.

At this point the interpretations begin. In *Gravity's Rainbow*, Thomas Pynchon relays one such interpretation, as delivered by one of the characters, a composer named Gustav Schlabone. Gustav presents Webern as "the last European," the final point in the evolution of both a musical tradition and a civilization. Raymond Norwood Bell is symbolic of the new barbarians from across the ocean who are destined to subjugate and dominate the Old World. European high culture is tipped into its grave by a cook from North Carolina, somebody who probably knew as little about *haute cuisine* as he did about *Kunstmusik*. Basically, in Gustav's version, America kills Europe, just as Bell killed Webern.

Thinking further on the subject, it struck me that Gustav's interpretation was wrong. Europe didn't die, after all. It was resurrected, in a different form, but it continued none the less. It may be true (as I've stated before) that everything is temporary. But it is also true that things we thought were dead can come back to life. The current crisis inevitably passes, until the final crisis that puts an end to everything occurs. But who can know how many years or how many centuries have to pass until that final crisis is upon us?

Other interpretations focus on the character of the composer himself. Webern had a conflicted, on-and-off sympathy for the Nazi regime. This sympathy did not seem to affect his relations with other people. As a personality, he comes across as solitary and isolated, confined within the small circle of his musical interests and the few people close to him, and consequently naïve about the outside world. Therefore, it's no surprise that he was unaware of the dangers of associating with a person like Bruno, with his SS and black-market connections. He probably had no idea that the sting was going on around the very house where he'd taken refuge. For many years, Webern's mind had been immersed in a crystalline, clockwork realm of musical arcana: Renaissance polyphony, canons within canons, miniature scherzos, tiny songs featuring weirdly leaping intervals. His was a mind singularly unsuited to dealing with the world of war, gangsters, and extremist ideologies.

I can add my own personal interpretation. Webern was a musician who thought he'd found a refuge in a small town, far from the collapsing world around him. He was accidentally killed by Raymond Norwood Bell, a person who was doing his job, and who screwed things up in a most unfortunate way. In my interpretation, Webern is analogous to Jackie O'Reilly, with Bell playing the tragic role later reprised by Alhamdullilah Jackson, the truck driver with the unusual first name, who may or may not have belonged to an Islamic splinter group. Jackson, although he was injured in the crash, survived it. I couldn't help but wonder about the man's mental state. I hoped he would not be plagued by guilt the way poor Raymond Norwood Bell was.

But why stop there? I asked myself. Let's consider what would have happened if Webern had been killed not by Bell but by Noodles Fontaine. In that case, scholars would have had to grapple with the formidable task of cutting through the thickets of Noodles' imagination. One can only marvel at what the great confabulator would have come up with in his own defense. The cigar Webern was smoking would have become no ordinary cigar, but a signaling device equipped with a special on-off switch, communicating messages to Bruno and his pals. Perhaps it really was a gun, and Webern intended to shoot at the alfreds and buckchucks running across his lawn, because they annoyed him beyond reason. Having any sort of gun without a permit made the composer a threat, so he had to be eliminated, and Noodles would have felt no guilt about doing that.

Why did Thomas Pynchon decide to include Anton Webern in *Gravity's Rainbow* in the first place? Once again, if you dig deeply enough, you can find some surprising connections. Pynchon began his career in Seattle, working as a technical writer for Boeing. He lived there long before that city became a byword for corporate feudalism, and companies like Jasher Creativity Partners probably didn't even exist in those days, but Pynchon hated Seattle, anyway. In 1962, he wrote to a friend that he'd found only one good thing about the city during his time there: the world premiere of a piece by Anton Webern, which he'd been fortunate enough to attend.

The deeper you dig, the more connections you unearth. Shortly after *Gravity's Rainbow* was published in 1973, Pynchon pulled an Onyx. That is, he disappeared from public view. This was not a great surprise. Pynchon had always been reclusive. Many writers are. Since writing usually requires you to sit still for hours on end in a room without distractions, and to shun social life for long periods of time, having an antisocial streak is a benefit for writers. Pynchon took his antisocial streak to an extreme level. He fanatically avoided photographers and media in general, gave no information as to where he lived, and stayed out of the public eye to the greatest possible extent. The lack of any concrete information about him led to wild speculation, including rumors that Pynchon was Ted Kaczynski (the Unabomber), or that he was the mysterious California writer known as Wanda Tinasky, who posed as a bag lady living under a bridge somewhere in Mendocino County. These rumors reminded me of the outlandish stories that circulated about Onyx. But in contrast to the situation with Onyx, it was generally assumed during this entire period that Pynchon was still alive.

Completing my chain of thought on this chilly day of early November, I contemplated all these refugees from the big and scary outside world: Anton Webern, Jackie O'Reilly, Lydia "Onyx" Douglas, Thomas Pynchon, and me. Two of them had met violent deaths, but one of them (Jackie) had enjoyed over twenty years of small-town peace and tranquility before her shocking demise. The others were still alive. Maybe they were happy; I could only speak for myself. Returning to my habitual academic mode of analysis and argument, I tried to derive some firm conclusion from these individual cases of escape, something to tie them all together, something I could apply in my own life. I couldn't come up with anything. I'd accumulated a lot of knowledge over the years, but I could draw no conclusion from it. I looked for a point to all these musings, but what if there was no point, other than "shit happens, and people cope with it however they can"? The only case I knew from the inside was my own, and while I couldn't save the world or even build a strong barrier to keep the world out, I could at least clean up and beautify my little corner of it.

As I mentioned at the beginning of this narration, Mrs. Van Dorp was my homeroom teacher in elementary school. I had her for more than one grade, so we got to know each other well. Apart from Mrs. Van Dorp, my memories of my elementary school career are hazy, as hazy as a hazy IPA. That's probably because I was in and out of several different schools, a result of my father's corporate job, which saw him transferred through several medium-sized metro areas around the country. All these schools felt anonymous and generic in character, and to my young eye, they were populated by anonymous and generic teachers, who instructed anonymous and generic students. But I have to admit that Mrs. Van Dorp was not anonymous and generic at all, which is why my memory of her is still vivid.

161

One day, she gave us an assignment that I still remember in detail. In fact, even though this happened way back in fifth grade (or perhaps it was sixth), it's an assignment that I've been thinking about and grappling with ever since. Mrs. Van Dorp told us to write an essay. The premise of the essay was as follows: "You will go blind exactly six months from now. There is no chance of saving your sight. This is a one hundred percent certainty. The question is: what are you going to do with your remaining six months of eyesight?"

I spent the evening pondering this gloomy assignment, and dutifully put down a few hundred words on paper about my future as a sightless person. The next day, we read out and discussed our essays in class. The key parts of my essay were as follows. Since blindness was inevitable, I should spend the next six months getting used to the idea and developing skills that would help me cope. I would buy a cane and learn to use it, practicing with my eyes closed. I would pick out a pair of dark glasses to wear if I had to appear in public. I would learn to read braille, so it would be easier to adjust when the time came. I would do some research on service dogs (or as we called them at the time, seeing-eye dogs). I would work hard on sharpening my remaining senses, to make the transition to total blindness easier.

My essay was followed by Linda Adamski's. As I recall, she was consistently the best student in the class, and it was no surprise that she delivered a polished and well-structured essay. More important was what she said. Her six months were going to be a visual feast. Linda had never visited classic European cities like Paris and Rome, but she was determined to do so. She would take in all the historic architecture that she could travel to, and she would visit as many of the great art museums of the world as possible. She wouldn't neglect nature—she had a list of natural wonders that she'd not yet seen, and her intention was to try to visit all of them before darkness closed in. She admitted that this would be difficult, but if she could see even a mere fraction of these sights, she would count herself happy.

Hearing Linda read her essay made me wish that I'd written a different one. All the preparations and precautions that I'd written about were important and reflected some good sense on my part, but shouldn't my last six months of eyesight encompass more than that? Where was the hope? Even if there was no hope, where was the fun? It was still possible. But I'd given it not an iota of thought.

There's no reason to be upset about things that are inevitable. You should take their inevitability as given and work out the best response to it. Linda and I had given two differing responses to an inevitable event.

My response was entirely practical, and to my way of thinking, sensible and laudable. Linda's response was that of a person who wanted to make the most out of life, and who realized that the pleasures of living were fleeting. Probably, the ideal response would have been a combination of the two approaches. But our differing approaches were merely manifestations of our divergent personalities. I acted negatively, in anticipation of the gloomy outcome that I accepted, because I had no choice. She acted positively, aiming to make the most of the time left to her.

Off and on, I thought about this during my life. Amanda never explicitly said so, but I knew that my persistent negativity and gloominess had driven her away to her European jaunt. Ethan had offered the sensible advice that I should follow my hopes rather than my fears. I concluded that his advice should apply not just to me personally, but to the entire country and, if it were possible, to the whole world as we entered a new time of troubles.

Meanwhile, it was late November, the first snow had fallen on Roverton, and our family life appeared to be solidifying. That is, it seemed to be taking shape, although that phrase is misleading, because all shapes taken in the course of time are merely temporary, except for death. What I really mean is that we seemed to have reached an equilibrium in our communal existence. There was a sense that we'd reached the endpoint of some phase in our lives, and a new phase was about to begin.

When I outlined the town's educational setup to Amanda, I neglected to mention something. I can't remember if I had known about it and forgot, or if I never knew in the first place, but Jackie's memorial service reminded me that the local Catholic church ran its own school. It was a smaller institution than the two secular high schools, and easy to overlook if you didn't have a connection to the church or a student going there. Since Amanda had been unable to find a job at the two larger schools and wasn't notably enthusiastic about joining the remote revolution, I suggested she look into working at the Catholic school.

She greeted my suggestion with skepticism: "You know I'm not a believer, Freddie. How am I supposed to work there if I'm not Catholic?"

I pointed out that, as far as I knew, Catholic schools didn't require you to belong to their church to work there. I was able to convince her to talk to the administration, and as it happened, they had a vacancy for a social studies and history teacher. With her excellent credentials (and I suspect, her high-IQ accent), she was able to get the job. The principal commented that he hoped Amanda wouldn't be bored and disappointed to be living in such a rural backwater after living and traveling in major cities and fascinating foreign destinations. Amanda assured him that she had chosen to plant herself in this backwater and looked forward to blooming in her new garden. Apparently, the principal was pleased by this poetic response.

Amanda was serious about what she said. Now that she had a job and a home, she was determined to make the most of her new environment, as was I. Our new life was turning out to be more unruffled and harmonious than our old one. Our goal was to cultivate our garden, Candide-style, while blooming in it, if that made any sense. (I probably shouldn't take these metaphors too literally.)

As if by osmosis via Amanda, Ethan found himself taking an interest in Catholicism, his investigations of Islam having failed to bear fruit. He admitted that his quest for a badass religion had been rooted in immaturity. But he was still taken with the idea of adhering to a strict, demanding religion, so he got interested in Traditionalist Catholicism. He started out, as usual, with online reading, and quickly graduated to actual books taken out of the town library. Books are better than websites—had he picked that up from his old man? It gave me a warm feeling to think so. But he didn't stop at books. He got in touch with Father Garcia, the priest at the church. In some cases, people can be even better than books. You can ask them questions, you can observe their reactions and their way of life, you can engage them in conversation. Our atomized world frowns on deep conversation, but we can't have real civilization without it. I was glad Ethan had taken that step, even though I was largely indifferent to his religious interests. Father Garcia was not a Traditionalist Catholic, but he was happy to discuss the religion with Ethan, addressing it from several angles.

"I hope you were straight with Father Garcia," I said to Ethan one evening, as we were having dinner.

"As opposed to what? Gay?"

"I mean honest," I clarified. "Straightforward. Meaning, you admitted you're looking for a strict religion that will allow you to continue to brew beer."

"Oh, I brought that up. He knows what I do for a living, he doesn't object. He's not anti-alcohol, just anti-alcoholism. Remember, this is a guy who has to slug down the Communion wine if there's any left over after the service. He's cool, an open-minded guy who's willing to listen but who's firm about what he believes."

"You realize that you've confessed to something. Your real religion is beer. Your theology has to accommodate itself to that."

He gave me a serious look. The condescending smile I expected was not there.

"You know what, Dad? You were a catalyst for this. You gave me some pointers."

"How do you mean?"

"Do you remember that summer night after dinner, when we were out in the backyard with Bruce? We were talking about the stars and the night sky and what it all meant to us. You said something about the metaphysical interpretation, or the theological interpretation—I don't remember exactly what term you used. I don't remember if it was Christian or Jewish or Islamic or whatever. But you mentioned that, if this interpretation was true, then we were on this earth for a purpose. There was a reason for us to be here, unlike in the scientific interpretation. There was also a time limit, because eventually everything would come to an end, and whatever we were meant to do, we should get it done by then. I don't know if this is true, or if I can prove it or not. But it feels right to me, because as a human being, it makes sense to have a purpose and a reason for being. You see what I mean?"

"Yes, I remember. Having a purpose is something that seems to be ingrained in us, and that's why we instinctively revolt at interpretations that are purely materialist or biological. But isn't brewing beer a purpose in itself? We also talked about Nietzsche, and you said that the proper way to become an *Übermensch* is to be the best brewer that you can. I don't think you were looking for theological support for your position back then."

"Yeah, well, my thinking is changing," he said. "I'm trying to align my way of life more closely with my beliefs."

"Beliefs should be based on the quest for truth, however. You shouldn't believe something because it's convenient for you to do so."

"How much of the truth can we really discover? Maybe we can find some fragments of truth to hold on to, here and there. But so much is unknowable and unpredictable."

It felt like I was talking to myself. I didn't know if I'd dropped a line like that at some point in our past conversations, and he'd picked it up from me. It was possible that he'd come to that conclusion himself. It didn't really matter. What was noticeable was that his thoughts were evolving. What the terminus point of those thoughts would be, I had no way of knowing. Possibly, neither did he. But it would be interesting to revisit the question in a year, or five years.

Then came the afternoon when I had come home from taking Bruce for a walk. We entered the house, and I was shaking the snow from both me and the dog when the phone rang. I fished the phone out of my coat pocket and answered it.

"Hello there," I said. "It's been a while since I heard from you, my mysterious telephonic friend."

"I suppose you want to know why I didn't call you earlier," said Lydia. "Like, right after Jackie's memorial service. To find out how it went."

"I admit that question crossed my mind." I sat down in the kitchen.

"I was traveling for a while. But now I'm home again. How did it go?"

I told her. I stressed what a moving event it was, and how I was sad that she didn't come. To avoid complicating matters, I said nothing about the brief conversation I had with Mr. Newman. But I didn't want to make her feel guilty, so I accentuated the positive. I told her about the concert at the Opera House, and how surprised I was to find out that she was a songwriter as well.

"I never knew you did that! With the singing and the instruments, I suppose that makes you a triple threat."

I got a chuckle in response. "I guess you could put it that way. The songwriting comes a distant third; I haven't written that many songs. But I'd like to get back to it. I didn't receive any royalties for your local performance as far as I know; they probably assumed I was dead. That's another reason I'm calling."

"Oh really?"

"Yes, really. I've worked out a plan. I'm going to reveal myself, but not all at once. I'm telling people around here already who I really am. There might be a story in our local newspaper soon. From there, it'll gradually spread. I'm easing my way back into the world. There's another reason for that. I want to be a musician again. I mean, this time in public, as myself, doing all the things I like to do. After Jackie's death, you know, first I decided to reveal myself, and then I decided not to reveal myself. Recently I've started hammering at the old dulcimer again in a serious way. I'm writing songs again. I was never that great a singer, but I can do it. I feel connected to what I used to be, at least to the good parts of it. I'm thinking maybe it's time for a new project. Not the McTaggart Family Creamery, that's dead and gone. This time it'll be me and maybe a few friends. Check in with me in a couple of years, Fred. You may be surprised by what you hear."

Perhaps it was the knock-on effect of talking to Lydia, but a couple of days later, I stopped dawdling and put my expanded, formidable plan for the oral history project into action. There was another factor that spurred me on. I thought about my doctoral dissertation, moldering away in a library across the ocean, in that picturesque university city. I thought about students, librarians, and professors walking past the stacks where it decayed, year after year. If none of those people picked it up and opened it, well, that would be par for the course for a doctoral dissertation.

I was thinking about my dissertation when I picked up my phone and called Mean Christine. Unlike my dissertation, the new expanded history project was destined to grow into a book that people would read. It would capture more of Roverton (and potentially the surrounding area) than any publication ever had. Assuming I could find the right informants, it would be entertaining as hell. Who knows, it could turn out to be a classic of the oral history genre. At this stage, I could allow myself to think so, because positive thoughts were a catalyst for inspiration.

Christine was a little surprised by the scope of my ambition.

"Are you sure you want to talk to some of the people I know? You might get a little more Noodles-style content than you bargained for."

"That's fine. All content is good right now. I'm on a quest for the raw material. From it, I make the book. I'm not much of a creative writer, but I think I'm a good editor. The more material I have to work with, the better."

"I know a lot of people. I taught some of them, years ago. I'm related to some of them. I'm pretty sure my daughter would be interested in this. You didn't have any younger folks on your project earlier. Hearing from her generation might be useful to you."

"At this point, the more the merrier." I looked forward to getting started on this revamped project after the beginning of the year, when the weather makes Rovertonians want to stay indoors, curl up with a hot beverage, and engage in conversation. First, I had to gather my informants. Then, I had to work out a schedule and a plan and adhere to it.

After I finished talking to Christine, I heard Amanda's voice, coming from downstairs.

"Who were you talking to just now?"

"That was Mean Christine."

"Are you having your amusing little get-togethers again?"

"Yes, but on a much bigger scale."

"You'll have to tell me about it, then. Oh, and Freddie: we've still got a few more hours of sun today. Why don't we take Bruce and go for a walk on the beach?"

An excellent idea, to which I acceded instantly.

During the cold months here, a sunny day isn't something you want to waste. Today, the sun was out, giving everything a nice, mellow sheen of warmth. On the beach, the pale sand was shining. Lake Michigan was behaving in its usual temperamental way. You could count on it to change its appearance every day, switching to a new color scheme about as often as I changed my clothes. One day it would be turquoise; the next, iron gray; the day after that, deep blue streaked with green. This afternoon, it was a brilliant sky blue, foaming with white where the waves came in.

"Hey, what's that?" asked Amanda. She pointed at something, off to the left.

It looked like a giant spider, or some massive black multilegged reptile, had crawled onto the beach. I felt a shock in my gut. Were we about to be attacked by this horrible creature? Already, Bruce tensed up, staring at the monster with suspicion. We stood there for several seconds, frozen in place. We approached it, cautiously.

"It's driftwood," announced Amanda.

"You're right," I said. "I've never seen a shape quite like that, though. Amazingly lifelike, isn't it?"

Amanda wore sunglasses, so I couldn't tell if she was regarding me with amusement or with contempt. She gave me that slight, crinkly smile I knew so well, so I concluded it was the former.

"Scared you, didn't it?" she asked.

"Only for a second. It's not just the shape—it's the size. You could build a shack out of that."

"Might make a fun little project for you."

"Don't know about that. Woodworking isn't really my thing. But did you know that, in Norse mythology, the first two humans were formed out of pieces of driftwood? Also, in the *Laxdaela Saga*, Hoskuld looks for driftwood along the shore. This answers the question of how Icelanders could build wooden houses even though Iceland has very few trees."

"That's fascinating," said Amanda—meaning, obviously, that it wasn't. "You should write a screenplay, *Attack of the Driftwood Spider*, or something like that. I'm sure it would be a huge hit."

"Thanks, but I've got other things to keep me busy." The conversation turned to the subject of what we should have for dinner.

Standing on the bright sunny beach with Amanda and Bruce, I couldn't say I had a lot of confidence in the future. But I was reasonably certain that we'd all stay here and bloom in place, come what may. We'd stay here even if it turned out that the scientists were wrong, and the climate apocalypse never drowned the cities on the East and West coasts. We'd stick around even if the wildfires didn't burn down California, even if the people of the Southern states weren't going to die like flies in murderous heat waves after all. This would be our home even if the United States remained intact as a unified entity and the Great Lakes Republic never came into existence. We were committed to this place even if Ethan's predicted Dictatorship would never be installed to save us from the coming chaos. We were going to hunker down and defend our patch even if the hostility between Nukes and Old-Timers broke out into a full-scale civil war. Even if the worst did happen, and Lake Michigan itself were to rise up and inundate and drown the town together with its craft beer, its emerging regional cuisine, and its whimsical stories, I'd stay here and die in my home, because if there was one thing I didn't want, it was to survive the end of civilization.

THE END

Acknowledgements

Thanks are due first of all to my beta readers: Bill Hinchliff, Tom Rand, and Alison Maillard-Parker. This book would not exist without their helpful critiques. Tom Rand, photographer extraordinaire, provided the cover photo. I also thank Darian Bianco and the team at Alternative Book Press for bringing this project to fruition.

Many towns went into the making of Roverton. They include South Haven, MI; Grand Haven, MI; Ludington, MI; Manistee, MI; Sturgeon Bay, WI; Bayfield, WI; Burlington, WI; Stillwater, MN; Woodstock, IL; Astoria, OR; and Port Townsend, WA.

The central incident in the story is based on an accident I personally witnessed in Lambertville, NJ, in May 2000. Details about this accident can be found in the article "Witnesses recall horrific truck accident," posted on May 18, 2000, at centraljersey.com. I thank the Lambertville Free Public Library for providing me with media reports dealing with the event, which refreshed my memory of it.

The story of Lydia "Onyx" Douglas was partially inspired by a real event: the disappearance of Christina "Licorice" McKechnie, of the Incredible String Band, who was last seen hiking in the Arizona desert in 1987. As of this writing, the mystery of her disappearance has yet to be solved.

There is indeed a *pupusería* on the Southwest Side of Chicago, at 63rd and Neenah, near Midway Airport. I highly recommend it.